Northbrook Public Library
3 1123 00843 4014

P9-CQA-804

Death's Door

A LEIGH GIRARD MYSTERY

DEATH'S DOOR

GAIL LUKASIK

FIVE STAR
A part of Gale, Cengage Learning

Detroit • New York • San Francisco • New Haven, Conn • Waterville, Maine • London

Five Star Publishing, a part of Gale, Cengage Learning.

Set in 11 pt. Plantin.

Printed on permanent paper.

LIBRARY OF CONGRESS CATALOGING-IN-PUBLICATION DATA

Lukasik, Gail.
Death's door : a Leigh Girard mystery / by Gail Lukasik. — 1st ed.
p. cm.
ISBN-13: 978-1-59414-714-2 (hardcover : alk. paper)
ISBN-10: 1-59414-714-0 (hardcover : alk. paper)
1. Women journalists—Fiction. 2. Serial murderers—Fiction. 3. Resorts—Fiction. 4. Door County (Wis.)—Fiction. I. Title.
PS3612.U385D43 2009
813′.6—dc22 2008049398

First Edition. First Printing: March 2009.
Published in 2009 in conjunction with Tekno Books and Ed Gorman.

Printed in the United States of America
1 2 3 4 5 6 7 13 12 11 10 09

For the courageous women, men and children who have battled cancer.

ACKNOWLEDGMENTS

The author wishes to acknowledge the invaluable assistance of the following people: breast cancer survivor, Bev Parker; Environmental Educator, Jean Weeg; *Chicago Tribune* Editor, Robert Davis; Conservation Ecologist, Mike Grimm; *Door County Advocate* News Editor, Joe Knaapen; Ranger Laura Hedien; Dr. Bill Ernohoezy; Linda Andrews and Nancy Cirillo.

ACKNOWLEDGMENTS

[illegible]

Prologue

April, Twenty-three years earlier: Des Plaines, IL

Carol Sandinsky stood on the stoop of her apartment building staring at the spot where her daughter was last seen. Smoking a cigarette, she seemed not to notice the chill winds that whipped past her.

"When was the last time you saw Ashley?" the reporter from the *Chicago Times* asked.

"Like I told the cops, Friday, around seven. I was just getting ready to make dinner. I looked out the window to check on her. She was over there by that tree." She pointed to a leafless tree near the curb.

"About forty minutes later the boys straggle in. Hungry, you know. I says to them, 'Where's Ash?' But none of them knew." She pushed back a strand of brown hair from her face. "I just had this strange feeling, and I said to my husband Mitch, 'Mitch,' I says, 'I'm calling the cops.' "

"Can you give me a description of Ashley? What was she wearing when she disappeared?" the reporter asked.

"Ashley's fourteen. She's five-five and weighs about a hundred and fifteen pounds. She has long blond hair, curly-like, and blue eyes. That day she braided it and tied it off with one of them rubber bands with those glass balls. Purple colored. She likes the purple ones. She was wearing a light blue T-shirt, dark blue jeans and white sneakers." Her voice had gone flat with the recitation.

"Did anyone else see her after you?"

"My husband, Ash's daddy. He said he saw her sitting in her uncle's car out front there by the tree. He told her to come in for dinner."

"Was there anyone else around at the time? Her uncle, maybe?"

"Bill, that's her uncle, my brother. He was inside watching a baseball game. No one else was out there."

"What about your husband? How do he and Ashley get along?"

She crushed the cigarette out with the toe of her sneaker before she answered. "He loves his daughter. That answer your question?"

The reporter shifted from one foot to the other. "What were, are Ashley's interests, outside of school?"

"Ashley's real involved with sports—basketball, soccer. She's also a member of the school choir. And she's a straight-A student. Make sure you put that in. She's a real good girl. I want people to know that about her. She's never any trouble."

"Sure. I'll do that. Do you have any ideas what happened?" the reporter asked.

"It's like she was sucked up into the sky. I'm just waiting here, hoping she'll fly back."

Chapter One

May 20, Saturday, Present

When the phone rang at 4:49 a.m., I knew it was bad news. For one minute I debated letting the answering machine get it, then reached for the phone. Bad news didn't get any better replayed.

"Leigh, it's Marge. Sorry to call so early, but we got a missing kid." Marge Lindquest was the *Door County Gazette*'s production editor, office manager and Jane-of-all-trades. Her versatility was only matched by her dedication. "Jake didn't happen to come by your place this morning?"

Though it was common knowledge at the newspaper, in Egg Harbor, and probably on the entire Door County peninsula that Jake Stevens, editor of the *Door County Gazette,* and Leigh Girard, the new reporter, were sleeping together, some sense of village propriety kept most people from saying it to my face. "As a matter of fact, he's right here." I nudged Jake, holding the phone out to him. He mumbled something and pulled the covers up over his head.

"It's Marge," I said, lifting the covers. "There's a kid missing."

He emerged from under the covers and took the phone. "Who's missing?" he asked, sitting up, suddenly all business. "Wait a minute, let me get a pen and paper." He shouldered the phone to his ear and picked up the pen and notepad I kept on the bedside table.

"How long has she been gone? Yeah, okay. What's that side

road? ZZ till Margate. Got it. I'll be there in a few."

Jake hung up the phone and threw back the covers, causing me a moment of panic, as I quickly managed to pull the top blanket over my nakedness. "Get dressed," he said, leaning over the bed to search for his jeans.

"What's going on?" I sat up, careful to keep the blanket over my chest. Already the bedroom was filling with early morning light. And though Jake and I had been lovers since last fall, when he'd convinced me that the absence of my left breast didn't matter to him, I still hadn't let him see the six-inch scar that cut across my left side from underarm to sternum in full daylight.

As he stood, yanking up his jeans, he looked briefly at my hand clutching the blanket, a strange expression on his face. "The Margarises' fifteen-year-old daughter disappeared late yesterday. They got a summer home on the Mink River. I want you over there. Talk to the parents. Kid'll probably show up before noon. Happens at least once every tourist season. Kid runs off, then turns up the next day. But just in case, we need to cover it."

"What about tonight's meeting?"

There was a town meeting at 6:30 p.m. in Sturgeon Bay. Next Monday the Door County sheriff's department was releasing a list of registered sex offenders living on the peninsula. The list would be distributed as a pullout sheet in the *Door Resort,* the Peninsula's free advertising weekly. To minimize the fallout from local businesses that wanted the police to wait until after tourist season, the meeting was a public relations ploy. Deputy Chet Jorgensen told me the list was going to be published on Monday, no matter what.

Although this was supposed to be the kind of thing that made a journalist go all sweaty, I wasn't looking forward to the meeting. Not that I don't enjoy spectator sports, but I had a hunch it was going to turn into the *Jerry Springer Show* with lots of incoherent shouting and maybe some chair tossing. It's hard to get a good quote when chairs are flying.

"If something else turns up on the Margaris girl, call me. I'll get Martin to cover the meeting. If not, I want you there."

"Hope there's no connection between the missing girl and one of the sex offenders," I offered.

"Leigh, don't go there," Jake cautioned. "Just do your job. Not the police's. Interview the parents. Get the story. Attend the meeting. Write it all up and go home. Like I said, kid usually shows up the next day."

"Don't I always," I said, bristling at his bossy tone. "Get the story, that is." For the past week Jake had been unusually distant. I'd chalked it up to cabin fever. We'd weathered a particularly long and brutal winter that had everyone on the peninsula out of sorts. According to the police stats, domestic violence was up ten percent from last winter.

He stared again at my hand clutching the blanket, then threw on a navy sweatshirt and started for the door. His graying hair rippled down past his shoulders—in defiance of any fashion trend. As far as I could tell, he hadn't cut it all winter. He'd also grown a goatee. He was looking less and less like an editor of a small-town newspaper and more and more like the poet he professed to be. Both personas made me nervous.

Salinger, my Shetland sheepdog, stirred from her bed by the window and followed him, snapping at his bare feet. To Salinger, Jake still bore watching.

"Jake," I called after him. "Are you going to tell me what's going on with you?"

He turned around. "You still moving into Joyce Oleander's place next week?"

I had one week until the snowbird who owned the cottage I rented reclaimed it. With the return of the summer people and tourists, and with them escalating prices, the only place that accepted dogs, wasn't booked, and even came close to my meager housing allowance, was a town house in Egg Harbor where Joyce Oleander had died. I hadn't known Joyce, but she had figured in two murders last fall. The vision of her bloodstained carpet still haunted me.

"It's not the dead you have to worry about, Jake," I said with more conviction than I felt, "it's the living. Is that what's been bothering you lately? My moving into Joyce's place?"

He shoved his hands in his front pockets and stared at his bare feet. Not a good sign.

"Look, I've got to take off for a while. I'm not sure when I'll be back."

I waited for him to elaborate. For all our bed time, Jake didn't talk much about himself or his life before Door County. He'd made it clear from the start that he didn't want to discuss his past, which I'd learned from Marge included an ex-wife and a nineteen-year-old daughter. Since I wasn't keen on discussing my past, which included an estranged husband back in Illinois, I'd let sleeping dogs lie, so to speak.

"There's something I've gotta take care of," he added, as if that explained everything.

"Okay. Well, thanks for letting me know." I leaned over and swiped my silk nightgown from the floor where Jake had thrown it last night. Keeping the blanket against my chest, I slipped into the nightgown one arm at a time.

"C'mon, Leigh, it's not like you're very forthcoming about yourself," he paused. "There's that husband of yours you never talk about."

I stood up and faced him, crossing my arms over my chest. For some reason, his mentioning my husband had ticked me off. "You know, Jake, all you had to do was ask."

He looked around the room as if he was seeing it for the first time. When his eyes came back to me they were tight with anger. "I thought by now I wouldn't have to."

"Yeah, well, I guess you were wrong about that."

When he didn't respond, I walked past him toward the bathroom, slammed the door, and turned on the shower, not sure why I was so angry. He had every right to take off and not tell me where he was going or why.

I slipped off the jade nightgown and stood in front of the medicine cabinet mirror. Over the winter the six-inch scar that cut across my left side from underarm to sternum had faded to a pale pink like the inside of a seashell. I ran my finger along the smooth suture line. Its shiny surface was numb to my touch.

A few seconds later I heard the front door slam. I continued staring at the flat, empty expanse where my left breast once was. Finally the steam rose, clouding everything.

CHAPTER TWO

May 20, Saturday

There was no street sign for Margate Lane. Instead, two yellow signs nailed to a dead tree marked the gravel road. The bold black letters read: *No Trespassing* and *No Hunting.* In case you weren't sufficiently warned, a Dead End sign was nailed to a utility pole a few feet away.

The signs matched my foul mood. I'd replayed our conversation as I drove north up the peninsula on Highway 42 and concluded that Jake didn't trust me. And I hated the fact that I cared.

I gingerly eased my battered pickup down the rutted road, rattling and bouncing through potholes fit for a Chicago street. Though the deciduous trees were still leafless, the woods were so dense with pines and cedars only shafts of light reached the road. It would be easy to get lost in these woods.

The few facts I had about the missing girl I'd learned from Deputy Chief Chet Jorgensen over the phone. Name: Janell Margaris. Last seen yesterday evening. Age fifteen. Missing persons report filed this morning. Family—summer people from Chicago. Father owns Margate Development Company. Mega bucks.

After snaking through the woods for half a mile, the gravel road ended abruptly in a clearing. In the distance stood a log cabin, the word cabin being a misnomer.

The two-story house was big and windowed and overdone.

Gables and balconies were in abundance as was Victorian bric-a-brac. Although the logs were a bleached blond hue, their thickness gave the house an oppressive feeling, as if at any moment it would sink into the earth from its sheer weight.

Standing guard by the front door was an honest-to-goodness wooden Indian, bare-chested wearing a headdress and a loincloth and holding a bow. He seemed to be looking out toward some imaginary distance. Everything about the house made me feel it didn't belong here.

I slammed the door of the truck and followed the bark-chipped path leading to the wrap-around front porch, my suede boots sinking into the mushy path. Scattered throughout the woods surrounding the house were green shoots pushing up through the soft ground. It all looked painful. I didn't believe in premonitions. But as I stood on the porch, pushed the lighted doorbell and listened to the chimes' hollow echo, I had a bad feeling.

Russell Margaris wore his wealth like an extra layer of skin that made me wonder what was underneath. Gold Rolex watch, gray linen shirt unwrinkled, leather loafers so supple they looked like they'd dissolve in sunlight. Even his thinning blond hair worked like another accouterment. While some men would have wistfully cultivated those long hairs to cover a balding scalp, Margaris's hair was short and neat and made no apologies. Its symmetry drew you to his aquiline nose and his glacial blue eyes. This was who he was, take it or leave it. He understood the power of wealth, but none of its ease and subtleties. For him, there'd never be enough.

He and his wife Janet sat on a maroon leather couch, looking rather meticulously groomed for parents whose only child had been missing since last night. But extreme duress affected people in different ways. Some people fell apart; others took comfort from structure and routine.

Behind them was a wall of arched windows that reached past the trees outside to the nether bluish morning. I could see two things clearly: the silver trail of the Mink River and a wooden pier reaching toward it. Neither sight gave me much comfort.

"Could we get this over with, Ms. . . . ? What did you say your name was?"

"Girard. But, please, call me Leigh." I perched on the edge of the twin leather couch whose massiveness was so overpowering that to sit back seemed like a form of surrender.

"I'm sorry," I began, "I can't even imagine what you're going through. So I'll try and keep this brief. Could you tell me about Janell?"

"Like what?" Margaris asked.

His question caught me off guard. After eight months as a *Gazette* reporter, I'd begun to approach reporting as a social call. I always got the story—eventually—as well as recipes for sour cherry pie, the best place to buy smoked salmon and where the perch were running. My reporter's notebook looked like the diary of a crazed tourist.

"I know this must be very difficult for you." I flipped over the page as if another more succinct question was written there. "But if you could lead me through what happened. Like, when did you last see Janell?"

Margaris started to get up from the couch, but Janet put her hand on his shoulder stopping him. She was still a pretty woman with soft, tastefully highlighted auburn hair and those tiny perfect teeth only dentists can give you. Her clothes were as studied as her husband's. But if his were workday casual, hers were urban country: black jeans; white silk blouse, V-neck; single strand of pearls peeking out from under a silk scarf—Givenchy. There was no doubt it was a Givenchy because the name was plastered on it. Although both parents wore the trappings of wealth, their demeanors were radically different. Whereas Margaris stared directly at me with impatience, Janet had yet to make eye contact. Her head was down and her eyes were closed, as if opening them would make everything real. Something about their demeanors didn't fit.

"It's our fault," she began, her mouth trembling.

"Janet," Margaris said, patting his wife's hand a little too hard. "Don't say that."

"No, Russell, it is." She stopped and looked up, finally making eye contact. Her eyes were such a light green they looked transparent. She kept blinking them as if she were having trouble seeing.

"Janell didn't want to come. But we made her." She looked sideways at her husband. "Russell said she had to. We always come up here the weekend after Mother's Day to open up the house." She took a deep breath and let it out. "We got this place about ten years ago. You know, to get away from the city. It's so safe up here, and the city . . ." her voice drifted off.

I waited for her to continue, hoping the recitation would ease her pain.

"Janell used to love to come up here when she was younger. She and Stephanie—that's the girl who lives across the road. They've been friends since they were five or six. The Eversons live here year round. I mean this is their home. They're some kind of artists or something. I can't think now. You know, Russell." She looked at Margaris.

He didn't respond.

She took another deep breath and continued. "I think Ben manages one of those hotels, too. The girls have always gotten along. They'd spend all summer together."

"Janet," Margaris said, squeezing her hand.

It was obvious that the stress was exacerbating a familiar family dynamic. I don't think I'd ever seen two people more strained and less able to connect.

"As soon as we got here yesterday afternoon, Janell told me she was going over to Stephanie's to see if she was home. And it was only across the road. How could this happen?" She appealed again to her husband, who ignored her. He was staring at me, watching me take notes.

"Anyway, it was starting to get dark. And I didn't see them by the river or out front. I mean, I had seen them earlier sitting on the pier. I remember walking past the windows and seeing them. I don't know why they didn't come in and at least tell me they were here. I guess Janell was still sulking."

"What time was that when you saw them sitting on the pier?"

"I don't know. It's all a blur." She pressed her lovely, long fingers to her temples. Her glossy brown fingernails looked like drops of wet mud against her pale skin. "But like I said, it was starting to get dark, and I didn't see them by the river. By then Russell was here. What time was that, Russell?"

"About seven," he answered, his mouth a taut wire. I couldn't tell if he was impatient, frustrated or angry. Maybe all of the above. Who could blame him?

"You two didn't come together?" I was trying to make sense out of the sequence of events. Janet closed her eyes again.

"No. Russell's hardly ever here. His business takes up all his time. It's just Janell and me. But like I said, we always come up after Mother's Day weekend. If the weather's good, we go out on the boat. Russell had the boat put in at the marina last week." Janet stopped and played with her pearls. "I called the Eversons to see if Janell was there. But she wasn't. Where could she be?"

He interrupted. "I went over there to talk to Stephanie. Thought I'd run into Janell on the way." He paused. "When I got there, Stephanie told me they'd been down by the marina sitting on the boat. Stephanie left when her mother called."

Margaris must have read the question on my face. "On the

cell phone," he said as if he were talking to an idiot.

"What time was that?"

"Five-fifteen." His answer was as clipped as his hair.

"And Janell?"

His chin jutted out. "She stayed there."

"Was that unusual, her hanging around the marina alone?" I instantly regretted my poor choice of words.

Margaris didn't answer. Instead he fixed me with a dead stare.

"What I mean is, did she have any other friends she might have met up with?"

"No."

"Do you know what they were doing there?" I asked. "She and Stephanie, that is?"

He glared at me again with those icy blue eyes. "What do teenagers do?"

"I wouldn't know, Mr. Margaris."

"Exactly."

I shifted in my seat, trying to get comfortable. "Did you walk down to the marina to look for Janell after leaving the Eversons'?"

"She wasn't there."

He hadn't answered my question. "Then as far as you know, Stephanie was the last one to see Janell?"

Janet slowly eased her hand out from under her husband's.

"That's what I said," Margaris answered.

"And Mr. Margaris, you arrived about seven. Right?"

"I already told you that." His stare was intense enough to shatter glass.

I studied my notes for a moment. "So that leaves about two hours between the time Stephanie went home and your call to the Eversons."

"What are you trying to get at?" He leaned back as if he were preparing to pounce. His hands fisted on his thighs.

"Nothing, Mr. Margaris. I'm just trying to establish a time frame for the article."

"Get on with it." His hostility toward me was palpable, a result no doubt of worry, frustration and helplessness.

"Sure thing. How far a walk is it from Rowleys Bay to your house?"

"About ten, fifteen minutes," Margaris said, looking over my head as if I wasn't there.

"Other than the walk from Rowleys to your road, it's pretty wooded. Any chance she could have gotten lost?"

He spoke very slowly, emphasizing every word. "Even if she didn't take the road to the house, which she wouldn't do, she wouldn't get lost. She knows these woods. She knows to follow the river. I told that moronic cop, what's his name, Jorgensen, the same thing."

"The cops have searched the two properties, then?"

"If you want to call it that. The two cops they sent spent more time scratching their heads than looking for my daughter. I want you to quote me on that."

"Did they find anything?"

"What do you think?" Margaris ran his fingers through his thinning blond hair. "You know what that cop asked me? Was it possible that Janell ran away? As if we're some kind of child abusers!"

"Somebody took her," Janet said. "I know it, Russell. You know it."

"Janet, don't say that. We don't know anything yet. Don't fall apart on me."

"Was there a ransom note?"

"For God sakes, if there was, don't you think I would have told you already?"

"Not necessarily, Mr. Margaris. You could have been

instructed not to."

"There's no ransom note. My daughter's missing and there's no ransom note." He was shouting. "Put that down in your little book. Make sure you get it right."

"Somebody has her," Janet cried. "I can feel it. Some sick bastard has my beautiful girl, doing God knows what to her." Tears were trailing down her face, making lines through her flawless makeup.

"Okay, that's it. We're done." He looked at his watch. "Where are those damned cops?"

"I'm sorry if I upset you," I directed my comment to Janet. "But I have to ask one more thing. Do you have a recent photo of your daughter? For the paper."

Janet Margaris got up and moved toward one of the floor-to-ceiling bookcases that flanked both sides of the flagstone fireplace. From one of the shelves she took a silver-framed photo and handed it to me. It was a picture of a sturdy blond girl dressed in a yellow and black soccer uniform. She was standing before a goalie net holding a soccer ball above her head as if she'd just made a save. The only trace of femininity were the two yellow ribbons dangling loose from her braids and the gentle swell of her prepubescent breasts. She had one of those big, open smiles that made you want to protect her.

"Janell loves sports." Janet stood over me, holding the picture by its edges. Her spicy perfume prickled my nose.

Before I could take the picture from her, Margaris sprang up and snatched it from his wife.

"She said recent. That picture's four years old." Margaris threw the picture down on the couch behind him, went to a bookcase and grabbed another picture.

"Here." He thrust the photo into my hands, nicking my thumb. "This is what you want."

It was hard to believe it was the same girl. She was still blond, but the open smile was gone. In its place were a pouty, defiant mouth and the seductive stare of a lingerie model. Her hair was long and straight and sleek. But the biggest change was her body. It was as if she had gone from prepubescent to womanhood without that awkward stop in between. She was wearing a black, satiny strapless gown that she had no problem keeping up and more makeup than I owned. Next to her stood a tall, gawky boy who looked as if he had walked into the photo by mistake and didn't have a clue what he was supposed to do. His hand hovered about her waist as if to touch her was some commitment he had no idea how to fulfill.

Janet picked up the first picture from the couch, ran the sleeve of her silk blouse over the glass, then walked back to the bookcase, carefully positioning the picture of her soccer-playing daughter. With the exchange of photos something had gone out of Janet—her shoulders were sloped and that closed-eyed, downcast posture was back.

Margaris looked at his watch again. "If you don't mind." He gestured toward the door as if he were dismissing the hired help.

I crossed my legs and leaned back into the couch, ignoring his dismissal. "I'd like to include some personal details about Janell, her interests, hobbies, things like that. You never know what might help."

He took a deep breath. "Let's cut the crap, okay? When does this rag of a paper come out? Huh? If memory serves me, not until Tuesday. By then, it may be too late. The first twenty-four hours in a missing person's case are crucial. Am I right? After that the trail gets colder with each passing hour. If you really want to help, get some people over here and start looking for Janell."

Somewhere in the middle of his tirade Margaris had turned toward his wife, who was still standing by the bookcase. It was as if he were addressing his remarks to her and not me. Surely she knew all that. There seemed no point to his tirade, except cruelty.

I should have left immediately instead of walking around the Margarises' soggy woods in my suede boots and burgundy pantsuit. If he owned a gun, Margaris had every right to shoot me. That is, if he could see me through the snaggled evergreens, shrubs and budding trees.

I needed to walk off some steam. I'd kept my cool with Russell Margaris, but now my brain was seething with a cauldron of snide things I wanted to say to him—starting with "This rag of a paper just might help find your daughter" to "You remind me of my estranged husband, Tom, another blustering male." Margaris, like Tom, carried his maleness like the privilege that it was, expecting as his due all the perks that went with it. There'd be no reasoning with his tacit expectations.

Whoa, Leigh, let's not tar the entire male population with the same brush, I told myself.

Margaris's hostility, though misdirected, was understandable. His only child was missing and he couldn't do a thing about it. Helplessness was not a part of his vocabulary. But why did his hostility seem personal, as if I had done something to him? I'd never even heard of him before today.

Of course, his hostility could be a cover. Parents were sometimes a child's worst nightmare. Was I picking up some vibe from him? Under all the insults and impatience was there fear?

At the rear of the house I emerged into another clearing. As I walked toward the pier, I glanced back. The immense windows reflected the scene before me but in reverse. I couldn't see into the house, but if the Margarises were still in the great room, they would see me just as Janet had seen Janell and Stephanie yesterday.

I turned away and continued walking until I reached the pier. The river looked pristine and wild and isolate—swept clean of humans. There was no indication that a young girl had sat here yesterday talking to her friend about whatever teenagers talked about—boys, music, clothes.

Margaris was right about one thing. If Janell hadn't run away, which I wasn't as convinced of as Margaris, and someone had taken her, Tuesday's article would have little impact. Most children abducted by strangers are murdered within the first few hours. And if one of her parents was involved, the same held true. Either way it was an exercise in futility.

I started as a fish jumped from the water. It disappeared as suddenly as it appeared, leaving only a rippling circle of water. I felt a chill run through me. I flashed on Janell Margaris in that black strapless dress, the soft flesh of her new breasts, her defiant pouty mouth that probably had an answer for everything, that expected everything. I hoped I hadn't been looking at a dead girl.

Chapter Three

Before exiting Margate onto County Route ZZ, I called the Eversons' number on my cell phone. A woman answered.

"Mrs. Everson?"

"Yes?"

"This is Leigh Girard from the *Gazette*."

Before I could make my request she cut me off. "Stephanie doesn't know anything. Talk to the police. Okay?"

"It'll only take a few minutes. You can stay in the room if you like. It might help Janell."

"Look, Stephanie's sleeping. She's had a rough night." She sounded both annoyed and distracted.

I explained that I was sitting across the road from her driveway.

Her voice softened. "She's only going to tell you what she told the police. But seeing you're here, I suppose you could talk to her."

I wasn't complaining, but her change of mind seemed curious.

"You're doing the right thing," I said, looking at my watch.

"Yeah, right."

The Eversons' house, like the Margarises', was a log home lost in evergreens and leafing deciduous trees and shrubs. But that was where the similarity ended. The Eversons' log home, a one-story cottage painted barn red, was modest and unassuming—

typical of older Door County homes.

A few feet from the house was a small barn, also painted red. Over the barn was a white sign with dark green lettering: Annie Everson Gallery. There had been no sign at the entrance. Unless you knew it was there, you'd never find the gallery.

A bony, angular woman opened the door. "Russell calm down yet?"

She walked ahead of me into the cluttered room, not waiting for my response. I placed my muddy boots by the door and followed the faint trace of patchouli that trailed behind her.

"Thanks for letting me talk to Stephanie," I said to her back.

She turned and held up a large ceramic mug. "I'm on my third cup. You want some?"

"Just some water if it's no trouble."

"Have a seat, I'll be right back."

I sat down in one of the two worn chairs cluttering the small room.

Annie called from the kitchen. "Stephanie's getting dressed. She'll be out in a minute."

There was a feeling of chaos about the room. None of the furniture matched. The chair I sat in was brown corduroy. The other, occupied by a sleepy tabby cat, was green tweed worn through to the stuffing on both arms. The couch, which was meant to pull the room together, was splotched with large pink peonies on a green and brown background. One wall was spattered with children's photographs at various ages—all the boys were dark-haired, all the girls were blondes.

What the room lacked in order, it made up for in dazzling rugs. An assortment of hand-woven rugs covered the pine floor and draped the two walls. The rugs depicted medieval scenes of dragons and maidens, rivers and unicorns, castles and knights. There were so many conflicting colors and patterns in the room it made me jittery.

"I haven't gotten to last night's dishes yet." Annie handed me a silver goblet. "That's the only clean anything. Sorry. And sorry about my crack about Russell. That was real insensitive. Just that he upset Stephanie so much last night she cried. He was so angry, you'd'a thought she had something to do with Janell's disappearance."

Annie stood in front of me holding her coffee mug and nervously tapping her bare foot. She was so thin; she seemed weighted by her white fisherman's sweater and long denim skirt. Deep creases scored her face and neck that a little weight might have filled in. Despite her wrinkled skin, she had a quickness about her that made it impossible to guess her age.

"I recognized your name even before you said you were from the paper."

That might explain her not wanting to see me.

"You're that new one. The one that . . ." She paused for half a second. I knew she was rewording her sentence. ". . . I've seen at town meetings." She sat down in the other chair, tucking her skirt around her bare feet. She cradled the mug in her hands.

"That's me," I said, settling back in the chair. "Are these yours?" I pointed to the rugs.

"I've been weaving since forever. You'd think I'd be rich by now." She laughed easily. "No such luck. But I'm not interested in that. Trish, you know, who owns that rug shop, Dream Weavers, between Fish Creek and Ephraim. She sells them for me. Charges too much. At least that's what I tell myself when she only sells one a year. But hey, every little bit helps, especially with Jimmy away at college. He's my second youngest."

"How many children do you have?"

"Five. Besides Jimmy and Stephie, there's Carrie, Billy and Teddy. They're all grown up. I'm just waiting on grandkids. Listen, I only let you come over here because of Janell. I don't want Stephanie more upset than she already is, okay? I mean the police were bad enough. But Russell, he was just out of control."

"No problem."

She put her mug down on a side table and turned toward the other doorway. "Stephie, honey. That lady from the paper's waiting."

She turned back toward me. "I gotta protect her. Sometimes Stephanie's too nice for her own good."

"What did he do that upset her so much?" Not that I couldn't guess.

"It's just the way he talked to her. Like he was accusing her. Police have any idea where Janell is? They wouldn't say anything last night." Something about the way she asked made me suspect she had her own theory about Janell's whereabouts.

"No, not yet. You have any ideas where she is?"

She massaged the palm of her right hand and then her left. There was a plain silver band on her left hand that could have been a wedding ring except that it seemed too slender. "I don't think anyone's kidnapped her if that's what you're asking."

"Why's that?"

She shook her head. "No reason. Just don't."

Okay, she wasn't going to share.

"Janet Margaris told me Janell and Stephanie spent the afternoon together."

"Yeah, I was kinda surprised when Janell showed up like that. Sort of out of the blue."

"I thought Janell and Stephanie were friends."

"*Were*. They *were* friends. 'Course I saw that coming. Surprised it took so long. Last summer they had a falling out about something. You can ask Stephanie about it. I think it was over some boy. Stephanie says it wasn't." She made a dismissive gesture with her right hand. "Teenagers. What can I tell you? Thank God, she's my last."

Either Janet Margaris didn't know her daughter very well or someone was lying.

"Did she tell you what it was?"

"No, not really. She just said people change."

"Had Janell changed?"

"From what I could see, yeah. She had a hardness about her I hadn't seen before. She always was kinda mouthy. I figured it was her way of getting attention. Her parents don't pay her a lot. She pretty much does whatever she wants. She started dressing different. No more baggy jeans and T-shirts. More bare midriff, clothes too tight and too short. Not that any of that means anything. Hey, you're only young once. Right?" She stopped and shook her head. "Sorry. I don't mean to make light of this. The Margarises must be going crazy. I'll bet she turns up all safe and sound."

The same thing Jake had said. I hoped they were right.

"Is Janell the kind of girl who'd run away to get attention or to punish her parents?"

Annie considered the question. "I could see her doing that."

She picked up her mug and took a sip of coffee. I waited. Something was on her mind.

"You didn't hear if there'd been a ransom note? I asked the police, but they wouldn't say anything."

"I thought you said you didn't think Janell had been kidnapped?"

"I don't, not really. But Russell made some enemies last summer. You remember, about his developing his land. You know, because it's near that dragonfly's habitat. All of us who live near the river protested, but he still got the go-ahead. Money talks. What can I say?"

"As far as I know there's been no ransom note." Living here was making me soft. Why hadn't I asked Margaris if anyone had a grudge against him?

"Like I said, she's probably run off. Mark my words, she'll show today." She stretched out her long legs.

"You said you were surprised the girls' falling out took so long. What did you mean by that?" For all her frankness, there was something contradictory about what Annie was saying. One minute she was suggesting Janell'd been kidnapped, the next she was saying she was a runaway.

"Let me put it this way. Janell is fifteen going on twenty-five and Stephanie's fifteen going on thirteen."

"Hi." Stephanie Everson stood hesitantly in the doorway. She was barefoot and wore a University of Wisconsin sweatshirt and those baggy pajama bottoms girls use as pants. A tall girl, long and lanky, she had blond wavy hair and large blue eyes that dominated her round face. Though she was tall, maybe five-eight or five-nine, she was also small-boned, which gave her that same aura of fragility her mother had. But unlike her mother, her thinness seemed full of potential. It was a matter of youth, not circumstances. And given time, a softness, evident in the roundness of her face, would assert itself and ground her. She would be an interesting-looking woman, handsome with lots of character.

"Don't stand there gawking. Come sit down. I've got some weaving to do. So you two have a talk. Stephanie, when she leaves, call your father and find out what time he plans on coming home tonight, so I can plan dinner."

With that, Annie went into the kitchen. I heard the back door shut. I must have won her trust, because she'd decided not to stick around.

Stephanie picked up the tabby cat from the chair and sat down on the lumpy couch.

"What's your cat's name?" I asked.

"Baby," she answered, stroking the cat. "My mom named

him. She said that's the last one she's having. Have they found Elly?"

"No, but they will. I'm sure."

She nodded her head yes.

"Tell me what happened yesterday from the time Janell—*Elly*—came over to when you went home."

Stephanie repeated what Margaris had told me.

"Weren't you surprised when she came over yesterday?"

"No. Why?" She stopped stroking the cat and pushed her hair behind her ears. She had a small dark mole on her left cheek near her hairline.

"Well, your mom says you two had a falling out last summer. That Elly changed."

"That's not what happened." She rolled her eyes and let out an impatient sigh. "She always gets it wrong. She's just saying that 'cause she doesn't want to admit she doesn't like the way Elly dresses. She thinks it gives boys the wrong idea. As if they don't already have those ideas." She rolled her eyes again. "Does she think I don't know that? Besides, I think a girl should be able to dress how she wants. Don't you? I mean, you should be able to express yourself."

She was so sincere and earnest it was heartbreaking.

"Sure, I'm all for self-expression, long as you can handle the consequences."

"Gosh, you sound like my mother."

"That bad, huh?"

She laughed.

"But something did change between you and Janell last summer. Am I right?"

She put her head down and her hair fell forward over her face. Her blondness went clear to her roots—a silky yellow color.

"It was no big deal, really. Just this guy thing. I mean I didn't like him or anything. It was Elly. She thought he was cute and sort of dangerous. That's what she said. He's kinda older and got a boat. So I had to cover for her a lot with her mom. I was scared I'd get caught. So finally, I told her to forget it. She wouldn't talk to me for about a week. It was like the end of summer."

Her words rolled out like a confession.

"Do you know this boy?"

She put her head down again. This time when she raised her head, her cheeks were flushed. "No. I never saw him up close. She met him down at the marina. He's probably a summer kid."

She said the last a little too fast.

"Are you sure you don't know him, Stephanie?"

Her flush deepened. "I said I didn't."

"If you knew his name, would you tell me?"

"You know I don't have to talk to you."

"You're right, you don't have to. But we both want to help Elly. Right?"

She put her head down again.

I backed off. If she knew this boy, she wasn't saying. My haranguing her was only going to shut her down completely. "Did Elly ever call this boy by name?"

She looked up at me. "Yeah, she called him Brad. But I don't think that's his name. 'Cause she'd always laugh."

That sounded like it had the ring of truth.

"Why didn't you tell Mr. Margaris this or the police?"

"I didn't really think about it. Mr. Margaris was so mad. He scared me. Then later I remembered, but I didn't want Elly to get in trouble. I know I should have. But you don't think this guy has anything to do with her being missing? I mean, he was older, but not that old." Stephanie sounded like she was trying to convince herself.

"I don't know, Stephanie. But I want you to call Deputy Chief Jorgensen and tell him what you told me. Okay? Here's his number." I wrote Chet's direct number down, tore out the sheet of paper and gave it to Stephanie.

"I'm real sorry," she said, taking the paper. "I didn't mean to do anything wrong. I just didn't think." Again, the words were for herself.

"You'll call, right?" I asked, feeling like the teacher I used to be.

"Yeah, sure."

I followed County Route ZZ west, then north. The morning's crisp blue was gone. In its place clouds splayed the sky white. All along the road mud fields stood open and waiting, their dark brown monotony broken occasionally by patches of butter yellow dandelions. Everything looked tenuous.

I turned on the radio. Mike, WPEN's swap jock, was predicting a partly cloudy day with continued below-normal temperatures. Seventy percent chance of rain by evening, possible sleet.

"Same ole, same ole, folks," Mike said, his voice full of empty enthusiasm. "Okay, then, Gareth's got some wood he wants to swap for lawn mowing. There's an optimist for ya."

It had been an excessive winter even by Door County standards. Storm after storm had dumped snow in double-digit numbers. The only respite came with below-zero temperatures that froze the snow into intractable barriers and kept everyone indoors except for the foolhardy and the desperate. And now spring was two weeks late. The whole peninsula seemed to be in a state of expectation. And it was making everyone edgy.

I turned the radio off, picked up my cell phone and punched in Chet's number at the police station.

On the second ring, Chet's voice message kicked in.

"It's Leigh. Janell Margaris had a boyfriend. Ask Stephanie Everson about it."

Chapter Four

May 20, Saturday

The Sturgeon Bay Town Hall sat two blocks from Green Bay on Third Avenue in the older section of town. Built of native limestone in shades of cream and tan, the building exuded warmth and stability, unlike most of the older section of Sturgeon Bay, which had a feel of slow decline and better times.

As I trudged up the stone steps I looked at my watch—6:10. My stomach grumbled a reminder that I hadn't eaten since three o'clock when Emily, or the girl playing Emily, in the high school production of *Our Town* had offered me a stale donut. I'd spent most of the afternoon at Peninsula High School watching the dress rehearsal and interviewing the director and some of the leads. After that I'd stopped briefly at home to let Salinger out. Then I drove to the *Gazette* office where I worked up the Margaris article. The girl still hadn't showed up.

As soon as I opened the door, the temperature shift hit me. The meeting room was muggy and smelled of too many bodies clad in winter wool. The temp had fallen to the low thirties, so the radiators were hissing and spitting out a syncopated tune that punctuated the low rumble of conversation.

Every folding chair was occupied, and people were standing along both sides of the room and in the aisles. Over the crowd I could just make out the slightly elevated stage area at the front of the hall on which sat Skip Conroy, the mayor of Sturgeon Bay, and Deputy Chief Chet Jorgensen.

As I made my way down the aisle, a waving arm caught my attention. It was Lydia Crane, who had saved me a seat—front row center.

"Long winter, no see," she said as she moved her coat off the wooden folding chair next to her. Lydia, who was an RN at Bay Hospital and owner of the Crystal Door in Fish Creek, had spent the winter in Florida. Though she didn't flaunt it, she was from old Chicago money, which allowed her the freedom to escape Door County winters every year.

"When did you get back?" I asked, unzipping my down jacket. "You missed quite a winter."

"So I've heard. Got back late last night."

"You look tan and rested," I said, taking in her bronzed skin and sun-touched hair.

"What can I tell you? Sun and more sun and more sun. Not to rub it in." She smiled, shaking her short-cropped, chestnut hair.

"I like your hair." I resisted the urge to run my fingers through my curly dark mop that now crested my shoulders.

"Ramon talked me into it. He has a salon in the South Beach area." Her eyebrows went up and down suggestively.

"Must have been hard to come back."

"Yes and no. Oh, because of Ramon? No, he's gay. Not that I wouldn't have considered it. Very yummy." She laughed. "Anyway, had to open up the shop for the season."

I knew Lydia wasn't here tonight just because she was a concerned shop owner. She thrived on drama. It got her juices going. It was the same reason she couldn't bear the peninsula during the winter. She had a tendency toward melancholy. Drama kept her from depression's door.

"See that woman over there?" She pointed to a dark-haired woman in her twenties. "That's Don Stuart's wife. One of the guys on the list." Lydia handed me her copy of the registered sex offenders list. "They gave them out at the door," she explained. "Anyway, Don worked weekends and late hours at the shop for me last summer. I never had a clue." She raised one eyebrow. "Makes you think, huh?"

"Hiring him this summer?" I asked, staring at the mug shots of Door County's registered sex offenders. There were eleven offenders ranging in age from twenty to seventy-four. Most looked like the guy next door. And I guess that was the point. The *Gazette* had received advance copies last week. I'd already checked to see if I knew anyone on the list. I didn't.

"Please!" she gave the word two syllables. "Not that he ever did anything." She almost sounded disappointed. "But still."

She dropped her voice to a whisper. "Can't believe his wife showed up. She must have a death wish. And this guy, Parks, he's on the list." She pointed to a heavily bearded man sitting across the aisle. "He used to be a psychotherapist. What's he trying to prove?"

Before I could comment, Mayor Conroy, a stout middle-aged man with gray politician hair and large steel-framed glasses, stood up and moved to the podium. His tie was so tightly knotted his neck bulged over his collar.

"Okay then, as you all know that list of registered sex offenders we passed out will be released on Monday. I know some of you business people aren't too happy about that there."

A low buzz rose in the room. Conroy put up his hand.

"You'll have a chance to talk in a minute. Timing's not the best, but we wanted to get this thing out there as soon as we got the go-ahead. I stand by the police and the sheriff's department on this. Just so you know, we aren't the only Wisconsin county who's doing this. It's a good decision for our community and for our families and kids. Like I said, maybe the timing could have been better. But the police don't want to wait till after the tourist season."

"Why the hell not?" someone shouted from the back of the room.

"Okay, there's no need for that," he said. "I'm turning this meeting over to Deputy Chief Jorgensen. Who you all know. Some better than others." He paused and smiled, waiting for a laugh. It didn't come. "Okay, then. Deputy Jorgensen."

Chet walked up to the podium like a prisoner about to be executed. A massive man, he seemed shrunken into himself. His normally ruddy complexion was pale and blanched. He tried several times to raise the microphone to meet his Viking height but failed. On the last try he yanked so hard it came off in his hand. A ripple of laughter broke out. Chet didn't seem to notice. Instead he was looking at the microphone as if it smelled bad. Finally he grabbed it with his other hand. From my front row seat I could see trickles of sweat running down the sides of his face.

"Now then, I'm here to say we don't want any harassment toward them men on that there list. I'm not defending them. But if you do anything against them, the police'll have to arrest you. We got no choice."

A loud booing erupted. For a moment Chet stood speechless. "Okay, okay," he finally said. "Let a man finish. These . . ." He struggled for the word.

"Perverts," a guy shouted a few rows back.

Chet squared his shoulders. "Hank Smythe, now you just shut up. Don't matter what all you think of these here men, you can't break the law. You can keep an eye on them. You can call us if you think there's something funny going on. But you can't break the law. Because then you're no better than them."

Lydia leaned toward me and whispered, "Like that'll work."

I was feeling sorrier and sorrier for Chet. He looked about as uncomfortable as I had ever seen him. I wondered why Chief Burnson wasn't here. He was a practiced speaker who had aspirations to be mayor. Chet was a cop who was putting in his time until he could retire and do what he really liked: hunt and fish.

Conroy got up from his chair and took the microphone from Jorgensen, replacing it in its holder. "We're gonna take questions. But one at a time and no shouting."

An older woman who owned one of the antique shops in Carlsville stood up. "This isn't a question, but a comment. You guys are showing bad judgment. There's no good reason on God's green earth why you have to release that list right before tourist season. It's gonna hurt my business and all the other seasonal businesses who rely on tourists. That's all I have to say."

A few people applauded. Conroy pulled at his tie. "We thought if we could save one person from being victimized, then that was worth it. We weren't thinkin' about business."

"If you say so," the woman said, shaking her head as she sat down.

"I don't think it's fair neither." Don Stuart's wife stood up. Her voice trembled. "Most of you here know Don and me. Don's been in no trouble since that one mistake. He was a dumb kid. Eighteen years old and she was fourteen. They were both kids. He knows it was wrong, but there was no forcing. Now he's going to be afraid to go out. It's just not fair," she said, her voice trailing off, "to lump him in with those other criminals. It's like you're punishing him all over again."

The only sound in the room was the hissing of the radiators. I think everyone was thinking what I was thinking: this woman has guts.

Suddenly Chet's cell phone rang. He turned his back to the audience as he answered it. When he turned around, he looked shaken. He said something to the mayor and then walked through the crowd to the exit.

Only one thing I could think of would call him away from this meeting. The missing girl: Janell Margaris.

I grabbed my purse and jacket and ran down the aisle after him. By the time I caught up to him, he was getting into his police car.

"Chet, what's going on? Did they find Janell?"

"This don't concern you, Leigh."

"Just tell me if it's about Janell."

He slammed the door and started the car. As he pulled away the light was whirling red.

It was 6:50 p.m. If I drove really fast, I'd be at the Margaris house before the sun set.

Janet Margaris leaned into the tall cold window as if she were on a storm-tossed ship. Her sobs had subsided into a silence more frightening than her husband's habitual ranting.

Deputy Chief Jorgensen held the paper bag containing a wet, muddy white cloth in his hand like a letter bomb.

"What I want to know is how the hell did you miss this?" Margaris pointed to the bagged cloth. Before dissolving into tears, Janet had confirmed that the material was similar to the white T-shirt Janell had been wearing yesterday.

Jorgensen ran his hand across his sturdy jaw. "Now hold up there, Mr. Margaris. Didn't necessarily miss it. Like I told you outside, this river's tricky. It's got a seiche. Changes direction every thirty minutes or so. This here coulda been up- or downstream. Coulda got caught in the brush there."

I was sitting once again on the mammoth maroon couch wondering why I hadn't spotted the cloth that morning when I walked behind the house near the river.

Margaris batted his hand in Jorgensen's face as if he were swatting at a fly. "Then why aren't you men out there on the river now?"

"We know what we're doin' there." Chet looked over at Janet, then bent toward Margaris. "Chief Burnson's briefing the task force right now. Boats'll be here shortly. Till then, like I told ya, we're doin' another spiral search of the woods. Got some volunteers helping out as well."

"Didn't you do that last night?" Margaris's teeth were clenched so tight his voice sounded gravelly.

"Mighta missed somethin' in the dark. Now why don't you go over there and be with your wife. Let us do our job."

"If you had done your job, my wife wouldn't have found that." His finger jabbed at the bag. "Maybe you should send her out on your spiral search. She seems better at finding things than your so-called police force."

Chet Jorgensen flinched as if he'd been punched. Margaris had just inadvertently hit a sore point. Last fall I'd solved a double-murder without the police's help. Afterwards Chet had taken a lot of ribbing. Normally good-natured and easy-going, I'd seen him lose it a few times. To suggest that the missing girl's mother was more capable of locating her daughter than the police was bringing it all back.

But standing in Margaris's posh summer home scratching his head, Chet seemed determined to remain the same slow, plodding cop who knew more about deer hunting than crime investigations. Chet clung to the belief that people were basically good. Usually that was an asset on the peninsula. Where I came from, it was a decided liability no one could afford.

"Okay, then, Mr. Margaris, no need for that." Chet held up his hand.

Before Margaris could respond, the doorbell rang. Margaris strode out of the room like a man pounding nails with his shoes.

I came over to Chet. "So how's it look to you?"

He glanced back at Janet, who was staring out the window as if she expected her daughter home at any moment. "Whatta ya think," he said in a low, edgy voice that didn't sound like the Chet I knew and liked. In fact, this close his blond hair looked dingy and his khaki uniform exuded a musky scent. "Don't like it," Chet continued. "If a kid don't turn up within twenty-four, then it's usually bad news." Chet didn't seem to share Jake's optimistic view of missing teenagers.

"Chet," I said, keeping my voice low and even so Janet wouldn't look up. "Did Stephanie Everson contact you today?"

"You know somethin', you better tell me then," he said, his face reddening.

"Didn't you get the message I left on your voice mail this morning?"

"I got it."

"Well, don't you think it's worth looking into? Stephanie Everson told me this guy is someone Janell met at the marina last summer. It sounded like she was keeping it from her parents."

His jaw went rigid. "You stay outta this."

Before I could defend myself, Margaris came back into the room followed by a much taller man. I hadn't seen Joe Stillwater all winter. He hadn't changed much: same commanding physical presence—broad shoulders, barrel chest, black hair shot with white. Except his usually short-cropped hair was longer. I wasn't surprised he was here. When he wasn't nursing children at Bay Hospital or managing the Land's End Inn, he worked part time at the marina's boat rental.

"This guy claims he's here to see you," barked Margaris.

Joe Stillwater ignored Margaris's rudeness. "Chet. Leigh. Got four canoes out front on the trailer. Who's going?"

"Divers ain't here yet," said Chet. His face was still an angry red. "Gotta wait for 'em. Burnson's orders."

"How about I leave three canoes? You and the others can take 'em up to Rogers Lake. With all the rain we've been having, the river's high. It's already after seven. Sunset's around eight-fifteen. Divers aren't much good after dark. So you're better off starting up there. I'll put in downriver by the bay. That way we can cover the whole river before dark and meet you back here. Okay?" He didn't wait for an answer. "I'll head out now."

His dark eyes fell on me. "Leigh, how about you?" He looked me up and down, studying my clothes. I was still wearing my black suede boots, the wool burgundy pantsuit, and cream-colored silk blouse. "Can't wear that though. Got some extra clothes and boots in my dry bag that should fit you."

I glared at Joe as if he had asked me to eat glass. "You're kidding, right?"

"Never mind her. I'm going," said Margaris.

"No offense, mister, but parents don't make good searchers. Too close to the situation. Take my cousin's boy who went missing last summer. My cousin, he insisted on going with us to look for the kid. So we didn't argue with him. Kinda hard to argue with a Stillwater. Anyway he walked by this one cave twenty times calling the kid's name. Well, what do you think? The kid was in there all the time. If someone else hadn't gone in there, who knows what would have happened. Anyway, it seems my cousin was mad at the kid. So when my cousin came by, he stayed hid. You see what I mean. You have to leave it to someone else. Don't worry, Mr. Margaris, we'll find your daughter safe and sound."

"She's my daughter and I'm going," Margaris said.

Chapter Five

Rowleys Bay was as gray and turbulent as the sky. I stood on the muddy bank knee-deep in cattails looking out at the choppy, uncertain bay Joe and I were about to enter. Dark clouds bunched at the horizon, rain pocked the water and the wind swept it all toward the shore in a ceaseless curling and uncurling that mirrored my roiling gut.

Even the baseball cap I wore was no protection from the wind-driven rain that ran down my face. I licked a drop from the corner of my mouth. It tasted sour.

Though it was hard to tell by the sky, I guessed it had to be around seven-thirty. I'd left my watch in Joe's truck along with the rest of my clothes. In about forty-five minutes, what light there was would be gone. If Janell was anywhere along the Mink River, we had to find her fast.

"You sure this thing floats?" I stared at the dented and patched aluminum canoe Joe was loading with gear. There was a puckered seam along one side that was sealed with duct tape.

"It's unsinkable." Joe shoved a large, rubbery blue sack he called a dry bag under the canoe's struts.

"That's what they said about the *Titanic.*" Though I was layered in wool socks, windbreaker over life vest over fleece jacket, two pairs of gloves, and waterproof pants, I was cold—and afraid. Water terrified me. I hadn't said anything back at the house about my irrational fear of water, because a child was missing. If that shred of cloth belonged to Janell Margaris, I knew what it meant. The thought turned my stomach. I would do what I usually did when I was scared—not let the fear stop me.

"Leigh," Joe called.

"What?"

"I said we're not going into the water, okay? Too cold." Joe slipped the walkie-talkie into a plastic baggy, slid it shut and put it in the pocket of his windbreaker.

"If you say so," I said, looking upriver. The light was beginning to fade and a mist was rising from the water. I watched the silvery tip of Margaris's canoe grow smaller and smaller as it disappeared into the river's mouth. He had refused to wait for us.

"I know what I'm doing. I don't need your help," he'd said, slipping and dragging his canoe down the mud path toward Rowleys Bay.

When Joe offered to help pull the canoe through the mud, he'd waved him away. Once on the water Margaris's canoe had seemed to have a direction of its own in mind, which wasn't straight ahead. But Margaris's ferocity had won out.

"You see that spit of land on the left bank?" Joe pointed to a brown grassy area near the river's mouth.

"Walk out there and I'll pick you up. That way your feet won't get wet."

"You're kidding, right?"

"Okay, then, grab the end of the canoe and push."

The river's mouth seemed impossibly far as I doggedly paddled through the white-capped bay. Swells of water splashed into the canoe and pooled around the leather hiking boots Joe had given me to wear. They were two sizes too big for me, awkward and heavy. If we should capsize, I was convinced the boots would pull me down to a watery grave. But other than breathing water,

I couldn't imagine being any wetter. Already a chill had seeped into my socks.

Finally we neared the mouth of the Mink River. For a moment the mist thinned and on the right bank a sign materialized. It read: *No Wake*. Then it was gone, swallowed by the mist.

Like a last remnant of civilization, I told myself, bringing the wood paddle out of the water and shoving it back in. For the first time I didn't hit the canoe's side.

"See," Joe said, "you're a natural canoeist."

Yeah, just like Madonna's a natural blonde.

As we entered the river, the wide expansiveness of water and sky closed and the water flattened. Where the bay had felt open and unpredictable, the river felt primeval and foreboding. The thickening mist only heightened that feeling, making everything dreamlike and transitory.

The strange quiet made me feel I had entered another time and dimension. Though we were on a river searching for a lost girl with the dark coming on, I couldn't get over the clarity of the place. Not that I could see anything clearly but that everything was as it should be, as it was intended. Even the low rumble of thunder in the distance seemed right.

As a line of shaggy firs came into view, I forgot for a moment the tightness in my gut and breathed in the loamy earth smell of new life.

"It looks like the Canadian wilderness."

"Yup, that's what everyone says," Joe answered.

I waited for him to elaborate, but he didn't. Usually Joe was a pretty talkative guy. But since we'd unloaded the canoes, he didn't have much to say. His silence was making me even more uneasy. We both knew what we might find along this river.

Finally Joe broke the spell. "I've been watching your stroke. Not bad. You come over to the marina in June. I'll teach you to canoe."

Every summer Joe taught canoeing and kayaking at Rowleys Bay Resort. "Joe," I said, thinking about what Stephanie had told me. "Last summer, did you ever see Janell at the marina?"

When he didn't answer right away, I turned to look at him. He had the brim of his cap so low that it cast his sharply chiseled features in shadow, deepening the circles under his eyes. Somehow I had missed the gold navy insignia on the cap.

He shook his head no. "Why?"

For a moment I loosened my death grip on the paddle. "Stephanie Everson told me Janell had hooked up with an older boy last summer. And Janell was last seen hanging around the marina. There might be a connection."

I turned back and started paddling again. Suddenly the paddling got easier. "Hey. What just happened?"

"That's the way the river works. About every thirty minutes or so the current changes direction. Believe it or not this river has a tide."

With the current change, the ache in my right arm eased up. "How about we switch paddling sides?"

"Sure."

"There's Margaris." I pointed up ahead, spotting his silvery canoe through the fog. We had just rounded a curve in the river. Even with the current, Margaris still seemed to be having trouble keeping his canoe in a straight line.

"I'll let him know we're here," Joe said, giving two short blasts on the whistle around his neck.

Margaris turned around, gave a dismissive wave and continued paddling furiously.

"What a jerk," I huffed. "Why's he trying to outrun us? It's as if he's trying to get somewhere before we do."

"Yeah, it does seem like that." Joe's voice was cautious. "But that doesn't mean he's done anything."

"It doesn't mean he hasn't." Until I was proven wrong, Margaris was a suspect. "He's acting strange. Even considering his daughter's missing."

Joe picked up the two-way radio. "Mr. Margaris, turn on. Mr. Margaris."

There was no answer. "Mr. Margaris, wait there for us."

Again, no answer.

"Hell, you may be right. Let's see if we can catch him."

I felt the canoe's speed increase. As Joe paddled harder, water splashed into the canoe. My heart was pounding so hard in my chest I thought I might break a rib. I concentrated on matching his strokes paddle for paddle. We were gaining on Margaris. As he rounded a bend in the river, the mist cleared and something on the right bank caught my eye—something red.

I turned to tell Joe. Then I felt the canoe shift left.

"Turn around." Joe jerked his head quickly.

I turned. We were headed straight for a downed tree. Thick, tangled branches seemed to span the whole river. I stared at it in disbelief. The canoe was moving too fast toward it.

"Leigh," Joe shouted. "Back paddle."

I shoved my paddle in the water and brought it out faster and faster. But the tree branches were coming closer and closer.

"No," Joe shouted, "back, back."

I reversed my stroke, but it was too late. The canoe turned sideways. I scrambled left away from the tree branches.

"Leigh, don't."

The canoe struck the tree with a loud whack, pitching me over the side. Instantly my body was shoved down into the muffled, dark water. The only sound was my heart pounding in my ears. I opened my eyes. Everything was murky. I kicked my legs and pushed at the water with my arms, telling myself not to panic, not to breath in. I kept kicking my legs and pushing at the water, but I barely moved. The boots felt like bricks on my feet. I kicked harder. My lungs were burning. Suddenly my body rose and broke through the water. I gulped in air, spitting and coughing out water, still flailing my arms and kicking my legs.

"Take it easy," I heard Joe shout. "Take it easy. You're not going to drown. You've got a life vest."

I turned toward his voice. Joe and the canoe were a few feet away. I was about to shout, "Are you crazy?" when I realized he was right. I stopped flailing and kicking for a minute. Water lapped my chin, my feet hung down weighted by the boots, but I was floating.

"Okay, I'll bring the canoe around and haul you in." He hunched low in the canoe and moved forward toward the center, his hands inching along the sides. When he reached the center, he knelt down and started paddling toward me, shifting the paddle from side to side.

Breathe, I told myself. To keep down the panic I stared at the opposite shore as if memorizing its details: mud bank, tan reeds, yellowish-green fir trees.

Joe maneuvered the canoe beside me. "Here's what we're going to do. I'm going to lean the canoe toward you till the gunwale almost touches the water." He ran his gloved hand along the canoe's edge. "That's the gunwale. I want you to grab it and hold on. Then I'm going to lean the canoe in the opposite direction. That's when you haul yourself in. Got it?"

"Isn't there an easier way?" I didn't see how this was going to work. I had a vision of the canoe tipping over and hitting me on the head.

"Nope."

"Just get me out of here," I said through shivering lips.

He leaned the canoe so low in the river, water was lapping into the canoe.

"Grab the gunwale."

I reached for the gunwale, but my fingers didn't seem to be

working right. They couldn't hold on.

"Try again," Joe instructed.

I took a determined breath. This time I grabbed on and held tight.

"On the count of three. Ready?"

"Ready."

"One, two, three."

Just as he leaned the canoe in the opposite direction I threw first one leg, then the other leg into the canoe, and the rest of me followed. I lay in the canoe staring up at the gray sky, letting my heartbeat slow.

"You okay?" Joe asked, inching toward the back of the canoe.

I sat up. My clothes were so wet, I felt like I'd gained thirty pounds.

"Yeah," I said, crawling over the front seat.

As I sat down on the metal seat, cold shot up my spine right through the waterproof pants that hadn't kept me dry. The cold metal was as unforgiving as the water had been. My teeth were chattering. I wrapped my arms around myself. I could feel my wet underwear against my skin.

Behind me I heard Joe pull the dry bag toward him and open it. He unscrewed the thermos and poured something lemony-smelling into a cup.

"You'd better drink this."

"Joe," I said, turning and taking the cup in my shaking hands.

"Just drink. You need to get out of those wet clothes. I've got some dry stuff in the bag."

I gulped down the tea shaking my head at him.

"Why'd you do that? I had it under control. You have to learn to trust, Leigh. That's what canoeing is about, trust." He was moving the canoe around the tree and toward the left bank.

"Joe, I saw something." I pointed toward the right bank. "Over there. Up by those fir trees behind us. Something red. At first I thought it was a plant. But . . ."

Before I could finish, Joe had turned the canoe and was paddling hard toward the bank. Within seconds the canoe slid into the muddy bank and stopped.

He jumped out of the canoe and I was right behind him. The mud sucked at our feet. Though I made squishy, wet sounds when I walked, the warm tea was coursing through my body, staving off the cold.

"See it?" I pointed up the bank. Just at the edge of a line of trees was a splash of red.

"I'm going to radio Margaris. Let him know we're here." Joe pulled out the radio from the canoe. "Mr. Margaris, we've found something. Turn back."

No answer. "Mr. Margaris, respond. We've found something." Again no answer.

He slipped the radio into his jacket pocket. Then he opened the dry bag and pulled out a pair of pants, a hat, a fleece jacket and socks. "You need to get out of those wet clothes. Everything, even your underwear. And fast."

"Where am I going to do that?"

He pointed to a group of low-lying shrubs on the left. "Behind those."

"I'm not cold." I wasn't about to strip down behind some sparsely leafed shrubs.

Joe took a long look at my soggy clothes. I shifted from foot to foot trying to generate some body heat. The tea's benefits were quickly waning. I was pretty sure my hands were numb.

"Yeah, okay, water woman. Have it your way." He handed me a blue wool hat with a fringed tassel. "At least put this on. Wring out your hair first. And take off those gloves. Put your hands under your arm pits."

I took off the two sets of gloves and threw them in the canoe. Somehow the baseball hat had stayed on my head. I took it off and wrung out my wet hair. The wool hat smelled of fish, but I pulled it over my hair. I sat down on the bank and replaced the soggy socks and fleece jacket with the dry socks and flannel jacket. My underwear, shirt and pants would have to stay wet.

We had just started mucking up the bank when we heard Margaris shout behind us. "What is it?"

Joe stopped and turned toward him. "Maybe you should just let us take a look first."

Before Joe could finish his sentence, Margaris was out of the canoe and bounding up the bank. His feet made loud sucking sounds, and one of his sneakers came off.

"Damn," he said, bending down and pulling the sneaker out of the mud. He shoved his foot back into the sneaker and continued up the hill like a man being chased.

Joe reached the red object first. He picked it up and showed it to me. It was a small, red, microfiber backpack. The kind designed to be used as a purse. It had two straps and two Velcro pockets, both closed. Along both sides were long jagged slashes. It looked as if it'd been opened with a knife. The bottom was splattered with mud. This is what I had spotted right before the second river bend.

"This look familiar?" Joe extended the purse toward Margaris.

"No," he said impatiently.

"Mr. Margaris. Have you ever seen your daughter with this?" I asked. He had barely looked at it. How could he be so sure?

"I don't see everything she wears," he snapped. "Let's go. It's getting dark."

I didn't like his answer and I didn't like the way the purse had been slashed. I could tell Joe was thinking the same thing.

"Wait." Joe held up his hand. "Maybe we should take a look around here first."

"We're wasting time. My daughter could be out there tired

and cold and afraid." Margaris ran his hand over his thin, short hair as if trying to rid himself of something. Dark with rain, it stuck to his head.

"I think Joe's right. We can take a few minutes."

Margaris stared at me, the rings of his eyes so tight they looked black. I stared right back. "If anything happens to my daughter, it's on both your heads."

Joe ignored his threat. "Mr. Margaris, you go straight up into the woods. I'll go left. Leigh, you go right. We're about ten yards south of the Nature Conservancy's main trail. There's an offshoot on the right. Leigh, you should run into it. Look for the yellow circles nailed to the trees. We'll search for about fifteen minutes. If you get lost, just follow the river north till you hit the main trail and wait there. If anyone finds anything, blow your whistle."

I touched the whistle with my stiff, cold hands as I headed right into the woods. Almost immediately I lost sight of Joe and Margaris. For a few minutes I could hear their thrashing through the underbrush and then all was quiet except for the creaking of trees overhead and the slow drip of rain.

The forest was choked with vegetation struggling for light: tufts of emerald moss, blooms of orange mushrooms, bursts of marsh marigolds. Their earnestness made the woods even more oppressive. They were reminders of the struggle to live in a dark place where trees tangled overhead blocking the sky, making twilight night.

I found the offshoot trail Joe had mentioned. It oozed a soft dark mud that was the color of milk chocolate but had the consistency of quicksand. I stood for a moment, looking for the yellow tin circle trail marker. I found it just ahead nailed to a cedar. Slogging down the trail I fought the mud tugging on my damp wet boots. On either side of the trail, moss-slicked rocks offered some reprieve from the mud but required a deftness I was finding difficult—especially walking with my hands under my armpits. My nose twitched with the pungent smells of decaying leaves, cedar and profound dampness. Large raindrops plopped from tree branches, hitting my face, trickling down my neck. A deep coldness was settling on me, but I kept moving.

Suddenly I couldn't find the trail. All around me were trees and more trees, none of them with yellow tin circles.

"Get a grip, Leigh," I told myself. "You can retrace your steps. Or walk toward the river and follow it back." I figured I'd been walking about ten minutes. No one would fault me for going back.

"Or you could sit for a minute." I no longer felt cold, only sleepy.

I looked around for a spot. On my right was a small opening—a clearing where I could rest for a while.

I stumbled toward it. My desire for sleep so strong I wasn't sure I could make it there.

Even before I reached the clearing, I saw the body, lying face down in the open. I blinked my eyes and shook my head as if it was a hallucination that I could make go away. But it was still there. I walked slowly toward it, as if in a dream. There was no need to hurry because it was obvious she was dead.

Her right arm was twisted across her back in a position no one could sustain in life, the other under her head. And then there were the sickening smells of urine and feces that emanated from her soiled clothes.

She was wearing a white T-shirt and jeans. Her white skin showed where the shirt was torn. It seemed obscene. The skin was the color of ivory tinged blue. One leg was bent up beside her, the other straight. Both feet were bare. Her long blond hair rippled out across her shoulders and her face, the hair shimmering with glints of cold light. In the disarray of death the hair seemed tamed, as if it had been brushed. Though the body looked broken, it also seemed reassembled to mimic sleep, except for that one arm twisted across her back and the torn shirt.

I stood over the body, paralyzed. The word *no* was echoing in my head. Or was I saying it? There was no way to tell for sure who she was without disturbing her hair, without touching her. I fumbled for my whistle. Something shiny caught my eye. On her left hand, ring finger—a purple glassy ball.

I put the whistle in my mouth and kept blowing and blowing.

Margaris got there first. He came crashing through the woods like a man running from something. He stopped short when he saw the body and gave me a questioning look.

"I don't think it's Janell." I wasn't positive it wasn't his daughter. I'd only seen her picture. This girl was taller and thinner, her hair wavy. But it was someone's daughter.

Margaris bent down, reaching toward the body as if to turn it over.

"No. You better wait until the police get here."

He stood up and looked around like he didn't know where he was.

Then he walked around the body, bent down, and brushed the hair from her face.

"Oh," he said, standing up abruptly as if he had been burned.

"Is it Janell?" In the deeply shadowed woods, I couldn't see the face clearly from where I was standing.

He shook his head no. "How?" he whispered to himself. For a brief moment there was vulnerability in his eyes as they met mine. When he saw that I saw it, he blinked and turned away. His edge was back.

"Where's that other guy? What's his name, your partner?" Margaris pulled a radio from his jacket pocket, flipped the switch back and forth.

"Joe. His name is Joe." My eyes wanted to close. The adrenaline was seeping from me. I wanted to lie down, to sleep just for a minute.

He flipped the switch back and forth. "Come in, Joe. We found a body. Come in." There was no answer. Margaris tried again. No answer. He threw the radio into the trees, sending some crows squawking upward.

I was beyond cold. A numbness that felt quiet and peaceful was traveling up my body as I started walking around the periphery, edging my way toward the girl's face. My mind was taking quick, almost photographic glances at the body.

The bottoms of her bare feet were clogged with mud and leaves. The torn shirt didn't cover the soft swell of flesh that was too white, too blue. One arm was twisted across her back, the other under her head. A ring—no, a hair band with a purple glass ball—was wrapped around her finger. *She looks like she's sleeping. She* . . . I stopped, took a deep breath, then bent down.

Her eyes were open, blue and glazed, her mouth a terrible circle showing white teeth. There were dark stains round her upper neck and her face was bluish-red.

"Oh God, no," I said, my hand going over my mouth. "It can't be. I don't understand. Stephanie."

I tried to stand up but my legs wobbled and I fell back down into the leaves.

"Here," Margaris said as if from a great distance. I felt something heavy settle on my shoulders.

I tried to say something, but he slipped away into darkness.

"Leigh." Someone was calling me. I moved my mouth to answer, but no words came out. "Leigh," someone said again.

"Go away. Leave me alone," I kept trying to say, but no words came.

I moaned instead. I felt a warmth running down my throat

and into my belly. I opened my eyes and saw Joe kneeling over me, his face unusually stern. He put down the cup and started to rub my hands, slowly, gently.

I turned my head sideways. She was still there. Stephanie. It hadn't been a dream.

"Don't move," Joe said.

"I'm fine." I sat up. A rush of blood made me dizzy. "Where's Margaris?"

"He's down by the bank waiting for the police. When I got here you were out cold. I told you about changing. You could have been in serious trouble if Margaris hadn't covered you with his jacket. I started a fire and gave you more tea."

Just then, Margaris, Chet Jorgensen and two other uniformed men stepped into the clearing.

"It's Stephanie," I whispered. "It's Stephanie Everson."

"I know," Joe said.

"How could this happen?" I asked, trying to stand up, as if I needed to get distance from her. A wave of sleepiness washed up and over me. I sat back down. Then it all went blank again.

Chapter Six

May 20, Saturday

By the time I reached Highway 42 the rain had turned to sleet. Big solid drops blotted the windshield. Not quite snow, but close enough to make me worry about black ice. I clutched the steering wheel tightly with both hands. It seemed to quell the shakes that had overtaken my body after I'd left Rowleys Bay Resort.

Though my truck's heater was cranked into the red zone and the blower was on high, I was still cold. But at least the sleepiness was gone. At Joe's insistence, I'd changed back into my own clothes, minus my clammy underwear, in the women's washroom at Rowleys Bay Resort and eaten a large bowl of fish chowder. After that Chet had questioned me for over an hour in one of the resort's conference rooms. Finally he'd let me go with the promise that I'd show up Monday at the police station and make an official statement. He'd warned me not to discuss any details about the murder with anyone. I'd been too tired to argue. There'd be time to sort it all out tomorrow, when my mind was clear.

I'd called Jake at the cottage—no answer—then at his house and finally on his cell phone. But he hadn't picked up.

"There's been a murder," was all I'd said. "Not the Margaris girl. It's Stephanie Everson. I'll fill you in tomorrow." For all I knew he'd already taken off.

But even my muddled relationship with Jake couldn't keep my mind from seeing the body of Stephanie Everson, her oddly bent arm, the torn shirt, and the purple glass ring. It was all I could do just to keep my foot on the pedal, my thoughts on home.

Just get home, I told myself. *Then you can deal with it.*

As I drove down the gravel drive leading to the stone cottage, I could see the outside light twinkling through the night. I rolled down the truck's window. As always, the sharp clean air stung my lungs and quieted my mind.

Before entering the cottage, I stood for a moment in the falling sleet and listened to the distant waves. Then a high-pitched howl shattered my tranquility. Then another. Salinger knew I was home.

"All right. I'm coming."

The house was dark except for the amber glow of a table lamp in the living room window. I barely got the front door open when Salinger bolted past me, out the door, toward the field behind the house. I'd chase her later. First things first. I shut and locked the door behind me. I still wasn't comfortable with this laissez-faire country attitude about unlocked doors. And after tonight, who could blame me?

Kicking off my suede boots but keeping on my jacket, I breathed in the house's dank, musky smell. Even the heavy odor didn't dispel this hollow feeling I felt standing in the old and tired room.

"What you need," I told myself, "is wine, food and sleep. And in that order." When the shock wore off, and it eventually would, I wanted to be numb.

I walked through the dim living room into the kitchen. After flipping on the kitchen light, I took a wine glass from the drying rack, uncorked a bottle of pinot grigio and poured myself a very full glass, splashing more on the counter than in the glass.

The first swallow was sharp and satisfying. After the second swallow, warmth flooded my body and steadied my shaking hands. Leaning against the counter feeling the wine do its lovely work, I noticed that the kitchen looked different. Cleaner? No. Less cluttered.

Jake's wok was gone from its usual place next to the stove as well as his one cookbook—*Literary Recipes of 20th Century Poets.* I walked into the bedroom. The closet door was open and what few clothes he'd kept at the house were also gone. I switched on the bathroom light. Toothbrush, electric razor, brush, comb, deodorant—all gone.

There was no note in the bedroom. I went back to the kitchen. There on the counter under a coffee cup was a torn sheet of paper.

Leigh,

Cleaned out my stuff. When I get back, we'll talk. Check out poem on back.

Jake

P.S. I let Salinger out at 5.

I turned the paper over. On the back was a draft of one of his poems. The poem filled the entire page. From what I could decipher, it was about wolves and skin and two women. One line read: "skins fold out into themselves, even now/her scent, their scent everywhere." He'd entitled it, "Extinct." It was dedicated to L.

"Well, I guess that's that," I said, crumpling the paper and throwing it into the trash. I didn't need any reminders about extinctness or this relationship.

As I turned away, I noticed the answering machine light was blinking red.

"What now," I said, pressing the play button. Would this day never end? I took another swallow of wine.

I could hear the deep inhale and slow exhale of someone smoking. A short cough, then a scratchy, low voice I hadn't heard in months.

"Look, I'm leaving for Chicago tomorrow. Got hired as a chef at this new Pacific Rim restaurant called Jimbo's." She laughed. "Go figure—Hawaii by way of Wisconsin. Anyway, heard you're looking for a place. Can't guarantee how long you can have it. But if you want it, the key's under the mat. Pay the utilities. We can do the rent thing later." There was a long pause in which I could hear her take another deep drag on her cigarette. "I guess you can bring that dog of yours. Long as you keep it out of my stuff. That applies to you too."

I replayed the message again. Sarah Peck was leaving Door County and she'd offered me her place. I hadn't seen much of Sarah over the winter. Even in a group of villages as close together and sparsely populated as Door County, it was possible not to see someone for months. Last November I'd saved her life. I kept her painting, *Destroying Angels, by S. Peck,* over my bed as a reminder of how close we'd both come to dying that horrible night.

I finished the glass of wine, poured another and opened the back door. It had stopped sleeting. I called Salinger. There was a stirring in the field.

I called again. "Salinger, come." Obedience wasn't her strong point. Devotion was. It was a good tradeoff.

As I remembered, Sarah's house was an Airstream mobile home circa 1950. It stood on a bluff that had an incredible view of Lake Michigan. I'd never been inside the mobile home, but I'd been in the outbuilding where she painted. A mobile home would have none of the hominess of the cottage. But as far as I knew, no one had ever died there. It was a big incentive.

"Salinger, come on. We've got packing to do." Salinger emerged from the field wet and smiling.

I sat facing the fireplace and ate my microwaved turkey dinner, watching sparks shoot up the chimney. Luckily, I'd discovered the dinner at the back of the freezer. There had been a layer of permafrost over the plastic covering that I told myself had kept it extra fresh. The turkey was a little dry, but the mashed potatoes were pretty good. It's hard to mess up mashed potatoes. All in all, it didn't taste too bad, especially after half a bottle of wine.

I leaned back in the green velvet chair and nestled under the two blankets I'd dragged off the bed. While my dinner was being nuked, I'd stripped off the day's clothes and put on a flannel nightgown, terry robe and wool socks. Finally, my tight, tense muscles were starting to uncoil, and my body had lost that deep chill I'd had since I fell in the river. The chair once again seemed to outline and hold me. I would miss it. Salinger was sleeping in front of the fireplace. Every once in a while her body twitched. Probably dreaming about whatever she chased through the field behind the house every night but never caught.

I picked up the wine bottle and turned it in the firelight. There were maybe one, one and a half glasses left. It had been a brutal day that had ended on a ghastly note. I poured the wine to the top of the glass. Its pale blondness shimmered in the firelight.

Stephanie Everson, murdered. Janell still missing, maybe alive. Probably dead. What was the connection? Chet had reluctantly promised when he dropped me off at my truck that he would call if they found Janell.

I didn't want to go where my active imagination was headed—the men on the sex offenders list. I imagined every one of them right now was accounting to the police for his whereabouts in the last twenty-four hours.

I flashed on Stephanie's body. It didn't look like she'd been sexually assaulted, which was small compensation.

The wine's sting had dulled my senses and my head felt too

full. I picked up the empty plastic tray and fork and went into the kitchen. I stood for a long time looking at the phone. Jake never went anywhere without his cell phone. It was only 12:45 a.m. I could try him again.

I turned off the light and headed for the bedroom. It had been an impossible day and I wanted it over. I stood before the bathroom mirror combing through my tangled hair. Slowly, very slowly, tears made their way down my face. Then jagged, ugly sobs shook my body. She was only fifteen. That handsome woman with lots of character I'd imagined would never be.

Chapter Seven

May 1, twenty-three years earlier

"I spotted the body on a sandbar," said the canoeist, Ted Anders.

"In what condition would you say the body was?" the *Chicago Times* reporter asked.

Ted pushed his baseball cap further back on his head. "Condition? What do you mean? She was dead."

"Were there any visible wounds? Was the body clothed?" The reporter made a mental note to remember that exchange for the next staff meeting.

Ted looked at Bud expectantly, hoping he would answer. Bud hunched his shoulders. "I didn't see any wound," Ted said. "But you've got to remember that girl was covered in mud. She barely looked . . ." He struggled for the right word. ". . . human. Yeah, she was barely that."

"What about the clothes?"

"Just a T-shirt. I told Bud right away it was that missing girl."

"What made you think it was her?" the reporter asked.

"Well, who the hell else could it be? It was in all the papers about her. Though she looked older than fourteen."

"How do you mean?"

"Bigger like. She was a big one. For her age, that is."

The reporter winced at Ted's fishing metaphor. "You guys canoe the Des Plaines River a lot?"

Ted pulled his cap down over his eyes. "What's a lot?"

The reporter rephrased his question. "How often do you

canoe the river?"

"Once spring's here, pretty much every chance we get," Ted answered. "But I got to tell you, it's the first time we've found a body. I mean a human body."

Bud leaned down and picked up his fishing gear. "I hear they think the uncle did it."

The reporter closed his notebook. "That's what they're saying."

Chapter Eight

Sunday, May 21, Present

"Hello," I groaned into the phone.

"Leigh? It's Joe." He sounded surprised to hear me answering my own phone.

"Joe?" I stared at the digital clock—4:19. The room was shrouded in darkness.

"Yeah, Joe Stillwater. Man, you sound terrible. You sick? You shoulda' listened to me yesterday by the river and gotten out of those wet clothes."

My throat felt raw and there was that familiar tightening at the back of my head that always preceded one of my migraines.

"I'm fine," I said, trying to clear my throat. "How do you sound when someone wakes you at four in the morning?"

"Okay, okay. Chill. Listen, I'm only calling because I thought you should know. Someone found Janell. She's here at the hospital. The police are trying to keep it quiet, but I figured you had a right to know. Seeing how you helped."

I sat up so quickly I knocked Salinger off the bed. She let out a complaining bark.

"I'll be there in fifteen minutes. What floor is she on?"

"I didn't call so you'd come here. I thought I'd get your machine. I didn't think you'd pick up. Anyway, I wouldn't have called so early but I get off shift in an hour, then I'm leaving straight for my sister's place in Fond du Lac. We got a big family thing going. Elliott's flying in, and guess who's picking him up? So I didn't know when I'd get a chance to call you. But I wanted to put your mind at rest, at least about Janell. It was a pretty rough day yesterday. You finding Stephanie. Besides, I don't think the cops are letting anyone near her except her parents. You know, because she was with Stephanie the night before. So you should go back to sleep."

Shouldering the cordless phone to my ear, I'd already pulled on a pair of black wool trousers and was looking in the medicine cabinet for my migraine pills. The tightening was banding my head. Damn, why did I drink an entire bottle of wine last night?

"Just tell me the floor, Joe." I filled a glass of water, threw back two pills and washed them down. The label on the bottle read: *take with food.* But I had to derail this migraine or I'd be marooned in a dark room all day.

"Okay, okay. Four. I know you'd get it out of one of the nurses somehow anyway."

"How bad is she hurt?"

"Not sure. Might be just an observation deal." Joe had suddenly gone quiet.

"Who found her? Where's she been?"

"Don't know."

I let out an exasperated sigh.

"Joe, what do you know?"

"I know I was right about this. Didn't I say she'd be found alive?"

There was an uncomfortable silence.

"Yeah, that you were right about."

I punched four on the elevator panel and watched the numbers light as the elevator ascended. My headache had eased, but my throat still hurt and my stomach was grumbling over the chocolate chip breakfast bar I had scarfed down on the way over. It was 5:05, and the day shift would be coming on soon.

For a moment I felt lightheaded as a barrage of hospital smells and images overcame me: the antiseptic scent of fresh linen, the interchangeable faces of the nurses and their endless poking and assurances, Tom patting my bald head, making some lame joke about bald women being sexy.

My two-year anniversary was next week, and I hadn't made an appointment with my oncologist in Chicago for my yearly checkup. I knew all the psychological tricks cancer survivors play on themselves, and I was back to playing the most elemental one—denial.

The doors opened to the subdued quiet of the pre-breakfast hour. In the dim light the pale green walls appeared anemic and sickly. Across from the elevators was the nurses' station with its familiar warning sign: *Only family members are permitted to visit patients.* As I walked toward the station, I glanced down one corridor and saw Chet Jorgensen standing outside one of the rooms, looking wired. Although his head was down and his arms crossed over his chest, he was shifting from side to side. He was so lost in thought, he didn't even notice me approach.

"Chet," I kept my voice low. "How's Janell?"

He started as if I'd materialized out of thin air. "How'd ya get past the nurse?"

"There was no nurse," I answered, taken aback by his abruptness.

"You can't be here now, Leigh. So you better turn around there and head back home." There was a guardedness in his voice I'd never heard before. His normally clear blue eyes were bloodshot and darkly circled. He looked like he'd been up all night. Which was supported by the fact that his uniform had the same grease spot on the pocket flap that was there yesterday.

"C'mon, Chet. I just want to know what you've got so far. Is there a connection between Janell's disappearance and Stephanie's murder? Then I'll go."

"Didn't Joe tell you not to come here?"

"You knew I'd come. It's my job. Why are you acting like this?"

He took my arm and led me down the corridor to the elevators. When we reached the elevators, he let go of my arm. I still felt the pressure of his grip through my down jacket. "Look, I don't need your interference this time. I'm handling it. Okay, then?"

"Can you at least tell me if she's going to be all right?"

"Can't tell you nothin'." His jaw muscles tensed.

"You can tell me how she is."

He punched the down button and folded his arms over his massive chest. "She hasn't said nothin'. Now get goin'."

"What do you mean?"

He stared at me a full minute, as if he were trying to put a name to my face. The sound of the elevator doors opening broke his trance.

"She says she don't remember nothin' about it. What happened, that is. That's enough for the paper. And I'd better not see any details about the murder in there. Now get outta here."

He was holding the doors open with his hand, but I didn't step inside.

"There's something else, isn't there?" I didn't know if there was something else, but in my experience there usually was.

Chet was about to say something when the sound of a raised voice drew his attention. Chet let the elevator door close.

Margaris was walking stride for stride with a tall, dark-haired man in a white coat who was ignoring him.

"Don't think I don't know what you're implying," Margaris said, jabbing his finger at the man's back.

The doctor stopped in front of the nurses' station, looked behind the counter and then down the hall. As if on cue, a nurse came scurrying on squeaky white shoes from the other corridor and fluttered behind the desk.

"Sorry, Doctor Risner, but we had a problem with one of the cardiac patients who didn't want to take his meds. But everything is fine now. Are there any instructions for our special patient?"

The nurse smiled one of those professional grimaces at Margaris that was meant to indicate that the proverbial "we" had everything under control including you.

"No. Just have Mr. Margaris fill out the discharge papers," Risner said "and they can be on their way. Here's her chart. Can you hand me Mr. Fields's chart?"

"Did you hear me, Risner?" Margaris said in a low menacing tone. "If my doctor finds something wrong, I'll be talking to my lawyers."

Other than a slight flush deepening Risner's olive skin, there was no indication that the doctor was irritated. He didn't even turn to address Margaris, but read the open chart as he spoke. "Mr. Margaris, as I told you and your wife earlier, there's nothing medically wrong with your daughter. Why she says she doesn't remember what happened, I can't say. But the MRI and brain scan were all normal. She has sustained no injury to her head. In fact, she had no injuries at all," Risner turned toward Margaris, "except what we discussed." He looked over Margaris at Chet and me and lowered his voice. "When you get back home I would advise you to have her see a specialist." With that Risner took the chart from the nurse, scanned it quickly and turned to leave.

Margaris's fisted hands went slack by his sides. He looked as if he'd been punched. For a second I almost felt sorry for him, then he opened his mouth. "We'll see about that, Risner," he shouted at the doctor's retreating back. "I'll sue this whole damned hospital if there's anything wrong with her." Even his threat sounded sad and diluted.

"Mr. Margaris," I said, walking over to him. "How's Janell? Is there anything I can do to help?"

"I'm taking her home now," he spat in my face. "We'll see who needs a psychiatrist."

Up close, the strain of the ordeal was evident on his face. His skin was a sallow yellow color and his eyes were unfocused and blurry.

"She doesn't remember anything," he said to me. "Nothing. She remembers Stephanie leaving the marina and that's it. That's it. God knows what happened to her." He stopped, put his hand across his forehead and rubbed his temples.

"Mr. Margaris." Chet had come up beside me. "Don't you think it would be a good idea to go see how your wife's doin'? She didn't look too good earlier."

You would have thought Chet had told him to go kill his wife. "Listen, you and your whole damned police department bungled this thing from day one. My daughter's friend is dead and my daughter was right under your noses. And you couldn't find her."

"We did a thorough search as best we could."

Margaris laughed. "Yeah, that's the problem."

Chet had gone a nasty shade of red. "You know she wasn't there as well as I do."

"The fact remains that my daughter was missing for two days and you didn't find her. If it hadn't been for that mechanic guy, she might still be out there. You know where this guy found her?" Margaris asked me, not waiting for my answer. "Inside the engine room on one of those ferries to Washington Island. How the hell did she get there, I want to know. Huh?"

"It's hard to say about that, Mr. Margaris. That's what we have to find out about. And that's why it'd be a good idea there if you let me do my job," Chet said.

"You know I could have you fired. Just like that." Margaris

snapped his fingers in Chet's face.

"I don't know about that. But even if you could, that wouldn't change what happened to your daughter, mister. Now would it?" Chet was about as mad as I'd ever seen him.

For a long hard minute they did that male stare-down thing. Eye to eye like two stags I'd seen once on one of those nature shows. If they'd had antlers, they'd be locked right now. Margaris raised his fisted right hand. And though Chet outweighed him by at least a hundred pounds, I thought Margaris was going to take a swing at him. Then Margaris turned abruptly and walked back in the direction he had come.

I looked down at my shoes, not wanting to meet Chet's eyes. The nurse, who'd heard the entire exchange, busied herself shuffling charts.

Chet strode toward the elevators and pushed the down button. I followed him.

"Can't you hold Janell here?" I asked Chet. "She might remember something about Stephanie."

"Leigh, why don't you go home like I told you?"

The door opened and we got in. Chet pushed B and L. His way of making sure I was getting off in the lobby. He was probably going to the cafeteria in the basement.

"Just answer me one thing. Then I'm outta your hair. Who's the guy that found Janell?"

The door opened on the lobby. I didn't move to get off. Finally, Chet pushed the open button and let out a deep sigh. "Andy Weathers," he said, not looking at me.

I got off and watched the doors close on Chet. I wondered why he had relented. After all, there were only two ferry lines that went to Washington Island. It wouldn't have taken me much effort to track down the guy. I didn't like it or the defeated look on his face.

Chapter Nine

Sunday, May 21

The sun was an orange disc slicing the horizon when I pulled onto Highway 42 and headed north to Gills Rock, the departure point for all Washington Island ferries. I needed to talk to Andy Weathers. He wasn't listed in the Door County directory and when I called the ferry line, a recorded message told me where to buy tickets.

The roads were still wet, but the heavy cloud cover had dispersed and the air had a lightness to it. If the weather held, it would be a fine day. For the Margarises, I thought. But not for the Eversons.

I slowed for the steep descent into Egg Harbor just as the bells of St. Patrick's church rang out. As I passed the gray-brick, gothic church, I saw the cemetery behind the church and said a silent prayer for Stephanie and my mother.

Last Sunday had been the first Mother's Day since my mother's death I hadn't visited her grave. As the last bell sounded, I wondered if my brother had remembered to bring flowers. I knew my father hadn't. If he had even gone.

What had he said last year? "She wasn't my mother."

Since my father had moved in with my brother Zach and his family, he'd almost made a religion of punishing all the women in his life. Somehow we had all let him down—my mother for dying, and me for leaving.

When I reached Gills Rock, the morning sun was arching

over the trees. I parked the truck by the ferry dock, got out, and breathed in a mingled scent of cedar and new earth. Surely a good omen that spring was resurrecting itself once again. I walked toward the ticket booth. The first ferry to the island was at eight. It was now seven-ten.

The tastefully weathered booth was empty. A sign read *Tickets can be bought at Death's Door restaurant.* I'd been to Washington Island enough times to know that the ferry had to pass through Porte des Morts strait or Death's Door to reach the island. A daring feat when Native Americans crossed in birch-bark canoes, but quite safe in a car ferry. Still, the sign did give one pause.

The restaurant, Death's Door, overlooked the harbor and the ferry launch. It, too, was tastefully weathered a silvery gray. Its exterior was festooned with fishing nets and buoys. An "Open" sign was in the window. I pushed on the door and a bell tinkled.

"Just have a seat and I'll be right with you," someone called from the back of the restaurant.

I sat down on one of the red leather stools by the counter. The restaurant had continued its nautical theme on the inside as well. Again, fishing nets were strung around the walls. They held starfish, seashells and a few life preservers, like you find on a commercial ship. The décor befitted a restaurant near the ocean. I doubted there were any starfish in Lake Michigan or Green Bay. And the only shells I'd ever seen were mussel shells. But I was hardly an expert on northern Wisconsin marine life.

"What can I do you for?" A woman walked toward me from the kitchen area wiping her hands on a white cloth. The best word to describe her was voluminous. She had to be close to six feet tall. Her body was big-boned, solid and waistless. She was wearing a V-necked red and black striped sweater that showed a lot of cleavage and black stretch pants that did nothing to subdue her full hips. Atop her head was a yellow ponytail held in a blue denim scrunchie that bounced when she walked. In the middle of one of her ample breasts rested a black-lettered nametag that read *Roz*. A web of wrinkles creased her eyes and mouth. She looked about forty, a hard forty.

"Cup of coffee," I said. My throat was longing for a cup of mild chamomile tea. But I needed the adrenaline, and this didn't look like the kind of place that served anything but straight Lipton—one bag still wrapped beside a cup of hot water.

She took a plastic-clad menu from behind the counter and placed it in front of me. Her only concession to restraint was a lack of makeup. But her ruddy complexion didn't need any help.

"We just opened," she said, pouring me a cup of coffee. "You takin' the eight o'clock ferry to the island?"

"That depends. I'm looking for Andy Weathers."

"Then you're takin' the eight o'clock ferry." She scratched the back of her neck with the tip of her pen. "What do you want to eat? Nothin' fancy, I hope, 'cause I'm the only one here today. I let my cook off for family business." She shrugged her shoulders. "Whatta you gonna do?"

"Where exactly can I find Andy?"

"Who wants to know?" She gave me one of those looks I'd become familiar with since living in Door County, a mix of suspicion and honest curiosity. "You're not one of his friends, 'cause I know all his friends. Unless he's been holding out on me."

I held out my hand. "Leigh Girard from the *Gazette*. Maybe you've read some of my stuff?" I asked, hoping to allay her suspicions.

She shook my hand, but there was some hesitation. "Oh sure, I know who you are. Nobody killed, I hope."

I winced.

"That was something—about the Pecks. You know, I knew

Sarah in high school. I always thought she was a little . . ." She twirled her finger near her head. "You know, strange."

Apparently the news about Stephanie Everson's murder hadn't spread yet. And I wasn't going to tell Roz about it—or discuss the Pecks with her, for that matter. "What I want to see Mr. Weathers about is that girl he found hiding on the ferry."

"Girl hiding on the ferry? That's the first I heard about it. Some kid run away from home or something?" She hooked the pen on her sweater's neckline.

"Something like that. Where can I find Mr. Weathers?" She seemed to be evading my question. I wondered why.

"That's the third runaway I've heard about. It's like an epidemic lately. Kids can't take the isolation up here, I guess. Most of them end up going to Milwaukee or Chicago. Livin' on an island can be real tough."

"Where can I find Mr. Weathers?" I asked for the third time.

She looked down. She was considering whether to tell me.

Something won her over. "If he's not at the dock working on a boat or on a ferry run, he's at his house. It's on Green Bay Road, about half a mile down from the dock. Gray stone cottage with red shutters. It's set in a bit. Just look for the sign out front, says Weathers Boat Repairs. Tell him when you see him that Roz says tonight's okay. So he better get his butt back here. Tell him that ferry ain't the only thing needs lubricating." She winked at me, her friendliness back. "Now what's it gonna be?"

Though I wasn't hungry, I ordered two eggs over easy, hash browns and wheat toast. I had time to kill before the ferry, and Roz just had a way about her that made you want to please her.

Chapter Ten

Sunday, May 21

It was cold and the waves were running high with white caps, but I decided to stay on deck. I hadn't taken my car, and there was a chain smoker nervously puffing away inside the enclosed deck area. I only wished I'd worn a sweater under my down jacket. I sat huddled against the steel mesh fencing, watching the light glitter the green water. But the sunlight did little to warm me. Cold was beginning to be a condition with me.

By the time we docked, my throat had started to ache even when I didn't swallow. I pressed the glands on the sides of my neck; they felt swollen and hot. When I got home, I'd take some aspirin, the universal cure for most everything.

Andy Weathers wasn't at the dock, nor was he on a ferry run. The woman at the ticket booth told me he had the day off. So I walked up Green Bay Road, a cold wind in my face.

Though his place wasn't visible from the road, it wasn't hard to find. Just as Roz had described, there was a Weathers Boat Repair sign at the entrance to the grassy driveway. Below it was a black metal mailbox. The name Weathers was painted in white letters across it. There were no numbers.

As I walked down the narrow tree-edged drive, strains of classical music wafted through the air. I wasn't sure, but it sounded like the dense tones of Bach.

The red-shuttered cottage was set in a sunny clearing like a gingerbread house. I stood on the stone steps and rang the bell several times before the music dimmed and I heard someone moving around inside.

A tall, thin man with a cleft chin and black-rimmed glasses opened the door. If he was Roz's boyfriend, they were the most unlikely couple I'd ever seen. As full-figured and obvious as she was, he was fine-boned and subtle—almost delicate. His light brown hair waved gently back from his high forehead. He was wearing a black turtleneck sweater and khaki trousers. A pipe was firmly planted between his teeth. Just the thought of them having sex was so incongruent, I almost laughed out loud.

"Yes," he said, taking the pipe out of his mouth.

"Hi," I began. I took off one glove and offered him my hand. "I'm Leigh Girard from the *Door County Gazette.*"

He looked at me as if I were trying to sell him magazine subscriptions.

"Roz gave me directions to your place," I added.

As if I'd said the magic words, he shook my hand, then swung the door wide inviting me in. I followed him into a low-ceilinged, beamed room where a fire was crackling in the grate. Paneled in dark wood, the room was cozy and warm, like a nest. Two burgundy wing-backed chairs flanked the stone fireplace, each with a matching side table. There was a large bookcase against one wall, and between the front windows was a roll top desk. The only thing that seemed out of order was an open book on one of the chairs.

"You've come about the girl," he said, turning to face me. Light from a front window illuminated a white scar that interrupted his one eyebrow.

"Chet Jorgensen told me you found her," I said.

"You want some coffee? You look near froze."

"Sure." I was jittery with caffeine, but I was so cold I would have drunk motor oil if it was hot.

"Have a seat." He gestured toward the wing chairs. "Fire'll

warm you up."

He placed his pipe in an ashtray on one of the side tables and disappeared into the kitchen.

I sat down and slipped off my other glove. The fire felt warm on the side of my face. As I took out my notebook, I leaned forward to read the book's title: *Zen and the Art of Motorcycle Maintenance.* Mechanic maintaining self.

He returned with two mugs of coffee. He handed me one, then sat down in the adjacent wing chair, placing the book on the table.

"You know Roz then?" he asked, crossing his legs. He was wearing black leather slippers and argyle socks. His clothes seemed at odds with his profession.

"Sort of," I hedged. "She says tonight's okay. And something about getting yourself back tonight for a . . . a lubrication." I felt myself blush.

He smiled. "If I know Roz, it was my butt she wanted back. Am I right?"

"That's what she said. Now about Janell Margaris." I took a sip of coffee. It had a nutty taste, probably some special blend. I put the mug on the table and opened my notebook.

"What do you want to know?" He put down his mug and picked up the pipe.

"Where exactly did you find her?"

"She scared the hell out of me." He tapped the ashes from his pipe into the ashtray. "She was in the engine room. I didn't see her at first. Then I heard this noise, like an animal crying. It was coming from under one of the tarps we keep in there. When I lifted the tarp, there she was all huddled up and shivering. I couldn't get anything out of her. I couldn't even get her out from under the tarp. So I called the police."

"Did she say anything at all?" I took a sip of coffee. He was a reporter's dream—forthcoming and descriptive.

"She wouldn't even tell me her name."

"Was she hurt?"

"Not that I could see. But her shirt was ripped. From here to here." He ran his finger from his collarbone to his mid chest. There was smudged grease under his nail. "And her hair was matted and dirty-looking, like she'd been out in the rain."

"What time was this that you found her?"

"Nine-thirty or so."

"What were you doing on the ferry at that time?"

"Didn't Roz tell you?" He smiled. "I'm the mechanic. I have a contract with both ferry lines. Sometimes I even crew for them. They called me after their last run yesterday. They wanted me to take a look at the engine. It wasn't running right."

"Why so late?"

"When else was I going to do it? The line runs all day. If there was something I couldn't fix, they needed to know ASAP. Especially with the weekend tourist trade."

"Have you any idea how long she'd been hiding on the boat?"

He opened the table drawer and pulled out a long, white fuzzy pipe cleaner and inserted it into the pipe's stem. "Can't say. Though if she'd been on their last run at six, they'd a found her. They always do a check before docking the ferry for the night."

"Would it be hard for her to sneak on the boat without anyone knowing?"

"It's kept in the harbor. All she'd have to do is climb a fence." He pushed and pulled the pipe cleaner back and forth in the pipe's stem. Then threw the pipe cleaner into the fire. I watched it curl black.

"Did she say anything at all about where she'd been?"

"Like I said, she didn't say anything. She just kept crying and acting scared."

"Acting? What do you mean?"

"There was something about the way she kept pulling on her hair and twisting her hands. It seemed put on. Then there were her eyes. When she looked at me, I could tell she was gauging my reaction. 'Am I convincing him? Does he buy it?' I could see she didn't believe what she was saying. You know the best liars are the ones who've convinced themselves that the lie is the truth." He took a deep breath and let it out through his mouth. "Wherever she was, she probably doesn't want her parents knowing. Hence the act."

"Something could have happened to her," I said, even though I suspected he was right. "You said her shirt was torn and her hair dirty."

"That coulda been all part of the act. You didn't see her."

The image of Stephanie Everson's dead body flashed across my brain: the twisted arm, the hair across her face, that one arm under her head, her soiled clothes.

"Ms. Girard? Are you all right?" Weathers's voice broke through the image. "Ms. Girard?"

I looked at Weathers, then down at my notes. Then back at him. I read my last notation. It said, "Part of an act."

"The police," I began, "what happened when they arrived?"

"A policewoman talked her out and they took her away. You know, that one from Brown County, the African-American cop. What's her name, Hallaway? Whatever she told that kid, it got her out of there pretty quick."

I hadn't met Deputy Chief Celeste Hallaway, but I'd heard of her. She was both tough and ambitious.

"I made a statement," continued Weathers. "And that was it." He unscrewed the stem of his pipe and blew several times into it, making a whistling sound, then screwed the pipe back together. "Do you think this girl's disappearance has anything to do with that murdered girl?"

"How do you know about that?" My question came out a

little too sharp.

He pinched some tobacco from a black, leather pouch, filled the bowl of his pipe, and lit it, puffing slowly as clouds of smoke rose. "I overheard the police saying something about the girls being friends."

I didn't answer. Was he pumping me for information? He wouldn't be the first person to try that.

"They also said something about the murdered girl being the last person to see that girl I found. Before she disappeared."

"Stephanie Everson," I said. "Her name was Stephanie Everson." The room suddenly felt claustrophobic, choked with the cloying smells of burning wood, furniture polish and coffee.

Again the image of Stephanie Everson flashed across my brain. This time sitting in her living room stroking her cat, Baby. I blinked to make it go away.

"Did you know her?" He stared at me, searching my face. I held his gaze. Then something registered in his eyes.

"You're the one the police were talking about, aren't you? The reporter who found the body." He almost seemed gleeful about his discovery. "Chet mentioned it was a reporter. He didn't say the name."

Anger was coursing through my body along with his designer coffee. I didn't know whom I was angrier at: Chet for being such an idiot or Weathers for prying.

"Unless you have something to add, I'll be on my way. And thank you for your time."

I shoved the notebook in my purse and closed the flap.

"I'm right, aren't I? I can see it in your eyes. That must have been horrific finding her body that way."

"What you see in my eyes is lack of sleep." His pity felt voyeuristic.

"Sorry. I don't mean to upset you. It's just . . . you look like you need to talk to someone." He was like a dog with a bone.

"You don't have a clue what I need." As I zipped up my jacket, my hands were shaking again.

He drew on his pipe and exhaled a perfect ring that wavered between us. "Maybe not. But I do know one thing. Keeping something like this bottled up only makes it worse. It'll eat you up. That's why you came here, isn't it? This need to do something, anything. Just to keep ahead of the pain. But the sad fact is no matter what you do, it won't take it away. And it won't change things. The girl will still be dead. And you won't feel any better."

"I'm writing a story," I told him, getting up from my chair. "Not trying to feel better."

"Sometimes," he said, blowing another circle, "it's the same thing."

Chapter Eleven

"Tell me how you found her." Annie Everson stood at her kitchen window with her back to the room, washing dishes and staring out at the green that was her backyard. As she picked up a glass, it slipped from her hands and fell against the counter, shattering. "I'm so clumsy. I don't know what I'm doing."

Ben Everson stood up. "Let me get that, honey, before you cut yourself." He was a big man, broad-shouldered and muscular, with jet-black hair, thick and straight like a horse's mane. He was wearing a plaid shirt, dark blue jeans and work boots. He had the look of a man who worked outdoors.

She turned from the window. "Why don't you get going? It must be time to pick up Teddy." Water was dripping from her hands. She wiped them on the front of her sweater. In the bright kitchen light, her gray eyes appeared overly large for her small gaunt face. Underneath them were puffy bluish circles. The imprint of grief was on her face.

This was what I had been avoiding since I found Stephanie Everson's body in the woods—this moment in the tiny kitchen, telling Annie Everson about finding her murdered daughter.

"Sure," Ben said, walking toward the wooden coat rack by the back door. "I guess I could leave now."

He slipped his coat from the rack. "I should be back in a few hours." He hesitated, looking at his wife expectantly. He wanted something, some sign that they would get through this together. When it didn't come, he closed the door behind him.

I doubt if Annie had noticed. She was looking at me, waiting for me to relate the awful moment I had found her daughter.

"It was in a clearing. Up an embankment near the Mink River," I started, not sure how much I should tell her.

"Was she . . . did it look like she'd been . . . ?" She rubbed her forehead with the palm of her hand. The unspeakable question hung in the air. "Ben identified her. He didn't say much, except it was Stephanie. No one will tell me any details. They think I can't handle it. They still have her. I want her home. But they still have her. They need to do tests. That's what they call it. Tests. Like I don't know they're cutting up my little girl." She seemed to drift away. I wished she'd sit down. Her fragility was frightening. She was wearing the same bulky sweater and skirt from yesterday.

"Annie, why don't you sit down," I suggested, gesturing toward one of the ladder back chairs.

She stared over my head as if she hadn't heard me. To sit down was to give in to the grief.

"Tell me what you saw. I need to know. My imagination is going wild. I have to know the truth. Don't spare my feelings." Clearly she was in shock. In my experience I'd seen two reactions to death. Either the person fell apart or the person went stone quiet as if a steel door had suddenly shut, separating them from the rest of the world. I could deal with the spent emotion. The quiet was a barrier I found impossible to breach.

I thought back to the scene, the horrible images rising up. "She looked like she was sleeping." I swallowed hard. It was a half-truth.

"Were her clothes on?" She crossed her arms tightly against her chest.

"Yes." There was no reason to tell her about the torn T-shirt.

"The police said they thought she was strangled. Is that what you think? Is that how it seemed to you?" She was squeezing her upper arms.

I nodded my head yes, seeing Stephanie's face, bluish-red and swollen, the open mouth, and the bruised neck. "That'd be my guess."

She took a long, hard breath as if surfacing from under water. "Who would do such a thing? For what reason?" For a moment I thought she would cry. Then she recovered herself.

She needed to talk. I was there to listen. "You know when the kids were little I used to be afraid of flying. Because I thought, if I died, who would take care of my babies? Sure, they'd still have their father. But kids need a mother. Once they got older I lost my fear. All those years I was afraid of the wrong thing."

For a moment she gazed up at the veined, white ceiling. When she spoke her voice was hard. "I want him caught. I want him to suffer for what he did to my sweet girl."

I gazed around the kitchen, trying to distance myself from this unbearable grief. A green and white viney wallpaper wove its way from floor to ceiling. Under the wooden clothes rack was a pair of muddy boots. There were two unwashed plates, a baking dish and a pot beside the sink. One glass, one bowl and silverware were drying on a rack. The rich smell of cooked meat lingered.

I reached in my purse for my notebook, flipped it open. Maybe I could do something to give her grief an outlet. "Tell me about yesterday. After I left. What did Stephanie do?"

I watched her eyes fill with tears. She swiped at them so hard she left two red marks on her cheekbones. "I'm not going to cry," she said. "Stephanie wouldn't like that. It would embarrass her."

She pulled out a chair and finally sat down. "That's what's eating me up inside. I worked all day on that damned rug. It was a commission, and the woman wanted it by Monday. Ben was in Green Bay for a DNR district meeting most of the day.

By the time I finished, it was after seven. When I came in, I asked Ben where Stephanie was and he didn't know. He assumed she was at a friend's house, because her bike was missing. Then Chet showed up. They found her bike and the canoe at Rogers Lake."

"Canoe?" I hadn't heard anything about a canoe. That might explain how Stephanie ended up on the other side of the river.

"We keep it on Conservancy land, near Rogers Lake." She folded her hands on the table in front of her as if in prayer.

"Do you have any idea what Stephanie was doing in the woods?"

"Probably looking for Janell. Around two, she stuck her head in the door. Said something about helping the police. All I said was, 'Did you call your father?' Nothing else. I didn't even look up. That was the last time I would ever see my daughter. And I didn't even look up."

She put her head down.

I resisted the urge to touch her arm in comfort. I sensed how that might cause her to fall apart. "Did Stephanie have a red backpack purse?"

"Why?" She raised her head.

"We found one in the woods." Chet didn't want me telling any details. But I figured Annie had a right to know. "It's what led to us . . . to *my* finding her."

"What do you mean?"

I explained to her about finding the purse, omitting the slashes and our search.

"Yes, she had one."

"Do you have any idea what she usually carried in it? Because it was empty, when we found it."

"The usual girl stuff. Brush, comb, a compact, wallet."

"What about her cell phone?" I asked. "Would she have had that with her?"

"Cell phone? Stephanie doesn't have a cell phone."

"Your cell phone. The one you called her home on. When she was down at the marina with Janell. Before she disappeared."

"We don't have a cell phone. Where did you get that idea?"

"Stephanie," I said. "She told Russell Margaris and me that you called her home on the cell phone. Didn't Russell mention it?"

"No. I don't know why she would say that."

I didn't know either. But it was curious.

"I think Stephanie might have been covering for Janell again." I wondered how much of her story had been a lie.

"What do you mean, 'again'?"

"Stephanie told me that she had covered a few times for Janell last summer so she could meet up with this guy. Then her conscience got the better of her. That's what caused the strain in their friendship."

She shook her head from side to side. "Isn't that the way, huh? Janell Margaris is running around with some guy behind her parents back and she turns up okay. And my daughter ends up dead."

A strong wind must have come up, because I could see the dense green moving across the window behind her. I listened to the slow, patient tick of the kitchen clock.

"You think there's a connection. Don't you? Between Janell's disappearance and what happened to Stephanie?"

I fidgeted with a ring on my finger. I wanted to say no. I wanted to walk out of her kitchen with my story and be done with it. "I don't know. There could be."

"You'll find out for me. Please." It wasn't a question.

"Annie," I began to protest. I had stuck my neck out once before and nearly been killed. But in the end, I had been right. "Sure. I can do that."

She put her hand over mine. "She must have liked you to

have told you those things. I'm glad you're the one who found her."

I crossed County Route ZZ and drove down the long, winding road to the Margaris house. Annie Everson was right; I did think there was a connection between Janell's disappearance and Stephanie's murder. I had to talk to Janell. Maybe I could get her to tell me what had really happened to her. Andy Weathers's assessment of Janell only confirmed what Dr. Risner had said. They were both skeptical about her memory loss.

I hadn't called because I didn't want to give Margaris a chance to hang up on me. As I pulled into the clearing, the house seemed too still.

I stood beside the wooden Indian and rang the bell. No one answered. Even as I rang again, I knew they were gone. I trudged around the house, destroying my suede boots for good. When I reached the tall windows, I cupped my hands and looked in. All the furniture was draped in white sheets. It looked like the house had been closed up for the season.

I pulled my cell phone from my purse and called the Bay Hospital.

"I'm a family friend," I began when the ICU nurse answered. "I want to bring Janell some flowers."

"Janell Margaris was discharged this morning," the nurse told me in a measured tone.

"Did her parents say if they were taking her back to Chicago?"

"Why don't you give them a call and find out. Since you're such good friends."

I hung up and walked down to the pier. The water was moving toward the bay, the chill wind ruffling it as if it were brushing the water. I looked upstream as if I could see Stephanie from here, as if she were still there, lying so still in the woods, waiting to be found by me—so carefully arranged, her hair across her face as if it had been brushed that way. Had I told the police about that? About how Margaris had moved it. I couldn't remember.

I walked back to my car. I had until Friday to move into Sarah's place. I'd be back before then. But before I left, I needed to talk to Chet. I called the station and was told he had the day off. I didn't want to delay my trip. And what I wanted to tell him couldn't wait until I got back from Chicago.

Chet Jorgensen's truck was parked on Highway 42 in front of Bailey's Roadhouse, a battered claustrophobic bar and restaurant in Egg Harbor just south of County E. Its white paint was grayed, chipped and peeling away. The back of the bar overlooked the bay, but the tangle of weeds and trees obscured most of the view. It was the last authentic holdout to pseudo-rural renewal and boasted the only all-smoking dining room. No one came here for the view.

Chet was sitting at the dark, gleaming bar that dominated the room, staring at the collection of beer bottles from around the world that lined one wall. I wasn't surprised to see him here, just surprised to see him here on a Sunday with an empty shot glass and half-filled beer mug in front of him. He usually spent Sundays at his mother's in Jacksonport. Why wasn't he with her?

"Irish coffee," I said to the bartender.

Chet had merely glanced in my direction when I sat down on the bar stool next to him. An unfocused look made me wonder how many boilermakers he'd had.

"So, Chet, what are you doing here?" I took a slow sip of my drink.

"Come to keep me company while Jake's away?" He kept staring straight ahead.

How he knew Jake was gone, I had no idea.

"There's something I need to tell you. About Margaris disturbing the body."

"You told me that," Chet said.

"Yeah, well. It's not just that he moved the hair from Stephanie's face. It's that when I found her, her hair covered her face. Like it had been brushed that way. Considering how she died, there's no way her hair could have been like that."

"So?" Chet answered.

Was he purposely being dense? "That means the killer took the time to arrange it that way."

Chet downed the rest of his beer. "Go play those detective games of yours with someone else, okay then."

"What's the matter with you?"

"Hey, Paulie, how about another round?" he shouted at the bartender.

Paulie nodded his head.

"What's going on, Chet?"

"What goin' on? I'm on leave, that's what's goin' on. And if you know what's good for you, you'll go home there and curl up with that dog of yours and forget about Margaris and his daughter."

"What about Stephanie Everson? Should I forget about her too?"

He turned his head toward me. "You're not a cop, okay Leigh? You're a reporter. You got lucky once. You won't get lucky again."

"Who's handling the investigation?" I asked, anger burning my skin.

"Chief Burnson and that task force. So you can tell him about that hair business. When you make that there formal statement you're supposed to make tomorrow."

"Do you know of any other killings in the area where the body's been arranged like that?"

"Why don't you lighten up there, Sherlock Holmes?"

I didn't think Chet was capable of sarcasm.

"I know my little gray cells aren't as good as yours, okay then."

"That's Hercule Poirot, not Sherlock Holmes."

"Maybe Martin's right about you." Chet was sweating. "You are kinda a bitch, Leigh."

Rob Martin, a columnist for the *Door County Gazette,* and I had issues. His issue was me and my issue was him.

"Chet, look, I'm sorry Burnson put you on leave. But it had nothing to do with me."

Chet shook his head from side to side and smirked. "It never does, and yet somehow, some way, you got your nose stuck in it. Isn't it about time you headed back to where you come from?"

I chalked that remark up to a bad day followed by too much to drink. This wasn't the Chet I knew.

"The Margarises are gone. Did you get anything out of Janell?" I asked.

He didn't answer.

Chet flapped his arms up and down like he was doing the chicken dance. "Squawk, squawk," he shouted. "Flew the coop, just like you should. Back to Chi-ca-go."

On my way down the peninsula I stopped by the police station. Burnson wasn't in, but Officer Ferry was. I made my formal statement and told him how Russell Margaris moving Stephanie's hair from her face had changed its arrangement. How perfectly it had been arranged. He said he'd tell the chief. But something about the way he kept nodding his head and looking away made me wonder if he would. I had a suspect reputation with the police. They saw me as a meddling reporter who hadn't learned the laid-back rules of rural existence. What had been their response last fall when I tried to convince Chet and his fellow officers that a murder had been committed?

Something about Door County not being Chicago. That maybe murders were as common as ticks on a deer in Chicago but not here. And now Door County was faced with another murder. Ferry looked a little too happy when I told him I was heading for Chicago.

Chapter Twelve

Monday, May 22

I was parked across the street from Margaris's brownstone on Astor Place, a one-way street that had as many trees as luxury cars. It was on the north end of the city, known as the Gold Coast, where old money gave way to new. You couldn't see Lake Michigan from here, but it was just close enough to smell it. Rich people didn't worry about lake views when they could live among their own. Lake views were for the bourgeoisie.

I sipped my motel coffee and stared at the marble stone steps, the Frank Lloyd Wright stained-glass windows of prairie sumac, and the black lacquered door with the gold door knocker, wondering how I was going to talk to Janell. After the five-and-a-half hour drive last night, I had pulled into a University Inn around 1:30 p.m. The one-story motel was just off the Dan Ryan and near one of the universities where I used to teach. I always thought that anyone who stayed there must have a death wish. The rooms faced the parking lot and had those dingy white drapes that never quite meet in the middle. At least one window had duct tape running from one end to the other, holding it together. But I couldn't afford the posh loop hotels, and I wasn't in the mood to deal with family. Besides, I had Salinger to protect me from gang members, drug dealers and local politicians.

As I squeezed my truck between a silver Land Rover and a black Jaguar, I'd decided to use the direct approach with Margaris. I wasn't going to appeal to his good nature, because I didn't think he had one. I was going to threaten him. With what, I wasn't sure. Tampering with a body, bad parenting, lousy attitude. I'd think of something.

Salinger's low growl interrupted my thoughts. She sat in the passenger seat, nose against the glass, perusing the street for any suspect movements. A man in black running shorts and T-shirt and those high-tech cross trainers with plastic heels that were supposed to assure you that your foot could withstand any punishment your health club could hand out, was walking his dog—a slobbering Rottweiler. He wasn't holding the leash, which dragged along the street behind the dog. If a cop happened upon the scene, he could always say the dog was on leash, he just wasn't holding it.

"Easy, girl," I said, petting Salinger's head. "You don't want to be someone's breakfast."

Just as the dog came abreast of the truck, Salinger lunged at the window, sending the lumbering dog into attack mode. The Rottweiler flew against the truck window, jarring the truck. Now Salinger and the Rot were nose to nose, growling and barking. Mr. Cross-trainer grabbed the dog's spiked collar and yanked, trying to pull the beast away. I grabbed Salinger and held her growling body in my lap. Finally the guy was able to dislodge his dog from my window. As he walked away pulling, yanking and cursing, he flipped me the finger.

I rolled down my window. "There's a leash law, buddy," I shouted. In the commotion coffee had spilled on my best gray slacks.

"Great," I said, watching the man round the corner and dabbing at the brown stain with a crumpled tissue from the bottom of my purse.

Once the man was out of sight, I got out of the truck. I was about to cross the street when the front door opened and Janell

Margaris emerged. I walked back to my truck as if that had been my intention and fumbled in my purse for the keys, keeping an eye on Janell.

She was dressed in a parochial school uniform—navy jacket with gold crest, white blouse with navy bow tie, navy-and-white-plaid pleated skirt, white socks, and saddle shoes, also navy and white. On her back was a very full backpack. A blue headband held her sleek blond hair off her face.

You've got to be kidding, I thought. I wanted to put my finger down my throat. The universal barf sign.

She slouched down the steps, making sure she scuffed the backs of her shoes. I locked the truck, left the window open for Salinger, pointing out a particular worrisome squirrel to her as I moved to follow Janell.

As soon as she turned onto the cross street, she slipped off her backpack and reached into one of the compartments. She dug out a pack of cigarettes and a matchbook. Standing on the street, she lit the cigarette, her blond hair falling forward, close to the flame. She took several quick puffs, then headed toward the El station on the next block.

I followed her down the steps, inhaling that familiar smell of urine, pollution and stale bodies. After going through the turnstile, she boarded the red line. I kept my distance, sitting in the same car but a few seats down. She got off at State Street. I couldn't imagine what school was on State except a cosmetology school, which I'm sure required a different uniform. But instead of exiting the station, she went into the women's rest room. I stood across from the entrance waiting.

When she emerged a full thirty minutes later, I almost missed her. Not only was the uniform gone, but an entire transformation had taken place, as if she had gone in a caterpillar and emerged a butterfly. Though the aptness of the analogy depended on one's viewpoint. In place of her demure schoolgirl outfit were denim shorts riding well below her belly button and cinched with a wide leather belt, a strapless white tube top, the better to display budding nipples, and spike heels of such height I was sure they were banned by chiropractors. Her hair had been braided into a mess of braids that hung around her face like limp snakes. The only restraint was her makeup: pink lip-gloss, mauve blusher, eyeliner and mascara. She didn't look older, just ready to be older.

As I gaped in utter astonishment, she walked right up to me, her spikes making a clicking sound even the passing El train didn't cover.

"What's your problem, bitch," she said. "You've been following me since I left home."

I didn't answer. I was mesmerized by her tongue ring. It was a silver ball near the tip of her tongue that gave her a slight lisp.

"My name's Leigh Girard. I work for the *Door County Gazette.* I'm not here to bust you. I just want to talk to you about Stephanie Everson."

For a second her hard veneer fell away and she looked like a kid playing dress up. "Stephanie? Why do you want to talk about her? She's got nothing to do with anything."

Her response seemed genuine. She put her backpack down so she could adjust her tube top, which was slipping downward and revealing a small rose tattoo above one breast. I wondered which parent had given permission for the body hardware, or if Janell had convinced the body artist that she was eighteen.

"Maybe we could talk somewhere? I know a place on Adams," I suggested.

She tilted her head to one side and pursed her glossy, pouty lips. "Sure, why not? You look normal."

We were seated in a booth at Milner's Tavern, a darkly paneled restaurant on Adams with fake stained-glass windows. Photos of famous people were plastered everywhere. The booth we sat in had a picture of Frank Sinatra. "My kinda burger town," he had written. "Best, Frank."

I'd ordered a cheeseburger; Janell a coke and fries.

"About what happened to Stephanie," I began.

"She get in trouble because of me?" she asked, playing with the silverware.

"Stephanie's dead," I said, looking directly into her doll-blue eyes.

For a moment I didn't think she'd heard me. Her face was a total blank. Then she put her hand to her chest as if to check if her heart was still beating.

"What? What are you talking about? I saw her Friday." Her pupils had narrowed to dark specks.

"Didn't your parents tell you?" I couldn't believe her parents hadn't told her. What was their motive for holding back this information?

"Tell me what? Listen, lady, I don't like this. Was Stephanie in a car crash or something?" Her cheeks were pink with emotion.

"It wasn't a car crash. She was murdered." I stopped and let that sink in. "She was found in the woods off the Mink River where we were searching for you."

Her eyes looked toward the exit. In another minute, she'd be out the door.

"You've got to tell me what you know," I demanded. "Anything that could help find her killer."

"I don't know anything," she snapped at me. "I don't remember anything."

I knew she was lying. She wouldn't look at me. But I wasn't going to probe Janell's mysterious memory loss right then. She'd only dig her spike heels in deeper. "Stephanie told me she was covering for you last summer. When you were sneaking around with that older guy."

"That's a lie," she said, jerking her head side to side. "Stephanie wants to get me in trouble. She's always been jealous 'cause I get to do stuff. And she's stuck in Dork County her whole life."

I must have had a horrified look on my face.

"Okay, that sounded bad. Anyways, why would I sneak around? My parents let me do pretty much what I want. Get a clue." She stuck her studded tongue out at me.

"Then why did you change clothes after you left home?"

I watched her face harden, as if she were assuming a part—jaw thrust forward, her eyes squinting.

"I thought it'd be funny. The Ps got me seeing some shrink this morning. I thought I'd make the guy earn his money."

"Where were you for two days, Janell?"

Her face went soft. It was like watching an actress at a rehearsal—falling in and out of her part. Only I wasn't sure which was the role and which was the real person.

"I wish I could remember," she said, her eyes wide and appealing. "I really do. But it must have been pretty traumatic, or I would remember. Right?"

I'd had students like her. There was only one way to deal with them. Call their bluff. "Cut the crap, Elly. I know you were with this older guy and that you probably had sex with him. I was at the hospital and I heard what Dr. Risner said. I'll make you a deal. I'll keep your little secret. Just tell me if you know anything that could help find Stephanie's killer."

She looked away. It was taking her too long to speak, which meant she was composing an answer.

"Honest. I don't know anything. I saw Stephanie that Friday down by the marina. Then I don't . . . I really don't remember anything. I gotta go. The shrink's waiting."

She grabbed her backpack and headed for the door.

I left a twenty and hoped that covered it.

Driving back to the motel through the city streets, I was sweating in my teal-blue knit sweater and coffee-stained slacks. Salinger's head was hanging out the window, her tongue trying to catch a nonexistent breeze. The bank clock on LaSalle and Adams flashed eighty-five degrees. And it wasn't even noon yet. I switched on the A/C. Lukewarm air that smelled like dust fluttered from the vents.

Janell was lying about not remembering. There was no doubt in my mind. She and Stephanie had concocted the marina story, probably when they sat on the pier behind Janell's house. Janell had arranged a tryst with this guy to spite her parents. And Stephanie had covered for her. There had never been a call from Annie; there had never been a cell phone. The hitch came when Janell didn't return the next day. Stephanie must have panicked. But why would she be looking for Janell in the woods by the river? And how did all this figure in with her murder?

I needed to talk to Janell again, shake loose the name of that guy. It was a slim lead, but at present it was all I had. But how was I going to do that?

I turned into the asphalt motel parking lot and parked in front of my room. The door was open. There was a cleaning cart out front. I could hear the TV set blasting over the vacuum cleaner.

While I sat in the truck waiting for the maid to finish, I dialed Tom's work number.

After two rings, I hung up and stared out at the empty parking lot.

I punched 4-1-1 into the phone.

"Could you give me the number of the University of Chicago Hospital?"

"What city?"

"Chicago," I answered in disbelief.

I dialed the number. "Oncology please."

"It's not like he knows we're here," I explained to Salinger, who had moved to my lap and was growling at the vacuum cleaner's steady hum.

Chapter Thirteen

May 23, Tuesday

The living room of the Margarises' brownstone was a display in cutting-edge design, literally. Everything was a geometric surface of glass, chrome or marble. Even the dark green Italian leather couch had a chrome frame encasing it like a twenty-first century sarcophagus.

The vast area rug that covered the gleaming wood floors was a black and white Art Deco design with lines and angles that went nowhere.

To my surprise I hadn't had to use any wiles to gain entrance. Janet Margaris, looking a bit drawn around her collagen lips, had answered the door and invited me in. Her hospitality had my hackles up.

I was balancing a cup of coffee in a gold-rimmed china cup so thin it chimed when I put it down on the saucer. Besides the coffee, Janet Margaris had offered me bagels and fresh fruit. I'd refused the food because my head was throbbing and my throat was still raw. Of course, sitting in the motel bar last night drinking wine and inhaling secondhand smoke until the wee hours hadn't helped. But my indulgence had the desired effect: I'd fallen asleep instantly and slept dreamlessly until morning.

"I'm so sorry to hear about Stephanie," she began. She wore a pale blue silk blouse, loose fitting with frog closings and a Mandarin collar, and beige linen slacks. There was a deep crease between her perfectly waxed eyebrows. "We've sent flowers to the family. Just let me know if there's anything I can do. That's why you're here, isn't it—to interview me about Stephanie? She was such a sweet girl."

Was this woman daft? She thought I had come all the way from Door County to interview her for an obit article on Stephanie. I could have done that over the phone.

"Not exactly, Mrs. Margaris."

"Please, call me Janet." There were those perfect teeth again, like little Chiclets.

What an awful burden, having to be so perfect. I wondered if she did it out of pride or fear or both. My guess—fear. After all, she wasn't getting any younger. Russell seemed like the type who'd trade up when the old model lost its luster.

"Janet, has Janell said anything about those two days she was missing? Did she give any hint about where she'd been?"

"What does that have to do with Stephanie?" She stirred her coffee slowly, her head down.

"Maybe nothing. But Stephanie was the last person to see Janell before she disappeared. There could be a connection."

She placed her cup and saucer down on the jagged glass table and sat up straighter, as if she were about to deliver a recitation.

"I can only tell you what the doctor told me. He said she might never remember." Her hand actually went to her throat. A diamond as large as an agate caught the light; surrounding it was a cluster of sapphires.

"And you believe that?" Was I being given yet another performance by one of the Margaris women?

"Of course. Why wouldn't we?" Her hand slid down to her lap and under her ringed hand. If Margaris ever gave her the boot, she should try a career on the stage.

"Because I don't think Janell is always truthful. Did you know she was seeing an older guy last summer? And that Stephanie was covering for her?"

Janell was fair game.

"Who told you that?"

"Stephanie, the day she was murdered. I talked to her that morning. She said that Janell had met this older guy last summer and was sneaking around behind your back with him."

"You did say you're a reporter." She suddenly looked as sharp as her furniture.

"Janet, look, I'm sure you've thought of this. But in case you haven't, there's every possibility that if things had gone differently, if Janell had been in those woods, she could have been the one murdered."

"That's ridiculous."

"Is it? And if that had happened, you'd be planning her funeral right now, not thinking about going to the opera or whatever it is you do."

She stood up. "This has nothing to do with us. Russell told me it was probably someone Stephanie knew. It didn't even look like she put up a struggle."

"How would he know that?"

"He was there. He found the body." She was pacing up and down that dizzy rug.

"No, *I* found the body. He came later and messed it up." I was shaking I was so angry with this stupid, vain woman. "Janell knows something. I followed her yesterday on her way to the doctor's. Did you know she changed her clothes in the El station before her doctor's appointment? She put on these provocative clothes. She's sending some message and no one's listening."

"What does that have to do with her memory loss or Stephanie's murder? She's a teenager. She's rebelling. It's what they do. You sound like Russell. He thinks the only way to handle her is to be stricter. That doesn't work with Janell. It just makes things worse. You have to let her do some things. What does it hurt if she pierces her tongue or gets a tattoo? In a year she'll outgrow it."

So she condoned Janell's behavior. "I want you to think about Annie Everson. I want you to think about what she's going through. She'll never have the chance to see her daughter grow up. That could have been you."

She sat down as if all the air had gone out of her, staring at her hands, her head down.

"I don't know where she was," she began. "You have to believe me. I asked her and asked her. She says she doesn't remember," she hesitated and looked at me. "But I think there was a boy last summer. She didn't tell me, but I suspected. Since she's turned twelve, she hates going up north. Thinks it's boring. But last summer, about the middle of July, her attitude changed. I was so glad not to have to look at her long face, I didn't question her. If there was a boy, I figured she'd get over it once she came home."

"Did she get over it?"

She ran her French-manicured fingers through her auburn-lighted hair. Every strand instantly fell back into place.

"How would I know?"

"Let me talk to Janell. If you want, you can be there. Maybe we can get her to open up."

"But what if it's real? What if she really can't remember?" There was little conviction in her words.

"Then where's the harm?"

Neither of us mentioned telling Russell Margaris. I think for Janet, deceiving him had already become a reflex.

Cook County Forest Preserve Picnic Shelter A was a short distance from Lake Michigan in Wilmette. I had arrived early and was watching a teenaged couple huddled together under a flowering crab tree make out. Every once in a while a breeze shook the white petals down around them, just like in the movies.

Their backs were to me. Both wore the official teen uniform—faded jeans and T-shirts. Her arm was around his waist and his was draped forward over her shoulder. I couldn't see it, but he probably was copping a feel, because she was giggling and squirming. Every once in a while a "No" drifted toward me on the sticky breeze.

Janet had chosen the meeting place and the time. Wilmette was far enough north of the city that she wouldn't run into any of her hoity-toity cronies from Chicago.

After leaving the Margarises' brownstone this morning, I had driven over to the U of C Hospital to keep my appointment with the oncologist. Because I was an add-on, I'd sat in the holding area for two hours, stripped to the waist, covered by the all-too-familiar green hospital gown, the old dread back in my gut.

As far as Dr. Aldrich could tell, everything looked fine. After a radiologist read my mammogram, they'd know more. She had reminded me that I needed to have checkups every six months and if it was too hard driving back, she could recommend someone in Green Bay. I said I'd stick with her. She also suggested I see someone about my cough.

Once outside I'd taken my first real breath since walking through the glass revolving doors, a labored breath, but a breath just the same. It had felt good.

"You tricked me!" Janell said as she entered the shadowy shelter and saw me. She turned to walk away.

Janet grabbed her by both her shoulders to stop her. Janell was disguised in yet another persona. If she weren't a teenager, I would think she had multiple personalities. This time she wore a spaghetti-strapped yellow sundress and cowboy boots. Her hair was in two braids. Heidi does Dallas?

"You know what I told you in the car. If you don't want your father knowing what you've been up to, you'd better sit down."

Score one for Janet. She had more gumption than I had given her credit for. If Margaris ever decided to trade her in, he'd pay for it big time.

Janell sat down on the edge of the bench clutching her beaded purse to her chest. "Yuck, this place is disgusting. There's bird poop and stuff all over."

Janet sat down beside her.

"Here's the deal, Janell," I began. "Your mother and I think you've been lying. We think you do remember what happened." A girl was dead and I was sick of Janell's games.

"Whatever." She shrugged her shoulders. One of the spaghetti straps slipped down. She left it.

"In case it hasn't occurred to you. That could have been you in those woods. You could have been murdered." It had worked on her mother; it was worth trying on her. "Your mother would be making plans right now to bury you."

"Yeah, right." She let out a laugh, all bluster, no substance.

To Janell's and my surprise, Janet slapped her hard across the face. Janell didn't flinch. She sat very still. As if her body was burning up, I saw a deep flush travel up her chest to her neck and face. Where Janet had slapped her was the white imprint of her hand. Very slowly a line of tears scored her face.

"You think you can control me." She tilted her chin up. Tears were coming faster. "But you can't. Erik and I love each other, and there's nothing you can do about it."

"Who is Erik?" Janet asked. Her voice was cold with rage.

Janell looked at her mother and didn't answer. The tears had stopped. In their place was defiance.

"Did you have sex with this boy, this Erik?" Janet asked.

"We didn't have sex, Mother," she spat in her face. "We made love." Her chin was still out, as if begging for another slap.

"How old is he?" Janet was sounding like a prosecuting attorney.

"You can't do anything to him. He's not twenty-one. I saw his driver's license. He's eighteen. He's a teenager just like me. You can't do anything to him."

Janet shook her head in disbelief. "My God, Janell, how stupid can you be?"

"I'm not stupid. So don't say that. I fooled you and Daddy, didn't I?"

"And that was why you lied? To fool us?"

"I didn't want Erik in trouble. I know Daddy."

"What's wrong with you, Janell?"

"Elly, my name's Elly. How many times do I have to tell you? Stop calling me by that stupid name."

If I didn't step in, they'd be reliving their whole history together and I'd never find out what I needed to know about Stephanie.

"Did Stephanie help you? Did she know about this meeting?"

Janell turned toward me. "Yeah, she knew the whole thing. She was my cover. I told her what to say, what to do. Stephanie thought we were friends. I let her think we were."

"So you were never down by the marina?"

"No. I hitched to Gills Rock. Then took the ferry. That's where we decided to meet. Washington Island. I wanted to make love above the tension line." She flung one braid behind her shoulder.

"Then what happened on the way back? Why were you hiding on the ferry?"

She dropped her gaze. She almost looked ashamed. "That was all part of the plan. It would have worked, too, except for what happened to Stephanie." She had the decency to lower her voice.

"Didn't you know the police would get involved? Do you know what trouble you caused?" I asked, incredulous of her narcissism.

"Daddy's got lots of money. He can fix anything. That's what he always says. There's nothing money can't fix. Right, mother?"

Except you, I thought.

Janet had gone very quiet. I wasn't convinced Janell was telling the truth. Something about her story didn't ring true. She was covering for this guy as she talked, purposely misleading us. I believed something sexual had happened to her. Whether by consent or not, I wasn't sure.

She slipped her purse strap on her shoulder. "Can we go now?"

Janet stood up and looked at me. "You've got what you came for. I don't want you bothering us anymore." She sounded exhausted.

"Just one more thing, Elly. What's his last name?"

She threw her head back. That smartass attitude was back. "He's not from that dorky place," Janell said. "So give it up. You'll never find him."

If I hadn't thought so before, I was convinced now. Erik was from that dorky place. I wondered how many eighteen-year-old Eriks there were on the peninsula and the island. If Erik was his name. If he was eighteen.

Swirls of mauve and tangerine were dragging the sun down. I was doing eighty on the expressway, hoping all the state troopers were otherwise occupied. It wasn't until I passed the 176 Exit for Libertyville that I slowed to sixty-five. If the truck had cruise control, I would have clicked it on now.

In fifteen minutes I'd be in Wisconsin.

Besides, I reasoned, Tom probably wasn't even home yet from work. Even if he were there, what would I say. "Just driving by, and thought I'd stop in. And by the way, how about a divorce?"

Did I even want a divorce? I sure as hell didn't want a marriage.

Just the thought of driving into that pretentious, overpriced subdivision made me itch.

"The A C house," I'd called our one-acre palatial estate in Libertyville. The initials stood for after cancer. The way I had divided my life. The way I was still dividing my life. And if Tom was honest, the way he divided our life.

What he'd told himself and me was that we needed a fresh start—everything new and shiny. As if that could cover up the six-inch fuchsia scar that cut across my left side from underarm to sternum. It was like trying to put a Band-Aid over the incision.

It was in that house I'd discovered how far apart Tom and I were. The street names summed it up: Trillium Lane, Heron Court, Goldenrod Avenue. And to make those streets, the developer had destroyed all the trillium, all the goldenrod, and he'd run off the heron. Tom wanted the names; I wanted the things they represented.

Why are the best kept secrets the ones we keep from ourselves? I thought as I turned on my headlights and crossed into Wisconsin.

Tom wasn't going anywhere. And I had someone named Erik to find.

Chapter Fourteen

Wednesday, May 24

"I'm not Jake," Rob Martin said. He was leaning back in Jake's swivel chair, jiggling a pen back and forth between his fingers. I was slumped in one of the green vinyl chairs, circa 1950, half listening to Martin ream me a new one. My chest felt tight and I was tired. I'd gotten home after midnight and hadn't finished the article on Stephanie's murder until two. Caffeine was the only thing between me and a comatose state.

"He may cut you slack because you're putting out for him, but I'm in charge now. You didn't meet Monday's deadline. You're off the story." His freckled forehead was pink like the skin of a baby white mouse.

Martin had left me a ranting message Monday morning on my cell phone. I hadn't called him back. Not a smart move. He had every right to take me off the story.

This morning I'd shown up for work at eight, ready to enter my article on Stephanie Everson into the computer. Martin had swiped the article off my desk and thrown it in the wastebasket, saying, "In case you've forgotten, the deadline for the story has passed." He'd already written the follow-up story—a dry piece of reporting that rehashed the facts.

"I have a lead on who Janell Margaris was with," I began, trying to appeal to his journalistic soul.

"What part of 'off the story' don't you understand?" He rocked the chair forward until his feet hit the floor. A fiery-looking guy with red hair and beard, his appearance matched his personality. The fact that Martin was the paper's nature writer was as congruent as my being a swimsuit model.

But even by Martin standards, he was enjoying this too much. Whether I liked it or not, he was in charge until Jake's return. Whenever that would be. I still hadn't heard from Jake. And I wasn't going to call him.

"Okay, Rob, what do you want me to do? Beg your forgiveness? Say I'm sorry? What? Just tell me." I was willing to grovel. I had to stay on the story.

"If something new comes in on the Everson murder, I'll handle it." He rubbed his hand up and down his red beard as if enflaming the color. "I want you to write an article on the release of the sex offenders list. Get both sides. Interview Burnson and at least two of the offenders on the list. There's been an incident. Someone spray painted Don Stuart's house. Go see him first. Then interview Monroe Parks. I've already set up the interviews for this afternoon. If you hadn't gotten back, I was going to do them."

I sank lower in the chair, gritting my teeth against the spiel of nasty things I wanted to unleash on him. "Jake assigned me the Margaris story. He's not going to like this."

"In case you haven't noticed, Jake's not here." That was meant to hurt. There was a malicious gleam in his dark green eyes. For the past seven months Martin and I had achieved a kind of peace that allowed us to occupy the same office space. His being in charge had disrupted that peace.

"And over Memorial Day weekend I want you to cover the Jacksonport Maifest." He leaned back in the chair. "Make sure you find an interesting angle. Something we haven't done before. Plan on being there all weekend. We'll run that article in Friday's paper. But the sex offenders list piece better be in the computer before Monday's nine a.m. deadline."

"Or what?" I asked. There was nothing he could do to me.

"Jake could be gone the whole summer. Wouldn't be the first time." He grinned. "But I'm sure you know that."

I didn't know that. "Okay," I said, standing up and leaning over the desk toward Martin.

He jerked back as if he expected me to take a swing at him.

I picked up the packet of pink phone message slips. "One more thing." I wrote down a phone number in big letters that a legally blind person could read. "Here's my new phone number." I tore off the top slip and placed it on the desk in front of him. "You can reach me there starting Friday."

He picked it up and glanced at the number. It took a moment, but it registered. He crumbled the paper and threw it in the trash.

"But of course, you probably knew that." I was pretty sure he didn't know Sarah had offered me her place. I had sunk to his level and it felt good.

My interview with Donald Stuart wasn't until two. So I drove over to Peninsula High School in Fish Creek in search of Janell's Erik. Shelley Mahoney, assistant to the principal, sat outside Principal Hendricks's office, talking on a headset while she typed on a keyboard. When she ended her conversation, she gave me the official bland smile reserved for parents—no teeth, lips drawn back slightly.

"Can I help you?"

"Leigh Girard from the *Door County Gazette*. I'm covering the Stephanie Everson murder. I was wondering if you could give me some information."

She took off her headset and put her hand over her heart. "I can't believe it," she said. "I just can't believe it. Stephanie was such a sweet girl."

I was concentrating on Shelley's pointy nose, pushing the image of Stephanie's dead body from my mind.

"How can I help?" Shelley asked, running her fingers over her nose.

"I need to know if you have any Eriks, age seventeen or eighteen currently enrolled."

She paused for a moment. "You don't think one of our students is involved?"

"No, not directly. I'm just following up a lead. I can't say more than that."

"I don't think I can give you that information without checking with Principal Hendricks."

"Listen, you know I'll eventually get the information. It'll just take me longer to check through the yearbook. Why don't you help me out here? I'm sure Stephanie's parents will be grateful."

She tsked a few time and then relented. She told me there were three Eriks currently enrolled as seniors. She gave me their addresses and phone numbers. None lived on Washington Island.

I thanked her profusely and left. If Janell hadn't lied to me about his age or name, one of them could be the guy. Short of asking each one if he'd had sex with Janell Margaris last weekend, which if he was smart he'd deny, I didn't know how I was going to find this guy. But I was going to try.

After leaving the high school I had two hours to kill before my interview with Stuart. I drove north on Highway 42 to the Peninsula State Park's Ephraim entrance and parked by the tower. A monolithic leggy structure made of wood, the tower afforded a view of the Green Bay Islands. Some tourists were milling around taking pictures of the spectacular vista. Kids were running up the gazillion steps, calling down to their parents to join them.

I chomped on a blueberry breakfast bar and started jotting down questions for the two interviews. Gee, what do you ask a sex offender? "How did you get started?"

I threw the notebook on the seat and stared out at the bay, bluing itself against the sky. I'd wing it.

I didn't want to do the sex offender story and I especially didn't want to interview registered sex offenders. Whatever the circumstances, as far as I was concerned the police department could put their names in flashing red neon outside their houses and it would be okay with me. But I had covered the meeting and, as much as it went against my nature, I needed to work with Martin. When information came in about Stephanie's murder, I didn't want him cutting me out of the loop for spite.

Before leaving the office, I'd shoved the list in my purse. I took it out and once again perused each offender's criminal bio. Martin had assigned me sex offenders lite. Don Stuart had had sex with his fourteen-year-old high-school sweetheart when he was eighteen. Monroe Parks had been convicted of fourth-degree criminal sexual conduct. No circumstances had been given. But I knew from Lydia that Parks had been a psychotherapist who'd had sex with one of his patients. What was Martin's motivation in choosing these two? Certainly not to protect my sensibilities. He probably couldn't get the hardcore offenders to talk to him.

I pulled out the phone directory from under my seat. Only one of the remaining nine offenders was listed—a Chuck Bayer. He'd been convicted of two sexual assault charges—one for molesting a seven-year-old girl and one for sexual assault of a twelve-year-old girl. I called his number.

"Yeah," a male voice answered.

I explained that I was doing a piece on the release of the sex offenders list and asked if he would be willing to talk to me.

"What's in it for me?"

"Your side of the story."

"I'm at the Bide-a-Way apartments in Little Sturgeon. Number thirteen. My lucky number. I'll be here till six."

Chapter Fifteen

Wednesday, May 24

Don Stuart lived inland off Route A in Liberty Grove. The modest white ranch house stood in an open field. There was wash on the line out back and the word Perv in big, black uneven letters across the front of the house. He must have heard my tires crunch on the gravel drive, because before I turned off the engine he came out of the house.

"You gonna take a picture?" he asked as I joined him on the concrete slab porch. "I left it like that. Figured you'd want it for the paper." Donald Stuart had a high, soft voice that clashed with his wrestler's build and his tough-guy attitude. He had on faded Levi's and a white, short-sleeved undershirt.

"Let's talk first," I said, waiting for him to ask me in. But he just stood there next to Perv as if he was proud of it.

"Nothing to say. This says it all." He jerked his thumb at the word. "I made one mistake when I was eighteen. Eighteen. One mistake and they won't let me ever forget it. Ever." He folded his arms across his chest. "How's a man supposed to move on?"

He was short and stocky with big, raw hands that looked like they made his living for him. Though he couldn't be more than thirty, his dun-colored hair barely covered his head. I could see the individual roots. His eyes were a washed-out blue. There was a coiled power in his build that made me uneasy.

"I told Cheri not to go to that meeting. 'You're asking for trouble,' I told her. I told her she'd just be drawing attention.

She wouldn't listen. She said she had to explain my side. Sure enough." He jerked his thumb again at the word.

"Why don't you tell me your side of it? How did it happen?"

"Came home from work and there it was. Damn cowards."

"No, I mean how did you end up a sex offender?" I couldn't help myself.

He ran his tongue back and forth over his front teeth as if something was caught there. "I'm no sex offender. Okay, lady?"

If he was mad, he was doing a good job of containing it.

"She was my girlfriend. We'd been going out for about a year. Her parents didn't like me, especially her old man. They wanted to break us up. So they accused me of having sex with their daughter."

"And did you? Have sex with her?"

"It was consensual."

A big word for a little guy.

"But she was fourteen and you were what? Eighteen?" I had my notebook out, but I wasn't taking notes. I was watching Stuart try to put a good spin on his crime. "That means, according to what you just said, you started dating her when she was thirteen."

He had the decency to appear sheepish. "Ma'am. She wanted to do it. Honest. I didn't force her." His voice hit a high, whiny note.

"She was underage and in the eyes of the law you weren't." Why didn't he tell me to get out of his face? He was being much too tolerant.

"I did my time." He had a wary look. "That give some moron a right to spray paint my house?" He ran his thick fingers over his wispy hair.

"Maybe not. But you can see how they would feel." I was pushing this guy. I wanted to see what shook out.

"You defending these creeps? I thought you were suppose to be impartial?"

"Well, Mr. Stuart, you don't seem very remorseful. You don't think what you did was right?"

He put his hands on his hips. "Look, I gotta get to work. You gonna take a picture or what?"

I took the picture, purposely blurring it. I had no intention of using it in the article. This guy wanted the paper to paint him as a victim. I didn't see it that way.

On the way up the peninsula to my interview with Monroe Parks, I stopped by the three Eriks' houses. Each had an alibi for Friday and Saturday, supported by a family member. Each looked sweet and young and a bit befuddled by my questions. I wondered if that was how Don Stuart had looked at eighteen.

Monroe Parks, unlike Stuart, was well dressed in black trousers, white short-sleeved dress shirt, and tie. He was a printer for the *Door Press* in Sister Bay. Ironically it was the *Door Press* that had published the list. He'd allotted me twenty minutes for the interview. His exact break time.

We were across the road from the *Door Press* in an Icelandic restaurant called The Viking. The entire restaurant was a sea of blue and white. All the waitresses were blond and buxom, which I was sure broke some labor law. A mural of a fleet of Viking long ships surrounded by icebergs covered an entire wall. I had no idea what constituted authentic Icelandic décor, maybe horned helmets and fur clothes, certainly not delft china and blue vinyl tablecloths.

"You want my version or hers?" Parks asked.

Parks's broad shoulders strained against his shirt. His black hair was slicked with gel that created deep furrows. He had a lush dark beard that hid most of his pockmarked complexion, which was the texture and color of sand paper.

"How about the truth?" Did any of these guys ever think they were at fault? I wondered.

A sly grin played around his wet, hairy mouth. "Already got your mind made up. All men are scum, right?" His long fingers circled his coffee cup.

"I'm on deadline, Mr. Parks." My crossed leg was pumping up and down under the table in impatience.

He raised one dark eyebrow. "I was a psychotherapist. Dr. Monroe Parks. Had my practice in Whitefish Bay. Wealthy area north of Milwaukee." He paused waiting for my reaction. "Right on the lake."

"Uh-huh," I said.

He continued. "I made the mistake of falling in love with one of my patients."

Falling in love. Abusing patient trust. I could see where it might get confusing.

I waited for the rest. It wasn't coming. "And?" I said impatiently.

"And she pressed charges. Or rather, I should say her husband found out and he convinced her to press charges. I lost everything. My license, my house, my kids, my wife." He turned his coffee spoon back and forth on the blue paper napkin. A brown stain spread across the blue. "I might as well be dead."

I jotted down his exact words. His order of loss said everything.

"I was wrong to have breached the doctor–patient barrier. That I admit. But I've paid heavily for that breach. I won't try and make a case that I'm not like these other life offenders. That mine was a one-time deal. Though it was. It is. Because I can see it would fall on deaf ears. But take my word for it, publishing names in the paper serves no purpose. It doesn't allay people's fear. In fact, it makes them more fearful. They don't feel safer. And what are they going to do with the knowledge? Except be anxious. Or strike out."

Nice speech. I wondered how many times he'd rehearsed it. "What's the alternative?" I asked. "Ignorance? What about the citizens' rights to protect themselves and their families? I'd want to know if a sex offender was living next door to me."

"What are you going to do if you do know, move?"

My pumping foot struck his shin. "Oops," I said coyly.

He didn't even seem to notice. "Do you honestly think this 'outing' is going to prevent a real sex offender from doing it again? It won't work. It's a compulsion. All the science points to these deterrents as being ineffective. The offender can't help himself. That's the difference between someone like me and someone like them."

"Is this the therapist or the offender speaking?" I was sick of these guys' excuses.

"Like I said, I'm not a sex offender. I made one mistake. I have no intention of making that mistake again." He looked out the window at the blank field. "Not that I'd ever be in that position again."

"The police contact you about the Everson murder?" I was sure they had and he'd been cleared. Or we wouldn't be sitting here.

He looked at his watch. "Why don't you ask them?"

He put down a five and left. I sat for a long time, my eyes on the brown field, my mind back there in the woods kneeling beside the body so emptied of Stephanie.

The Bide-a-Way Apartments, formerly the Bide-a-Way Motel, were on Shore Road across from Green Bay in Little Sturgeon Bay. It was 4:45 when I knocked on room thirteen. After Stuart and Parks, I was primed for Mr. Bayer.

"I'd ask you in," he said, opening the door, "but maybe I won't be able to control myself, seeing how pretty you are."

Chuck Bayer was about six-two with a medium build. A black

stocking cap was pulled low over his forehead. The cap emphasized his dark, dense eyebrows. A shaggy mustache edged his prominent lips and ran up toward his nose. He was wearing a silver balled chain around his neck and a black and red, long-sleeved T-shirt and jeans. His eyes were heavy-lidded and secretive. Everything about him said menace.

"I'm not twelve. So I don't think I have to worry," I said, walking past him into the room. There was one twin bed, one television, one chair, and one picture on the beige wall—a painting of a vase of blue flowers on a yellow tablecloth. It's cheery colors clashed with the room's somberness.

I sat down on the chair. "So what's your story?"

"I'm a pedophile. What else you need to know?" Bayer stood in the doorway, blocking the light.

"How do you feel about the release of the list?"

He closed the door and sat on the bed. I checked out the bottoms of his shoes. They were clean as a whistle.

"It's a joke."

"How's that?"

"You think some piece of paper's gonna make a difference? A man wants to do something, he's gonna to do it."

Parks had said the same thing, though his grammar was better.

"So that list hasn't had any effect on you or your life?"

"You mean has anyone spit on me? Nah. I get some dirty looks, but I give 'em right back. But that's all I do. I'm learning to control my urges." He smiled slowly as if we were sharing the same joke. "They got me seeing a shrink."

"And is it working?"

"Must be. The police have been and gone. That's why you came here, isn't it? To check out the animal in the pen. See if he got out and killed that pretty little girl. Well, I'm still here. Enjoying the view." He looked me up and down.

I looked right back at him.

He broke eye contact first. "But far as that list goes, it don't bother me none. But I could see how it might push some men over the edge." His hands were kneading the inside of his thighs. "Not me, of course, but some men. 'Specially if he was having a lot of stress in his life. His old lady giving him a hard time. Boss on his back. Lady reporter hustling him. Might make him snap. Just like a friggin' tree." He snapped his fingers. "And when a tree snaps, somebody gets hurt."

"You think that scares me?" I said, a rush of anger shooting up my spine. "It doesn't. I'm not afraid of you. You know why? Because I'm not a seven-year-old child. You don't have any power over me. Isn't that what you're about? Power? You feel like a man with a child. It makes you come. With a woman you're impotent." I clutched the arms of the chair. "You're afraid of me."

A muscle twitched in his jaw. "Yeah. Well, you keep telling yourself that."

When I returned to the office, I called Mayor Conroy and Chief Burnson. Conroy reiterated what he'd said at the town meeting about the list's release. Burnson was more forthcoming. After letting him know what I thought of the scumbags I'd interviewed, he referred me to Jane McAdams, an advocate for survivors of sexual assault.

"About the Everson murder," I asked before hanging up. "Anything from the medical examiner's office yet?"

"Told Martin all that this morning. Talk to him." He sounded impatient.

"Well, he's not in. And I need to get this article written before five."

Martin was in his office right now. I glared at his closed door.

"The Everson girl died of strangulation. But you already knew that."

"What about fingerprints? Footprints?"

"You know I can't tell you that."

"Did you find anything from the crime scene?"

"Nothing I can tell you."

"Was she sexually assaulted?" I wasn't giving up.

"Can't tell you that either."

"Look, Chief, I'm the one who found her. This is personal. It'll be strictly off the record. But I need to know, was she sexually assaulted?"

He paused for a moment. I heard him take a deep breath and then let it out. "I better not see this in the paper."

"You won't," I assured him.

"No, there was no evidence of sexual assault."

"What about the offenders on the list? Any suspects?"

"We're following up on a few things."

"Those things, any of them have to do with Don Stuart, Monroe Parks or Chuck Bayer?"

"Stuart's wife alibied him. Parks and Bayer were at home alone. But we have no evidence linking them to the murder. That's all I can tell you."

I hung up the phone and looked down at my notes. Strangulation. No sexual assault. Just like I'd told Annie.

The image of two dark bruises high on Stephanie's neck suddenly flooded my memory. They were smudged thumbprints. I shook my head as if I could dislodge the memory.

I'd been telling myself that the killer had probably come up from behind Stephanie and put her in a chokehold causing a loss of consciousness. That's the way I had needed to see it.

But now, it was all coming back to me. His thumbprints had been on her throat. The killer had strangled Stephanie face to face.

I flipped my notebook back to the three interviews and started working on the sex offenders list story. Anything to stop seeing those smudged thumbprints.

It was after seven when I punched my final copy into the computer minus the Perv photo. I'd downplayed Stuart's and Parks's stories, threw in a few flagrant quotes from Bayer, and focused on the repeat offenders and law enforcement's reason for releasing the list. It wasn't a balanced piece, but it was one I could live with. McAdams had given me my angle for the article. The headline read: *Release of sex offenders list empowers victims as well as police.*

As I drove down the long gravel drive to the cottage, I rolled down the truck's window and listened to the water's steady roil. The evening was chill and crisp—more fall than springlike. But at least it wasn't raining.

Salinger was waiting at the front door, her tail beating a greeting. For once she didn't dart past me into the field, but sat staring up at me, her head tilted to one side.

"I'm fine," I said, ruffling her fur. "Go on." She paused, then tore out the door and disappeared in the field. Beyond the field were the woods where large, three-petaled white flowers had bloomed overnight. They nodded on emerald green stems so new and green they seemed too lovely to last.

I threw down my purse, shed my jacket and shoes, and went straight for the wine rack in the kitchen. Something dark and brooding, I thought, slipping out a bottle of Bordeaux, domestic from California.

I removed the wine glass from the drying rack, uncorked the bottle, and poured myself a full glass. I held the glass up to the light. Black deepened the red.

I took the glass and the bottle with me into the bathroom, placed them on the tub's edge, and ran the shower. Once the steam enveloped the room, I stepped into the shower and started scrubbing my skin until it hurt. In between ablutions, I drank. By the time I felt clean of those men, I was on my second glass. I slipped into my black moiré nightgown with the plunging back and my green velvet robe.

I put on water for spaghetti, opened a jar of pasta sauce and poured it into a pot. I shook the remains of a bagged salad into a bowl and sat down at the kitchen table.

Stuart's beefy hands, that overly muscled body, his soft spooky voice, the way his anger seemed too contained. Parks's slicked furrowed hair, the virulent beard, his conviction that he was different from the others, his saying he might as well be dead. And Bayer's defiance. His barely disguised threat, and those hands kneading away at his thighs.

Burnson had told me Stuart's wife had given him an alibi. And Parks and Bayer had been home alone that day. Burnson had said there was no physical evidence linking any of the men to the murder. That meant there had been no liftable fingerprints on her skin. And the ground must have been too trampled to isolate the killer's footprints and match them to his shoes.

Why was I focusing on these three? There were nine other men on that list. Burnson was following up on something. No names, no other information. But at least he had told me Stephanie hadn't been sexually assaulted. It was something.

By the time the water was boiling for the spaghetti, I was on my third glass. By the time I finished my salad and drained the pasta, I had opened another bottle.

After dinner I piled the dishes in the sink. And thought about moving.

"Just a matter of two truck loads," I told Salinger who was on the floor beside my chair.

I got up from the chair and headed for bed, the last of the wine sloshing around in the bottle, hoping the self-medication would work yet again, that sleep would be deep and long and silent.

The woods are both dark and light. The trees grab at me, their wet, heavy hands tangling around my body. I push and kick at them. But they won't let go. I can sense rather than see the Mink River, like a dull ache. The slow, gray water full of rain. But there is no sound.

My wet nightgown is cold. Mud oozes between my toes. But I keep moving forward, fighting the trees, the mud. Suddenly I see yellow. Up ahead. It seems to pulse with light.

I close my eyes but I can still feel the light, too warm and breathy, like gasping.

I try to turn but something is pushing me from behind, forward into the yellow light, into the clearing.

I know what I will see. But I don't look right away. Then I do. And there she is. Face down like before. One arm under her yellow-haired head, one arm twisted behind her. But this time her body glistens like marble. And she's naked, a sheen of blue flesh in the yellow light.

I kneel down beside her. The blond hair like silk covers her face. I reach down to move the hair, but the body turns by itself. The hair falls away. Then I scream. It isn't Stephanie. It's me. My eyes are open and fixed, almost green in the yellow light. And my naked body is whole. Like before.

I jerked myself awake. White rectangles of moonlight arched across the bed. My head throbbed and my mouth was dry. I looked over at the digital clock: 3:35 a.m. My nightgown and hair were damp and I was shivering. I got up and took off the wet nightgown. For a moment I caught my image in the mirror, half expecting to see the dream self.

Dark hair, slim legs, oval face, my impossible nose and that emptiness made all the more empty by the one breast. I flattened my breast against myself. Maybe reconstruction could take it all away. At least let me forget about my mortality. Not be reminded of it every time I saw myself naked.

I turned from the mirror, reached into a drawer, and pulled out the last clean nightgown. A blue watered silk with large straps like those 1930s movie stars wore. I slipped it on and walked into the dark living room. The smoky smell made my breath come short.

The moon slid into the corner of the window, white and shadowed, a sliver of herself. I sat down in the green chair. The velvet felt cold against my back. Only then did I let myself remember the dream. Me, dead in Stephanie's place.

I got up from the chair, went into the kitchen and started a pot of coffee. With coffee in hand I went into the living room, took the wildflower book from the shelf, sat down in the green chair, and looked up the three-petaled white flowers.

Common name: trillium. American Indians used the root of the plant as an eye medicine. What was I not seeing?

Chapter Sixteen

Friday, May 26

"Where you been? I must have left you a dozen messages," Lydia Crane asked, looking around the cramped mobile home for somewhere to put down the pizza and bottle of Australian wine she'd brought as a housewarming gift. There was no place to put my books, so most of them were still in boxes scattered everywhere. It had taken me all of three trips yesterday to move in.

"Jeez, how can you stand this place? It's like being in a sardine can with none of the ambiance." Lydia put the wine in the sink and the pizza on the stove burners, the only uncluttered spots.

"It has its charms. Like no rent and—"

Lydia chimed in, "And no rent." She located a knife under a box of books on the dinette table. "Where are the paper towels?"

I pointed to the built-in desk behind the dinette table. She grabbed the roll. "This place explains a lot about Sarah. She lives in this cubbyhole and has her studio in that beautiful building next door. The girl does love to suffer."

The silvery aluminum mobile home resembled a wide, beige-carpeted hallway. Bed at one end, bath at the other. Sandwiched in between were a stovetop, sink, dinette table, and desk with chair. If I were claustrophobic, I'd be downing anti-anxiety pills by the handful.

On the other hand, Sarah's studio was a large, spacious room full of windows with a view of Lake Michigan. I didn't know if it had a bathroom, because I'd only been there once and Sarah hadn't left me the key. She didn't want me or Salinger anywhere near her paintings.

"So when's Jake getting back?" Balancing a piece of pizza on a paper towel, Lydia sat down in an orange butterfly chair, her long paisley skirt ballooning around her petite figure. The thin silvery bracelets on her wrist made a tinkling sound like wind chimes. She was wearing her crystal snake earrings, which meant an assignation. Her black scoop-necked knit top showed just a hint of cleavage.

"Can't say." I took a piece of pizza from the box and sat in the matching butterfly chair.

"So it's like that, huh?" she said, taking a bite of pizza. "He always gets a little weird this time of year. It'll pass."

I let that go. I didn't want to talk about Jake. "Lydia, you know a lot of people on the peninsula." Though a transplant to the area, Lydia had lived here for seven years.

"Leigh, you've got that look. What are you up to?"

"You know any eighteen-year-old Eriks?" I asked, coughing. After moving my things, I had spent the rest of the day trying to track down Janell's Erik and hadn't succeeded. I was beginning to think she had lied to me.

"You gonna see someone about that cough? Or are you going to do what you usually do? Ignore it and hope it goes away. You know, that could lead to pneumonia."

"Yes, Mom." I rolled my eyes.

"You've got a bad attitude, lady. At least take some cough medicine so you don't infect the rest of us healthy people."

"Eriks? Know any?" I asked again.

"Yeah, one. But he's not eighteen. More like nineteen or twenty. Erik Ritter. He lives on Washington Island. He's an honest-to-goodness fisherman. At least that's what he listed as his occupation. I treated him last year for an infected finger. He said he cut it gutting a fish."

Could this be Elly's dream guy? A twenty-year-old would know the trouble he'd be in for having sex with a minor. But, of course, that hadn't stopped Stuart.

"Very yummy. If you like tall, dark, and brooding." Lydia ran her tongue around her lips.

"Honestly, sometimes you're so disgusting." I laughed out a cough that burned my chest. I did have to pick up some cough medicine.

This couldn't be the guy. Stephanie had said Elly called him Brad as in blond Brad Pitt.

"Some young guys like 'experienced' women, if you know what I mean. They don't have to play games. And we know what to do with the equipment. He was definitely one of those guys. But he was a little off."

"What do you mean off?"

"Off," she said emphatically as if that explained it. She dabbed at her mouth with the paper towel. "Besides, it would have been too easy. Like taking candy from a baby."

In Lydia-speak that probably meant he wasn't interested.

"You know where on the island he lives?"

"No," she answered warily. "Does this have anything to do with Stephanie Everson's murder?"

"Can't say." Lydia didn't support my investigative forays.

"Can't say or won't say?" She folded her legs under her skirt. "I saw Rob did the follow-up article on Stephanie. Trouble in paradise?"

"He's on some power trip." I leaned back and reached for another piece of pizza. One plus about Sarah's place: everything was at your fingertips.

"Leigh, you just don't know how to handle him. He's really a pussy cat." Her eyebrows went up and down. "If you know what I mean."

"Please, I'm trying to digest my food. Want another piece?" I said, imagining the things I'd like to do to Martin, none of which involved handling.

She got up and straightened her skirt. "This has been fun, but gotta go. Hot date."

I wasn't aware that Lydia was seeing anyone. "Someone I know?"

"Only too well." She patted Salinger on the head as she walked to the door. "Poor doggie, I'll bet you miss all that space."

"You can't be serious."

"It's just a date, Leigh. Not everything is life or death."

I didn't say anything. But if she thought Martin was ever going to forget Sarah Peck, she was more deluded than Elly Margaris about her eighteen-year-old lover, Erik.

As she reached into her purse for her car keys, something fell on the floor. "Oh, I almost forgot." She picked it up and handed it to me. It was a purple hair band with a small glass ball attached at one end. "You left this on the doorknob."

I held the ponytail band in the palm of my right hand staring at it as if it were a poisonous snake.

"This was on my doorknob?"

"Is something wrong? You look positively white."

"No." I closed my hand over the purple hair band. "Nothing's wrong. I'm just tired."

"Make sure you see a doctor. Okay?"

After she left, I wrapped the rubber band around my ring finger twice, positioning the glass ball on top. It was a duplicate of the ring that had been on Stephanie's finger.

Chapter Seventeen

Monday, May 29. Memorial Day

As I stood on Northpoint Pier waiting for the ten a.m. Washington Island ferry to unload, I thought again about the purple hair band. I had spent an uneasy three nights in my new home. I'd debated calling Burnson and telling him about the hair band, but eventually decided against it. After all, what proof did I have that the killer had left it? I could hear Burnson's carefully phrased argument delivered in a tone used on unruly children and mental patients.

"For all you know, Leigh, that could be Sarah Peck's."

It could be. Just like super models could be brain surgeons. Possible, but very unlikely.

On the upside, I'd found an E. Ritter listed in the yellow pages. After repeatedly phoning, I had finally reached Erik Ritter. I told him I was doing a story on the hardships of being a fisherman. He sounded wary, but he had finally agreed to see me Monday. But only after I assured him that Wally Thiery, an old-timer and former fisherman, had given me his name. I knew Wally by sight but had never talked to him. Sometimes I wondered if a tally was being kept somewhere of all my lies and if I'd have to account for them one day.

So that meant I wouldn't be covering the last day of Maifest. To my credit, I'd made two quick stops on Saturday and Sunday just in case something happened I should know about. But it was business as usual: craft stalls galore, a beer tent doing great business, an open barbecue pit billowing clouds of smoke, and lots and lots of aimless people milling around.

Martin wasn't going to like it, but my Maifest piece was a profile of Mildred Glaser, a longtime Jacksonport resident and painter. Mildred had the unique distinction of never winning an award at the juried art fair in the thirty years of Maifest. She was the only artist who had entered all thirty times and lost all thirty times.

"I don't think about winning anymore. I'm just happy to still be painting," Mildred had told me. "I'm kinda the Susan Lucci of art fairs. Oh, but didn't she finally win one of those awards? Well, you never know."

She'd also been a WAC during WWII. Since it was Memorial Day weekend, I reasoned, as I walked up the ferry ramp, I had Martin's "interesting" angle. I'd titled the article: *Maifest's Memorial Mildred.* The only hitch was the awards weren't given out until four p.m. today. Mildred had promised to call me if she did win. I just hoped nothing momentous happened. What could happen? Other than someone drinking too much beer and getting into a fist fight.

As the boat pulled away from the dock, I made my way up the steel stairs to the open deck at the ferry's rear, breathing in the smell of gasoline and exhaust. Overnight rain had brought a change in the weather for the better. The sky was crisp as a blue sheet with big puffy cumulous clouds riding the horizon. Standing against the silver mesh guardrail, I watched the ferry's wake trail behind. Though the sun felt warm on my skin, the inky green water looked heavy and cold and encompassing, thick like jelly or clotted blood. How much of winter was still held there, I thought, again marveling at the Native Americans who once made the treacherous crossing through Death's Door.

"Pretty soon we won't be able to see where we came from," a man said to his son who was standing next to me.

I sat down on one of the brown metal seats in the sun. Inside the glass-enclosed area all the benches were filled with families, except for a couple necking in a corner and a guy watching them. The guy was wearing a navy blue windbreaker and a beige baseball hat. His face had that soft, loose look that men get after a certain age. Though he had on sunglasses, I could tell from the angle of his head that he was mesmerized by the necking couple. If that was the right word.

Not wanting to spend the extra ten dollars to take my truck over on the ferry, I rented a bike at the dock—a cheaper alternative at three dollars an hour. The guy who thought he was a comedian gave me a pink bike with a white straw basket on the front and a silver bell. I threw my purse in the basket, rang the bell, and headed down Main Road—a winding uphill asphalt road. Erik Ritter lived on the other side of the island near Jackson Harbor. That was where you caught the Karfi ferry to Rock Island, an uninhabited spit of land famous for its massive stone Viking Hall. The 900-acre island had been turned into a state park where the more adventurous could camp.

As I biked up a particularly long grade, I was breathing heavily and felt a stitch in my side. The winter inactivity had taken its toll. But at least I wasn't coughing. I had taken a megadose of suppressant before I left home.

When I reached Swenson Road, I was sweating profusely under my sweatshirt. Ritter had told me he lived at the end of the road.

"There ain't an address. It's the only place there."

The gravel road ended abruptly and I biked down a dirt path. The house, which was shaped like a lighthouse with a cross on top, was an old church. Its limestone exterior had darkened with age. Ivy grew up the walls and over the windows. The shift of dappled sunlight cast a deep gloom that was intensified by the small cemetery beside the church. A narrow mud path meandered on the other side that I guessed led to the shore. I walked up the three crumbling stone steps and knocked on the silvery-gray wooden doors. There was a smell of rot and decay about the place. I could hear the heavy syncopation of rap music.

Erik Ritter was indeed tall and brooding, but he wasn't dark. At least not today. He had to be six-four with a swimmer's body—lean, long muscles and square shoulders. His dark hair had been dyed a startling white. He had small, slitty green eyes and a day's growth of dark stubble that looked cultivated. He wasn't wearing a shirt and his jeans hung low on his hips. I sensed what Lydia had meant about something being off about him. Nothing I could name, just a feeling.

"You the reporter?" he asked. He was holding a beer. It wasn't even noon.

"That's me." Behind him, I could see pews scattered around the room.

"So how's that old dude, Wally, doing?" The one corner of his mouth lifted in a half smile.

"Great," I said. I took out my notebook to indicate the interview was starting.

"Don't you want to come in?" He didn't wait for my answer.

I followed his shirtless back into the house. He had a small tattoo of a spider near his left shoulder blade. The spider had a human face and fangs. "Wanna beer?" he asked.

"I usually wait till noon," I said, pushing aside several stained throw pillows to sit down on the pew closest to the exit. An old brown dog slept on a bunch of blankets against the wall.

He walked over to the refrigerator and pulled out three beers. He handed me one; he kept the other two. "It's about noon. Saves me a trip."

I placed the beer on the pew. A rap artist was blaring out a colorful array of names for women and what he wanted to do to them. All rhymed, all terrible.

"Do you think we could turn that down?"

He looked at me with those slitty eyes. "Sure." He picked up a small remote and pointed it at the stereo, turning the volume down. Then he scraped one of the pews across the wood floor so that we were practically sitting knee to knee.

A thin line of sweat was traveling down my spine. This guy was giving me the creeps. And it made me feel reckless.

"It must be hard for a young guy living on the island." I shifted my knees sideways. "Finding women to go out with."

"I do all right." He gave me an appraising leer. Maybe Lydia had been right—it would be too easy.

"Why don't you tell me about being a fisherman. Let's start with, why'd you become one?" I felt like licking the tip of my pen to assure him that this was a real interview, for a real article.

He took a long draw on his beer. "It's a living."

I was doodling on my notebook, pretending to write down his comments. I had just drawn a tiny jackass and named him Erik.

"Did you always want to be a fisherman?"

"Ya got to do something to feed yourself." He smirked.

I wondered if he thought this strong, silent thing was alluring. Maybe to fifteen-year-old girls.

"Do you live here alone?" I scanned the room. The scattered pews took up most of the space. One was doubling as a makeshift bed. There was a table with three chairs, a hot plate, and a potbelly stove. The altar had been removed. In its place was a TV and stereo unit. For all the clutter of the room, his CDs were neatly stacked in a metal CD stand. Morning sun flooded the stained-glass windows, throwing green, yellow, and red shadows across the floor. The windows' motif was the Stations of the Cross. I had a good view of Veronica wiping the face of Jesus.

"Just me and Rufus." At the sound of his name, Rufus raised his head, looked at me hard, sniffed, then went back to sleep.

"How old are you?"

"Nineteen." He didn't hesitate.

"That's kinda young to be on your own. I mean how did you finance a boat?" I didn't want to make him suspicious.

"It was my dad's. He's gone. So I took over. I'm old enough."

It was the most information I'd gotten out of him.

"I'm sorry. When did he die?"

He looked puzzled. "He ain't dead. He's down in Florida fishing."

"And your mother?"

"What do you want to know about her for?" he asked warily.

"Just trying to get the whole picture. Have you always lived in Door County?"

"Since we come from Indiana." He crushed his beer can with one hand and tossed it toward the open garbage can. It hit the wall and went in. "Lady, I don't see what any of this has to do with fishing."

I picked up my beer and popped the top. I took a slow sip, pondering what to say. "You ever fish the Mink?"

"I'm a commercial fisherman." He was losing patience. "That's pleasure fishing." He opened the second beer.

I gazed at Veronica and dived in. "You know Stephanie Everson?"

He put his beer down. "That kid that got murdered?"

"Yeah."

"No."

"She was a friend of Elly Margaris."

I had to give him credit; he didn't even blink. "So. What's that got to do with me?" He leaned back, crossed his arms over his chest, his hands under his armpits.

"Elly claims she was with you last weekend."

"I see a lot of girls," he said coolly.

"You see lots of girls who are fifteen?"

A ripple of emotions crossed his face. He finally settled on surly. "You think I'm dumb enough to fall for that?" He snorted. "You tell that crazy bitch it's not going to work. I'm not interested. She got what she came for. What's with you chicks?"

He picked up his beer and drank the rest down in two gulps. I watched his Adam's apple bob up and down. When he finished, he tossed the can into the garbage can, then let out a loud belch. I could smell the beer fumes.

"She's fifteen, which makes her jailbait. She's under some illusion that you two are in love. Just so you know, so you're not under some illusion yourself, if her parents decide to have you put in jail, they can. So it doesn't matter whether you believe me or not. 'Cause you're still in trouble. That's what's with us chicks."

It was like watching a person slowly unravel. His arms uncrossed, his hands slid down to his lap, his mouth opened in astonishment.

"Shit." He said it so slowly, it sounded like a snake hissing. "She told me she was eighteen." His demeanor had switched from surly to innocent. "How was I suppose to know she was fifteen?"

I gave him my best you've-got-to-be-kidding look.

"Honest. I swear. And she wasn't no virgin. I can tell you that."

"Look, save it for her parents. That's not why I'm here."

"You don't have to say nothin'. Do you?" There was a threat in the *do you.*

"Like I said. I'm not here for that. Tell me about Stephanie. Did you know her?"

His head was down, so I could barely hear him. "Elly

mentioned some girl by that name. I never seen her."

"What did she say about her?"

"Nothing. Just that she was covering for her."

"What about last Friday? When you met Elly, did she say anything about Stephanie then?"

"Listen, bitch, I told you I don't know nothin' about that girl." He was back to surly.

I knew an exit line when I heard one. I closed my notebook and stood up.

He stood up with me. His bare chest was in my face. He had a dark mole under one nipple. The nipple had a hole in it for a nipple ring.

"They can't do anything to me. You tell her parents that. She said she was eighteen. There's no way I did anything wrong."

The beer fumes encircling me were making me nauseous. I wasn't going to let him intimidate me. "Really, Casanova? Then why didn't you bring her back? Why'd you dump her like that?"

He hesitated. "What are you talking about? Dumped her where?"

"How'd she end up hiding in an engine room on the Washington Island Ferry? You kick her out once you were through with her?"

He stepped back out of my personal space—a look of worry on his stubbly face. "I don't know what she said, but I took her in my boat to Northport Sunday morning. You tell her parents that. Tell them I didn't dump her." There was a hollowness in his protests.

"I'm sure they'll be impressed by your chivalry." I pushed past him and walked to the doors.

"You chicks are all alike," he shouted at my back. "Nothing but bitches."

I pulled open the heavy doors and walked down the steps. As I biked away, loud thumping music filled the woods. "Show da hoe, show da hoe, show da hoe da floor. Show da hoe, show da hoe, show da hoe da door."

I didn't believe a word Erik Ritter had said.

Chapter Eighteen

Monday, May 29

"So how was the Stillwater reunion?" I was nursing a lukewarm cup of coffee, sitting in the sunken seating area of the Land's End Inn. The Inn was a twenty-three-unit motel off Highway 42 at the foot of the hill that led into Egg Harbor. What it lacked in a water view, it made up for in trees. As long as your room didn't face the asphalt parking lot, you could pretend that you were in a pine forest.

Besides nursing children at Bay Hospital and teaching canoeing at the marina, Joe worked the front desk on weekends and some nights. As he had explained to me when I first met him, "Only rich people have two jobs."

"Loud," he said. "Couldn't get a word in." I noticed he wasn't drinking the stale coffee. "I've been looking for you over at the marina. Now that's it's warmer, you can start canoeing lessons. So next time we go out on the river, you'll know what you're doing. Though for a beginner, you did pretty good."

Joe had a way of making you feel you were his best friend. That you could do no wrong. In my worldview, that kind of unconditionality left you open to all kinds of hurt.

"Until I went for a swim."

"There was that." He chuckled to himself. "How you doing?" His dark stare made me nervous.

I knew what he was asking. "Fine. I'm fine." I stared at the empty fire grate. "I'm living over at Sarah's for the summer."

"Okay, you don't want to talk about it. But I am a good listener. Have to be in my family. What's up?"

"You know an Erik Ritter? Fisherman. Lives on Washington Island. Young. Tall guy. Surly attitude." I'd driven straight from the ferry to the motel, hoping Joe was on duty. I had been avoiding him, afraid seeing him would bring back some other forgotten horror from that night. But I was willing to risk it. Joe might know something about Ritter.

"That's him." Joe laughed. "But you forgot the part about—thinks he's a stud."

I laughed. "*Thinks* being the operative word."

"I know him only too well. He and I got into it a few times. He keeps docking that heap he calls a boat at the marina and doesn't pay the docking fee. Tells me he's not leaving it there, just picking someone up. Then he leaves it there. You know, I like to give a guy a break, but he really takes advantage. And he's not much of a fisherman either. Not far as I can see. What's he got to do with Stephanie Everson? That's why you're here, isn't it?"

It was unnerving the way Joe seemed to read my mind. "He's where Elly Margaris was when everyone was looking for her."

"Man, I knew it was something like that. I just had a feeling. Her parents know?"

"Not yet." I didn't know if I should be telling Joe about this considering that a crime had been committed. "This is between us. Okay Joe?"

"Sure, don't worry. Hey, I don't like that Ritter kid much, but I sure don't want to see him go to jail. I mean, that's the kind of thing could ruin a kid's life."

I was surprised and a little disappointed by Joe's attitude. "Don't you think *the kid* should have thought of that before having sex with a minor?"

"Yeah, I guess. Though I wonder if he knew she was a minor.

She sure doesn't look fifteen."

"He knows now. You know anything else about him? Anything about his background?"

"Why the big interest in him? You don't think he had something to do with Stephanie's murder? You just said he was with Janell."

"Hard to say where he was when Stephanie was killed. Janell was found on the ferry around nine-thirty Saturday night. Annie last saw Stephanie around one. It was after eight when we found the body. Whether Ritter was with Janell between one and eight, who knows? I couldn't get anything out of her but half truths, and the police don't seem interested in Janell."

He cocked his head to one side, considering my answer. "Unless he's some psycho, what motive would he have." It wasn't a question.

"I don't know. Hates women? Who knows? It's just a feeling I have about him. You know anything about his parents? He seemed pretty touchy about his mother."

"They came here a few years back. Father thought he was a fisherman. I don't think he ever made a living at it. Mother got fed up and left. Then a year or so ago the father takes off. Someone said he went down to Florida. There was a joke about the fishing being better down there."

"Why didn't the kid go with him?"

"If I had to guess, he probably wanted to be on his own. He's that kind—always proving himself. And the father was real hard on him, especially after the mom left. Smacked him around some. I saw him with a black eye a couple times. Told me he fell."

That explained a lot. "They always live in that abandoned church?"

Joe looked at me perplexed. "What abandoned church?"

"I don't know the name. But it's at the end of Swenson Road.

There's a cemetery next to it."

"Jeez, he's living at old Saint Andrews. I got to give him credit. There used to be stories about it being haunted. Passed down through the generations of Islanders. What's left of us, that is. Most are gone now, so that's probably why the kid's living there. He probably doesn't know about it." Joe shifted in his chair. "Last priest they had, a young guy back in the late nineteen-thirties, early forties, died real sudden. Nobody knew why. And back then, there was no doctor on the island. The story goes they found his body on the altar. No one could figure out why a young guy would just drop dead. After that, people claimed they saw him in the graveyard at night. I never believed any of it. But I sure wouldn't be living in that church. Not next to a graveyard."

"Joe, you were an Islander?" I realized how little I really knew about Joe.

"Yeah, my people go way back. We lived on the island before you white people showed up and ruined everything." He smiled, but underneath there was a sharpness.

I studied his face. It was too broad and angular to be considered handsome. He had a straight, determined nose and eyes so deep set they were impossible to read. But his mouth was full and generous. There was a bearish quality about him that was both comforting and powerful. Under his blue dress shirt his broad shoulders seemed confined. His long legs looked restless in his khaki trousers.

"Well, we white people have a lot to atone for."

"What are you atoning for, Leigh?"

The question caught me off guard. The playfulness in his voice was gone. "I think you're pushing it with Ritter. And I think it's because something else is bothering you. And it goes deeper than finding Stephanie's body. You look strung out like you haven't slept in a week. Or eaten, for that matter. What's going on?"

My face flushed. I bit the inside of my cheek. He had hit too close to the truth. "What could be going on? A girl's murdered. I find her, just hours after talking to her. I have every right to be strung out."

"What did you talk about?"

"Her cat. How she'd been covering for Elly, how she ought to call Chet and tell him about it." I clasped my hands between my legs to stop my shaking. "You know what Stephanie was doing when she was killed? She was out looking for Elly. Annie told me that. She said, 'I didn't even look up. It was the last time I would ever see my daughter and I didn't even look up.' Stephanie was out looking for Elly when she met her killer. And I think it was because of me."

"You tell her to go look for Elly?" He leaned forward resting his arms on his thighs.

"I pushed her too hard. It's what I do. It was so easy." My voice dropped to a whisper. "She never called Chet. Instead, she went looking for Elly. That's what Annie told me."

His eyes never left my face. "Did you kill her?"

"That's not the point. I caused her to go there. I put her in harm's way."

"You're not that powerful, Leigh. Besides, why would Stephanie be looking for Elly along the Mink if she knew she was with Ritter on Washington Island?"

"I don't know. Maybe because she thought Elly never made it to the Island. That something happened to her after she left her at the marina."

"If she ever was at the marina." Joe sounded angry. "How did Elly get to the Island? If it was by ferry, how did she get to the ferry? There are too many ifs for you to take this on. Wait and see how it turns out. Guilt is a waste of time."

"If you believe Elly, she hitchhiked to Northpoint, then took the ferry over."

"Do you believe her?"

"Some of her story sounds right."

"Like I said, guilt is a waste of time." He sat back in his chair. "You should let the police handle this."

"Not an option," I scoffed, getting up to leave.

"Risking your own life isn't going to bring Stephanie back." Joe stood up. "Let it go."

"I can't. Chalk it up to my compulsive nature. I can't help myself." I wasn't going to tell him about my promise to Annie. I had told him enough.

He walked me out into the evening. Trees were darkening against the night. From Highway 42 came the steady hum of traffic, people heading south, back to their everyday lives.

"Look." Joe had come up behind me. He put his one hand on my shoulder and held my body still. Its warmth radiated through me.

"Over there." His other hand pointed past me.

I followed where he was pointing to a burst of white, delicate flowers in a thicket beside the motel parking lot.

"Wood anemones. Windflowers. Spring's finally here."

"Why are you calling?" Janet Margaris sounded annoyed.

"I found Erik." I could hear a voice in the background. I was sitting in bed, Annie Dillard's *Pilgrim at Tinker's Creek* on my lap, looking out into the dark woods surrounding the mobile home.

"It's someone selling something," Janet shouted to someone.

"Janet," I said loudly. "Did you hear me? I found Elly's Erik. He lives on Washington Island. His name's Ritter. Erik Ritter."

"Don't call here anymore."

The line went dead.

My conscience was clear. I had tried to tell her. Now if only I could clear my conscience of that other matter.

Chapter Nineteen

Tuesday, May 30

"What's this?" I asked Marge as I read my article on the release of the sex offenders list. Below my article was an editorial by Rob Martin entitled, "A Plea for Tolerance."

"What do you want, hon?" Marge asked. She was working on Friday's layout.

As I read through the editorial, my body became tenser and tenser. At the conclusion I felt like tempered steel.

"Marge, you read Martin's editorial?"

Marge turned in her chair to face me. Today she was wearing a tie-dyed blouse in shades of purple, blue and chartreuse and a long, wheat-colored skirt that looked like it was made from used barley sacks. Her newly straightened long hair, though white, made her look younger than her fifty-one years. Ever since she had begun taking pottery classes at the Peninsula Art School last winter, she'd had a metamorphosis. From day to day I never knew who would show up. It kept the place interesting.

" 'Course I read it. Have to stay awake somehow." She turned back to her work.

"You agree with this?" Martin's editorial fell just shy of criticizing the release of the list. It asked not only for tolerance but understanding. It implied that these men had paid their debt to society and should be left alone to get on with their lives.

"I'm a woman and a mother, whatta you think?"

"What's he trying to do by writing this?"

"Can't say, hon. You think it might have something to do with your discussion this morning?"

"You mean Martin's discussion."

"If you say so, hon."

When Martin read my story on Mildred Glaser this morning, he had turned purple and called me irresponsible, arrogant, insolent and a ball-busting hack. Mildred Glaser had won the grand prize at the Maifest Art Fair. As promised, she had left me a message on my machine. But what she'd failed to tell me was that she'd fainted upon hearing the news and been rushed to the hospital. Martin had witnessed the presentation. When I tried to explain that I was following up on a lead on the Everson case, he told me to get out of his office before he fired me.

After my tongue lashing, I was so incensed that I'd called the police department to see if they had anything new on the murder. Ferry had informed me that Martin had already called.

"Don't you people talk to each other over there?" Ferry had quipped.

I did learn from him that they'd found the contents of Stephanie's purse—scattered through the woods like an aberrant trail of bread crumbs—everything Annie had named, except her hairbrush. When I'd asked him why it had taken so long to find her things, he repeated the word *scattered.*

I mentioned the missing hairbrush and reminded Ferry about the body's positioning and the brushed hair. His only response had been: "Ya told me that there already."

When I explained Erik Ritter's involvement with Janell Margaris, he'd said that was up to the Margarises whether Ritter should be charged with statutory rape.

"Best left to the involved parties."

"But what if he's lying? He could be a suspect in Stephanie's murder," I'd practically shouted.

"I'll pass it along to the chief then. His call."

If nothing else, the conversation reassured me of my decision not to tell the police about the purple hair band left on my doorknob. Right now it was in my purse, zipped safely in a separate compartment, tucked away like an evil thought.

After hanging up with Ferry I'd written another article on the Everson case. I didn't care if Martin printed it or not. I was giving it to him. And I would keep on giving it to him until he gave in.

Around noon, Martin had stormed out of his office, stomped past my desk as if I wasn't there, and told Marge he was headed over to the Ridges Sanctuary. Every season he wrote an article on the sanctuary. Nature, Martin understood. People, he didn't.

I hadn't seen him the rest of the day.

"Hon, there's a call for you on two." Marge held the phone out to me as I walked by her desk toward the door. I was headed home to Salinger and a cool glass of wine. It was warm enough to sit out and watch night fall over the lake. "Who is it?"

"Wouldn't say. But he asked for you."

I reluctantly took the phone from her and pressed the red blinking light. "Hello."

"This Leigh Girard?" The voice was muffled.

"Yeah, who's this?"

"I got it right this time. I want you to find her. You know the place. Where the circles end."

"Who is this?"

He hung up.

"What's the matter?" Marge asked. "You look like someone walked over your grave."

I put down the phone slowly. "I hope not."

Chapter Twenty

Tuesday, May 30

I should have called the police, but I didn't. This could be a sick prank. Besides, I was tired of them treating me as if I was an escaped mental patient. Instead I called Joe at the motel. He listened and then told me to meet him by the mud path off Rowleys Bay.

We were on the water by 7:30 p.m. The sun was already in the trees, making its slow, sure descent—deep shadows moving across the water like night spirits.

"We should put in at the Conservancy path. Then follow the yellow circles to the clearing. I'm sure that's what he meant by where the circles end," I told Joe as we paddled into the river's mouth.

"Yeah," was all he said.

The river's Canadian charm was gone for me. Instead the emerald-green trees felt ominous, full of secrets and terror. I touched my life jacket for reassurance. But I wasn't afraid for myself anymore.

Neither of us spoke except when we changed paddling sides. The silence was so heavy; I had trouble catching my breath. Occasionally a fish jumped from the water or a gull screeched overhead. But mostly the woods waited silently with us.

We landed at the path and dragged the canoe up the muddy shore. I practically ran down the Conservancy trail with Joe at my heels. The mud and rocks tugged at my running shoes.

When I reached the clearing I slowed my pace. The light was losing itself in the trees. But the dimness was humming, as if alive with something potent and unnamable.

"Why don't you let me go first." Joe had his hand on my arm. I could feel his gentle pressure through my sweater.

"No." I pulled away from him and walked slowly forward. And then I saw it as before. The smell of death's release turned my stomach.

"Oh my God."

Like some horrible play reenacted, there she was, exactly where Stephanie had been. Face down, one arm under her head, the other awkwardly behind her back. The yellow hair meticulously brushed around her shoulders. And the purple ring on her left hand.

I stood over her. There was no need to push her hair back or turn her over. I recognized the spiky heels, the shorts, the white tube top. If I pushed back the hair I knew what I would see—Janell Margaris, her swollen, pierced tongue protruding from her open mouth as if there was one last thing she wanted to say.

"I got it right this time." The words rose up.

I ran toward the edge of the clearing and vomited.

I stood behind the yellow tape watching Deputy Chief Celeste Hallaway do her job with the precision of a drill sergeant. She was a large-boned African-American woman with short-cropped, bleached-blond hair, light golden-brown eyes, and a doughy nose. Her skin was a warm caramel color. She had to be over six feet tall, because she dwarfed Ferry by a good three inches.

Her manner was as crisp as her khaki uniform. She was the lead officer of the task force team. Before coming to Brown County, Wisconsin, Hallaway had been a Cook County ranger policewoman and a Chicago EMT. She was certified in dive rescue and bomb detection. Joe and I had learned all this from Officer Ferry while we waited for the task force to arrive. As the closest patrolman in the area, Ferry had been the first on the scene.

"Just don't get on her bad side," Ferry had said. "She's like PMS in a uniform there."

It had taken the task force forty-five minutes to reach the scene of the crime. In that time I'd sat at the clearing's edge, going over and over in my mind what I could have done to save Janell Margaris. Joe had tried to talk to me, but after my succession of one-syllable responses, he'd given up and sat with me in silence. I knew I was in shock but guilt was eating away at it. And when it broke through, it would feel like I'd been skinned alive.

When Hallaway arrived with the other task force members, she'd ordered Joe and me to canoe back to Rowleys Bay Resort where we were to wait for her. I'd told her I wasn't leaving. She'd taken one look at my face and said, "Get yourself outside the perimeter then. And we'll need your shoes."

The task force was like a well-choreographed dance under Hallaway's direction. She seemed to have an uncanny sense of what everyone was doing and how their movements impinged on everyone else's movements.

Night had blotted the clearing. Because of the remoteness of the region, they couldn't bring in a generator to light the scene. Instead flares and lanterns formed a ring of light around the area, casting long shadows. Joe and I sat outside the light, in its shadow. I tried to focus on what the police were doing. But my eyes kept drifting back to the body. Hallaway and another officer named Lewis were ministering to it. If that was what you called it. Both wore latex gloves. Neither touched the body. They noted the body's position, took photos from every angle, then took more notes.

"Okay," Hallaway said, kneeling down beside the body. "Let's turn her."

Lewis knelt beside Hallaway. Slowly they rolled the body face up. For a moment everyone stopped what they were doing.

I stood up. "That's not her," I said, walking over the yellow tape.

"Get back," Hallaway shouted, gesturing with her hand. "Right now."

"That's not Janell Margaris," I insisted.

Hallaway stood up and came toward me, but I didn't move.

"Do you know who this is?" Hallaway asked, pointing back at the body.

"No, I've never seen her before."

"I know her," Joe said. He too had stood up but he hadn't breached the yellow tape. "I know who she is." He looked shaken.

Hallaway waited for him to continue. "Her name's Lisette. I don't know her last name. She's one of the grad students living at the summer camp across Rowleys Bay. You know, with that professor from the university, Kolinsky."

Hallaway turned back toward Lewis. "Bag her hands. The rest of you finish what you're doing." She pointed to Joe and me. "You and you. Outta here now. Ferry, take their canoe back to the marina. Wait there for Lewis. You two are coming with me."

"What were the caller's exact words?" Hallaway asked me for the hundredth time. She was seated across from me in a windowless gunmetal-gray room that had the ambiance of an underground bunker. The room was at the rear of the Sturgeon Bay Police Department. There were no windows. Just one light beat down on the table, making a harsh yellow circle.

I let out a heavy sigh. "I've already told you."

"Tell me again." Hallaway showed no signs of fatigue. There was a fierceness in her golden-brown eyes. Murder was her aphrodisiac.

" 'I want you to find her. You know the place. Where the circles end. I got it right this time.' Can I go now?"

"That's not what you said before."

"Which time?"

"Listen, Girard, we've got two unsolved murders. The killer contacted you. You're a material witness." Some time ago I had gone from Ms. Girard to Leigh. Now I was Girard. Maybe when I'd become nameless, she'd let me go.

I was bone weary. My nerves taut as Hallaway's attitude. "Let me think," I said, going over in my mind the phone call.

"He said, 'I got it right this time. I want you to find her. You know the place. Where the circles end.' Then he hung up."

"And you didn't recognize his voice?"

"No. Like I said, it sounded muffled. Like he had something over the mouthpiece." I ran my hand across my forehead. If I didn't get out of there soon, I'd have a full-blown migraine. A banding at the back of my skull had already started.

"Why didn't you call the police first?"

"Because frankly, I didn't think you'd take me seriously. Besides I wasn't sure if it wasn't some kind of sick joke."

She pushed back on her steel-gray chair. It had a back that resembled prison bars. "But if it was true, you'd have an exclusive. Could make a journalist's career."

A flare of anger shot through me. I crossed my arms over my chest and stared at her. "Or a cop's."

Hallaway smirked. "Okay. What made you think the victim was Janell Margaris?"

"The hair, the body type, the clothes. I'd seen Janell wear clothes like those."

"When you followed her from her house?" Hallaway was

drumming her fingers on the cold gray table. First one hand, then the other.

I'd told her everything I knew about Janell and Erik and Stephanie, implicating myself in the telling.

I shook my head yes. "This woman, Lisette," I said, "and Stephanie—they seem to fit a profile. And the bodies, the way they were positioned. And that purple hair band ring twisted around their fingers." I wanted to test her reaction as well as wrestle back a measure of control.

Hallaway gave me a stare that could melt paint off a wall. "You're not to reveal any details about this case. You got that? And I want your interview notes. All of them. Anything that relates to Stephanie Everson and Janell Margaris. And those interviews you did with Parks, Bayer and Stuart."

"I don't know if I can do that." I returned her paint-peeling stare.

"You'll cooperate with me, or you'll end up in jail. I got no use for you newspaper types." She leaned in so close I smelled the faint trace of garlic on her breath.

"I know all about you, Girard." She said my name like it was a dirty word. "If you mess with me, you'll find yourself on the short end of my temper. And I'm no Chet Jorgensen. You can be sure of that. You bring those notes by my office tomorrow morning. Or else."

If she thought that speech was going to win me over, she was wrong.

"You can't stop me from doing my job." In the back of my mind was the promise I'd made to Annie Everson.

She stood up so suddenly her chair fell backwards. She put her two hands on the table and leaned into my face. "I don't know exactly how you fit into all this. But if I find out your meddling in any way contributed to this woman's death, I'll have you up on charges."

"You do what you have to do." I didn't know if I was handing over my notes to her or not, I just didn't like being bullied.

She straightened up, walked to the door, and swung it open. "We're done."

"Not yet," I said, gritting my teeth. I reached down for my purse and opened the flap. I unzipped the inside compartment, pulled out the purple hair band, and placed it on the table. I was sticking my neck out far enough for Hallaway to take a clean swing at it. But she needed to know about the calling card the killer had left me.

"What's this?" Hallaway asked, approaching the table. The hair band sat in the center of the yellow circle.

"It was left on my doorknob last Friday."

She picked it up and examined it. Then stared into my eyes, trying to read the truth.

"Get out of my sight," she said.

When I walked out into the cool night, Joe was leaning against his truck staring up at the stars.

"How did you get your truck?" I asked.

"They sprung me over an hour ago. Drove me back to my truck. Thought I'd save you another trip in a police car."

I could have hugged him I was so grateful.

"You look beat. What did she do to you?"

"Tuned me up good. Isn't that what they call it on those cop shows?"

Joe laughed. "Okay, let's get your truck."

I climbed up into the passenger side. "I could use a drink first."

"Not much open this late."

"I know a place never closes. Great lake view."

Joe slammed his door and started the engine. "Long as you're buying."

★ ★ ★ ★ ★

The lake was running high, with silver waves rippling in the moonlight. Salinger, sensing my need for comfort, was sitting quietly between Joe and me.

I'd set up two lawn chairs on the bluff and opened Lydia's bottle of Australian chardonnay. The air was chill but clean and invigorating.

"I think I'm in trouble," I said to Joe, who'd taken two polite sips of his wine and placed the glass down in the grass. I'd told him about the purple hair band left on my doorknob, which was now in Hallaway's possession.

I poured myself a second glass.

"You thinking this guy may come after you?" Joe asked. There was real concern in his voice.

I hadn't thought of that. "No. I don't think so. He's not after me. Besides I don't fit the victim profile. You know, blonde, younger. He wants me as a witness. In the biblical sense."

"What do you mean?"

The idea had come to me during the drive to the police station. "To attest to what he's done. As if to authenticate it in some way. Or maybe my witnessing it makes it right somehow. You know, like when you sign a document to make it legal. Or you have witnesses at a wedding to make it right in the eyes of God. Something like that."

"There's no way he could have known you'd find Stephanie. That was random. Any of us could have found her," Joe countered.

"Maybe that's what set him off. I don't mean killing again. But involving me. I found Stephanie. I wrote the first article. For some reason he wanted me to find the second victim."

"So you could write about it. Get it right, like he said."

"Get it right," I repeated. "But I'm not sure if I'm getting it right for him or for the victim."

"Now, what does that mean?"

"I'm not sure. Something about this ritual placement, somehow I think it all goes together."

"He's going to do it again." Joe said what I've been thinking. "If he's not caught."

"I know." I downed the rest of my wine and reached to pour another glass.

"It's getting kinda cold. You want to go in?" He took the bottle from my hand and picked up his own glass. "Let me help you."

As we walked toward the mobile home, Salinger ran ahead and into the open door. Yellow light was spilling across the clearing, welcome and warm as day.

"Don't think I'll be getting much sleep tonight," I said to Joe as I walked up the steps into the mobile home. "I keep seeing her face. Their faces. It was so awful." I stopped myself before the horror overtook me completely.

Joe didn't follow me into the home but stood in the doorway holding the bottle and his glass.

"You gonna finish this?" he asked, raising the bottle.

I looked at the half empty bottle. Then I looked at him—his sharply angled face, high cheekbones, the deep-set eyes, his dark hair. "They say it's not healthy. You know, drinking alone."

" 'They' say a lot of things. What are *you* saying, Leigh?"

"I'm saying I'd like you to stay."

He stepped inside closing the door behind him. He put the wine and his glass down on the dinette table, took the glass from my hand and put it beside them. For a moment we stood very still facing each other. Then he ran the back of his hand up the side of my face. My head leaned toward the gentleness of his gesture. It'd been a while since anyone had touched me with such care, such exploration. As if I were a new place waiting to be discovered.

For a man who found such expression in words, Joe was amazingly silent. It was as if something had switched off inside him. His body seemed to rob him of words.

I wanted to warn him before we went further. I wanted to tell him about what he would find under my clothes. But I wanted the feel of a living person beside me more than I wanted to protect myself. I wanted Joe to erase the death that seemed to cling to me.

His mouth found mine. It was a sweet, tentative kiss. Our bodies still maintaining that distance. When we pulled away, he had a question in his eyes.

I answered it with my mouth on his, insistent and hard as if I had to erase not only the distance between us but myself as well.

I unbuttoned his jacket, his shirt. I pressed my mouth against his chest. I pulled him toward the bed. He let me.

Shoes off, we knelt side by side on the bed. I took his hands and guided them toward my blouse. He unbuttoned each button slowly, kissing my forehead, my eyelids, my mouth. He slipped the blouse from my shoulders and kissed the space between my collarbones. I reached around and unhooked my bra. I was shaking as it fell away.

My face was burning, but I kept my eyes on his face as he saw me. There was no pity, no shock in his eyes. He cupped my one breast as he kissed the scar where the other breast once was.

Wednesday, May 31

The acrid smell of coffee filled the mobile home. In the dim, filtered light I rolled over and looked around. No Joe, no Salinger. My body hummed like a well-played instrument. I felt like Scarlett O'Hara the morning after that infamous abduction up the red staircase. Only I had played Rhett's part.

I got up and grabbed my robe from the hook. Coffee in hand, I went looking for Joe. He was sitting in one of the lawn chairs from last night fully dressed, watching the sun rise. Salinger was sitting beside him. His strong brown hands were running through her fur, slowly, gently.

I flopped down in the other chair. The sun was cresting the water, a splendid rush of red.

"Joe," I began. "About last night."

He put up his hand. He didn't look at me. "Sometimes, Leigh, it's better not to talk. We did each other a favor. Last night was about washing off the death. You don't owe me anything. I was just filling in."

Some of what he said was true, but not all of it.

"Still friends?" I asked, looking out over the lake.

"Sure."

Chapter Twenty-One

Wednesday, May 31

A bluegrass band was warming up in the dining room of the River Supper Club. The harmonic melody was as jumpy and jittery as Professor Terrance Kolinsky, who sat across from me keeping rhythm on the table with his fingers.

The River Supper Club, like so many businesses in Door County, was a converted house. Situated outside Ellison Bay, the club was separated from Highway 42 by asphalt parking spaces whose yellow lines were barely visible. Not much had been done to the white clapboard exterior except to put a sign out front. The interior was a dark series of rooms with solid maple tables and chairs. Along the sides of the building and at the back were a few windows filled with trees or views of the highway. But it had a reputation for good food at reasonable prices. And Candy, one of the owners and bartenders, made the best Bloody Marys on the peninsula. It was where the locals and the more seasoned tourists went.

Professor Kolinsky looked nothing like any professor I'd ever known. He had stringy, straw-colored hair parted in the middle that hung past his chin. His jeans were worn through in the knees and his four-pocket khaki vest was mud-stained. At least it looked like mud. He had a broad, rubbery face and a fleshy nose that gave him the appearance of lasciviousness. His large eyes were his only attractive feature—morning-glory blue. They were magnified by gold-rimmed glasses that rested halfway down his nose.

But underneath the slovenliness was the zealot's gaze—intense, hypnotic, seductive. I could see him pushing into the wilderness in search of souls. I could see him returning with them.

"That was the hardest phone call I've ever made," Kolinsky began. The sleeves on his red-plaid shirt were rolled up, exposing dirty-blond hair that matched the tufts at his neck. "Thank God, the police broke the news to her parents. I still can't believe it. You expect that kind of thing in big cities. But up here . . ." He looked down at his coffee, shaking his head. "Times like this I wish I still drank. My poison was vodka martinis, straight up, with a twist. Classy, yet potent. I sure could use one."

Like Kolinsky, I was abstaining from alcohol. I needed my wits about me. Until I eliminated him, Professor Terrance Kolinsky was yet another suspect on my list.

"Or a cigarette. Gave that up too." He picked up the silver cream server and poured more into his coffee. He'd been pouring so much cream into his cup, by now it had to be mostly cream. "My only remaining addiction is Somatochlora hineana, the Hine's Emerald Dragonfly."

After dropping off copies of my "selected" notes to Hallaway in the morning, I'd spent part of the day writing up a sanitized article on Lisette Cohen's murder and the rest of the day at the computer researching serial killers, disorganized killers, organized killers, lust killers, child killers. All the men I'd talked to since Janell's disappearance, including Terry Kolinsky, could fit one or other of these profiles. The common denominator they all shared was that they were white and male. But none of it was an exact science. There was a real art to finding a killer. Sometimes exceptions proved the rule. It seemed to me the killers made up the rules. And technically, these murders weren't classified as serial killings. There had to be three or more. But the closeness in time, the similarity of the victims, all pointed to a killer who, as Joe said, would kill again.

Martin had grudgingly accepted my article. It was hard to argue with the killer's new best friend.

As I'd left the office to keep my appointment with Kolinsky, Marge had commented, "I'll bet you're glad Jake's back tomorrow."

So he was coming back tomorrow. And I had to hear it from someone else. I didn't think the day could get any worse.

"Tell me about this dragonfly. What's so special about it?" I recalled Annie had mentioned something about a dragonfly and Russell Margaris's plans to develop his land.

Kolinsky actually seemed to get taller as he began to talk, and his hands became animated. "Used to be called the Ohio Emerald Dragonfly. But there are none left in Ohio. None left much anywhere except parts of Illinois, Minnesota and the Mink. The Mink's their breeding site. The Hine's is federally endangered. Even I'm restricted in the sort of experiments I can do. Here." He dug into one of his vest pockets and pulled out a glass vial. "That's her. Quite a beauty, isn't she?"

I turned the vial in the dim bar light. Inside was a helicopter-shaped bug with enormous eyes. I handed the vial back.

"Russell Margaris's development, how's that going to affect your research?"

"Not good." He scrunched his nose, pushing his glasses up. It was not an attractive sight. "So you want to know about Lisette."

That was an abrupt change of subject.

Kolinsky's enormous blue eyes darted around the bar as if the information was wafting on the smoky air. "Second-year grad student. Full ride. She had great instincts. Is that the kind of information you're looking for? Not just facts. The whole person, so to speak." There were deep creases in his forehead I hadn't noticed before.

My notebook was open on the table, but once again I wasn't taking notes. I was watching Professor Kolinsky as if he were under a microscope. His abbreviated comments struck me as oddly cold. He showed more emotion describing his bugs. Of course, he could be holding back his emotions. Maybe he was in shock. Or maybe he had something to hide.

"Anything and everything you can tell me."

"Brian, that's my other grad student, was always kidding her about how young she looked. When they'd go out for a beer, she'd always get carded and he never would. Though he's younger, I think by a year."

"How old was she?" I'd also read that serial killers, if this was a serial killing, usually choose a certain type as a victim. But again, that didn't always happen. Evil was unpredictable.

"Twenty-five. But she appeared much younger. Not just because she was blond and had a baby face. But there was a certain naiveté about her, a kind of innocence almost. You see that in some grad students, especially the ones who go right from undergrad to grad. Even if they work summers, it's always something to do with education. You know, camp counselor, tutor. Lisette was like that. Her whole world was aquatic ecology. I don't think she thought about anything else. At least she never talked about anything else to me."

Why was that sounding off? "Never, huh? That's unusual considering all of you are living together in that cabin. You married, Professor Kolinsky?"

That threw him. "Terry, please. After all, if you're asking what I think you're asking me, you can drop the professor." He pushed his stringy hair behind his ears. "I don't sleep with my grad students, if that's where you're going with this. Lest you think I have anything to hide, the answer to your question is:

divorced. Three years, no children. What about you?" I couldn't tell if he was being flirtatious or evasive or both.

I wasn't going there. "Do you think she could pass for a high school student?"

"I could see that happening. Like I said, she was young looking. If you didn't look too close." His guard was up again.

"She ever dress . . ." I was struggling to find a way to ask the question without giving him too much information. ". . . provocatively? Tight clothes, too short, maybe too much skin."

He looked incredulous. "If you want to be taken seriously in the academy, you don't dress like a tart."

I hadn't heard that word since I was an adjunct professor. It was one of the things I liked about the academy, how you could make anything sound good with the right word or words. "Okay. Maybe not in front of you."

"Then how would I know? Why don't you ask Brian about that? I think she had a crush on him. It wasn't reciprocal though." He stuck his large lips out.

"How so?"

"We're living together, as you pointed out, in that cabin. It's not hard to spot. Even a coldhearted scientist like me couldn't miss it. That's what you think I am, don't you? Coldhearted." He scrunched up his nose again, moving his glasses up.

When I didn't answer, he continued. "I've never been good at showing emotion. But believe me, this has hit me hard." He took off his glasses and rubbed his eyes with the heels of his hands. When he put his glasses back on, his eyes were red. The gesture seemed overdone. "Why are you asking me all these questions about her physical appearance?"

"No reason."

A slow smile spread across his rubbery face, almost giving it definition. "Don't you want to ask me how she was dressed yesterday?"

He'd caught on. Hallaway wouldn't like it. But I hadn't told him.

"Well?"

"Standard field gear—jeans, flannel shirt, vest. At least that's what I'd guess. I didn't see her when she left. And I can't tell you where she was going. Nor does Brian know. The police already went over all that with us."

"Any guesses where she was going?"

"Could be any number of things. Check out some sites. Just get away from us for a while."

"Were there any problems that she would need to get away?"

"Usual stuff that goes on when you're all crammed together like lemmings. Just sick of each other's company."

"But you hadn't been in camp very long."

"No, but we worked together all year." He looked at me, then looked away. "Brian will probably mention it, so I might as well tell you. But I don't want this printed in the newspaper. Brian accused Lisette of using his ideas in an article she submitted to a journal. It was a gray area. I won't go into the details. Brian found out about it the day before we left to come up here. He made a huge deal out of it. Brian makes a huge deal out of everything. He's very driven. She was so upset, she wasn't going to come, but I talked her into it. Told her she couldn't let that stand in the way of her work." He put his head down. "I thought I was doing the right thing for her. For the project."

"You couldn't have known."

"You wonder about things like that, don't you? I mean, if Lisette had listened to herself and not me, she'd be alive right now."

"The only person to blame is the killer." It sounded good. Now if I could only convince myself.

"Right, right."

"Can you think of anyone who would want to kill her?"

"What reason would anyone have for killing Lisette? She was a great girl. I know it's not PC to call a twenty-five-year-old woman a girl, but I think of all my students as kids. She was very bright. I can't imagine anyone wanting to harm her."

"What about Brian? He was upset with her."

"Brian as a killer is absolutely ridiculous. Just as ridiculous as me being a killer."

His voice had assumed that snooty tone professors used to remind you of their superior intellects. I wasn't impressed.

"Where were you that day?"

He stared at me for a long minute. "At camp working."

"And Brian?"

"He left about noon to get groceries," he answered curtly.

"And returned when?"

"Look, I know you have to ask these questions. But whatever problems there were between Brian and Lisette were sorted out before we came up here. More likely she must have been in the wrong place at the wrong time. Maybe she saw something she shouldn't have seen. Then there are the cold facts. Two girls, in two weeks, both blond, both murdered in the same place. I don't think you have to have a Ph.D. to figure out that someone's targeting these women."

The bluegrass band had taken a break and were crowding the bar.

"I might have some questions for you later. Are you staying on for the summer?"

"Have to. Whether I want to or not. Grant runs out next year. And then there's Margaris's development." He was trying to sound conflicted, but it was obvious nothing got in the way of his work. Probably that explained the divorce.

"What about Brian? Is he staying on as well?"

"He's pretty shook up, but he's going to stay. I told him he didn't have to." A paternal smile parted his lips. The snooty tone was gone.

"I'll want to talk to him."

"You know," he began, shifting in his seat. His leg brushed briefly against mine. "You didn't answer my question."

I didn't move my leg. "What's that, Terry?"

"Are you married?"

I hesitated for a moment. "Not that it's any of your business, but I am."

He pointed to my left hand. "Didn't see a ring. Might give a guy the wrong idea."

I closed my left hand into a fist. "Never found a ring made any difference." I smiled "To guys getting wrong ideas."

As I pulled out of the parking lot onto Highway 42, I realized two things. Kolinsky hadn't asked how Lisette was killed and the professor was a letch.

Chapter Twenty-Two

Wednesday, May 31

The sun was an orange glare purpling the sky as I drove south on Highway 42 through Sister Bay. A group of camera-clad tourists were ogling and pointing at the goats lolling on the roof of the Swedish Restaurant. The tourist season had officially begun.

If I hurried, I could be home in fifteen minutes. Other than Salinger and a glass of something dry and cool, home held no allure. I missed the stone cottage. At least there my sense of impermanence hadn't seemed so obvious. Sarah's mobile home emphasized how rootless my life had become. How rootless I felt.

"Are you married?" Kolinsky had asked.

A simple question I couldn't answer for myself.

As I approached the road to the mobile home, I decided to keep driving. I needed to think. And White Fish Dunes was where I went to think. On the outskirts of Jacksonport I slowed for the left turn onto Clark Lake Road and followed the sign to the Dunes.

Spring was flashing past my windshield—yellow daffodils, white trillium, some purple flowers I couldn't name interspersed with fields of greening tall grasses like an invitation to awaken. Then trees narrowed the road and with them the sense of possibilities ending. All around me nature was coming alive and I felt nothing but rage. It was as if in discovering Stephanie and

Lisette something had been unleashed in me. Some wild force that made me want to break things.

I'd made a promise to Annie Everson to help find her daughter's killer. And I hadn't. Instead, someone else's daughter had been killed. And the killer had decided I was the one he needed to share this horror with. Some message was being given to me by a maniac who thought I would understand, that I would get it. And do what? Stop him? Write about him? Save him? I should be scared or sad or both. But I only felt fury, and that made me dangerous. I'd been contaminated by their deaths, drawn into this evil by the killer. Would there be any washing me clean of this? And last night with Joe had only added to my fury. I wasn't washing off the death. I was mudding Joe with it.

There was no one at the entrance booth. I pulled into the first lot near the beach path. From a distance I could see a few cars scattered in the next lot. I slammed my truck door with a little too much force and walked down the asphalt path toward the beach. I stood for a moment at the railing, looking out at the water blue and shimmering, the white sand.

Good, no one was on the beach. I was in no mood for humans.

I walked over the white plastic meshing that protected the dunes from erosion toward the beach. Gulls were fishing the lake, swooping down into the water and back up into the sky, their bodies riding the air currents, seemingly without effort.

I meandered along the shore. It wasn't summer warm, but the air was light and frothy on my face. I took off my jacket. The play of sun and wind ruffled my hair, my white cotton blouse. There was an ache in the beach grasses that matched the ache in me. I could feel my body unwind like the wind, like the gulls.

If only, I told myself, I could breathe it all in, then slowly let it out and the anger and the rage would go with the breath. But it wasn't that simple. Or was it? I could leave Door County. I could pack today, get in the truck and go. Where? Two young women were dead. No matter how far I went, there would be no getting away from myself.

The brown wooden lifeguard station stood empty. I climbed up to the seat and looked out at the restless water. Jake and I had sat here last fall, understanding for the first time that there was something between us—unnamable, maybe not lasting, but something. Whatever tacit understanding Jake and I had had was broken. What gesture, what word had sent him away that morning? What need in me had wanted it?

I looked down at my ring finger. The tan line had faded last fall.

I jumped down and walked farther down the beach. In the distance I could see a couple approaching me. The woman was holding on to the man's arm as if she couldn't keep her footing. They were ambling, engrossed in each other. The woman looking up into the man's face as if there was some answer there she needed.

It was too far away for me to make out their faces—just their body types and body language. There was something vaguely familiar about the man. He was tall and lanky, and there was a stoop to his shoulders that I recognized.

No, it couldn't be Jake. The man had short hair. And who was the woman?

They came closer.

It was Jake. His hair was cut and the goatee was gone. A very young woman, maybe eighteen or nineteen, was holding his hand. She had light red hair that flared around her square, determined face. Her long, thin body looked model chic in faded jeans and a peasant blouse. There was a wry intelligence in her cobalt blue eyes. Rossetti would have wanted to paint her.

"Leigh," he said slowly, that insolent grin spreading across his face.

A flurry of confusion was spinning in my brain—from *thanks for letting me know you're back* to *is this your daughter or your new girlfriend?* I settled on a subtler response. "New look?" I pointed to his hair but looked at the young woman.

"Zoe's idea." He indicated the woman who was now staring at me as if I'd just emerged from the lake wearing a tail. "Said I had to get with it."

I nodded my head, trying to remember if Zoe was Jake's daughter's name. "Don't want to get trapped in the past."

He laughed. The young woman dropped his hand. "You read the poem I left?"

Poem? He hadn't called me in two weeks to let me know whether he was alive or dead. The peninsula had two murders, which he must have heard about. And he's asking about a poem. He wasn't getting off that easy.

I put out my hand to her. "I'm Leigh Girard. I'm a reporter for the *Gazette* and Jake's former girlfriend." *Former* had just spilled out.

She took my hand and shook it firmly. "I'm Zoe Stevens, college student and Jake's current daughter. Nice to meet you." She had the same sardonic smirk Jake had.

I knew my mouth had dropped open, so I'd better say something. "Jake never mentioned you were coming. You here for the summer or permanently?"

Jake shrugged his shoulders as if to say what's the big deal. I actually think he was enjoying this.

"For the summer. And, well, Dad's told me all about you." Her head was slightly down and she looked up at me from under her eyelids. It was hard to know if she was shy or coy.

"Zoe," Jake said. "I need to talk to Leigh. Go on ahead. I'll meet you at the Nature Center, okay?"

"Sure, Dad. Nice meeting you, Leigh," she said, plopping up the beach in her flip-flops.

"She has your mouth." I folded my arms across my chest.

"Leigh," he began, taking a step toward me.

I stepped back. "Save it. A lot's happened since you left. You know about the two murders, I take it." I didn't wait for his response. "This guy is targeting young blond women. I found Stephanie Everson, the first girl. I'm convinced her body was ritually arranged. Joe Stillwater and I found the second girl, Lisette Cohen. Her body was positioned the same way. And I think the killer may have changed her clothes. Though I'm not sure about that. Got to talk to this Brian person. Lisette, Brian, and a Professor Kolinsky were living together in a cabin off Rowleys Bay. They have a grant to research the Hine's Emerald Dragonfly. This Brian might know something. And there's an Erik Ritter, who might be involved, as well as our resident sex offenders. And one more thing. I was tipped to the second body. Someone called me, probably the killer. That about covers it, boss." I was staring out over the lake, not wanting to make eye contact. The water holding me steady.

"Leigh, I really did try to tell you about Zoe."

I turned to face him. "I thought we were friends. Friends tell each other things. 'Oh, by the way, I have a daughter who's coming to visit.' How hard could that be? Huh, Jake?" I didn't know how mad I was until I started talking.

"You didn't answer me. Did you read my poem or not?"

"Poem? What poem? The poem you left when you cleared out your stuff as if the cops were after you? That stupid poem about women and wolves and pelts and skin and . . ." I was like a woman with two tongues, neither of which were saying what I wanted to say. "We've got a killer on the peninsula and you're asking about some poem. Really Jake, your ego is boundless."

"It was all there in the poem. About you and me and Zoe." It was infuriating how calm he sounded, as if we were discussing the weather. "I dedicated it to you and Zoe. Didn't you see that?"

"So let me get this straight. If I'd taken the time to interpret this poem, I would have known all about your daughter and that she was spending the summer with you. And I would have got what's going on between us?"

"Pretty much."

I turned toward him in disbelief. He was starting to look bruised around the eyes. "I threw your damned poem in the garbage." In spite of myself, I laughed. I didn't want to laugh, but it was so absurd, I couldn't help myself. His clean-shaven and shorn appearance made him look like a kid after his first hair cut.

"Your loss, Girard. What can I tell you? Greatness is never appreciated in its own time?" He put his arms around me and pulled me into him. There was his familiar smell—a hint of musk and washed clothes—the cove of his body.

"Look, the time just never seemed right to tell you about Zoe and the whole deal with my ex. I admit it, not my smartest move. But sometimes you are so distant, so difficult. And there's your husband, whom I know nothing about. I just figured we had an understanding when it came to stuff like this." He was bending down, brushing my cheek with his lips. "Zoe's a good kid. You'll like her. Just let her be herself. Okay?"

I stretched up toward his mouth and practically breathed into him as I pressed my lips against his open mouth. It was an angry hard kiss meant to wound as much as give solace.

When we pulled away from each other, he ran his fingers over his lip. "Now tell me about the murders."

"It can wait till tomorrow."

"We're having pizza tonight. Why don't you come by? Get to know Zoe."

"Got something else going on." I didn't have anything going on, but I didn't have the energy to deal with Jake and his daughter tonight. This was going to take some sorting out.

We walked in silence for a while just letting everything wash over us.

As we neared the Nature Center Jake asked, "How's Sarah's silver house working out? Marge told me you were living there."

I glanced up at the observation window. There was Zoe watching us, her glowing hair like a warning.

"Just fine."

Chapter Twenty-Three

Thursday, June 1

"I've written a letter to the killer. I want you to run it in Friday's paper. Front page. My follow-up story on Lisette Cohen's murder is already in the computer."

I flopped down in one of the chairs, putting my feet up on Jake's desk. I was just itching for a fight.

"How am I supposed to find anything?" Jake asked no one in particular. His normally messy desk was a study in order. He leaned over and turned on his computer. "How'd Martin work like this?"

I still couldn't get over his new appearance—clean shaven, spiky short hair. Even his clothes were different. In place of old jeans and blue work shirt were a pair of khaki trousers and a white dress shirt. All he needed was an Armani suit and he could be in *GQ*. It was amazing what a man does for his kid.

"I worked up a rough draft last night." I almost blew my cover. "After I got home from that other thing."

Jake pulled up the blinds on the window. There was the bay. It had a greenish-gray tint this morning. The sky mostly clouded over. By noon we'd have rain.

"You see Martin this morning?" Jake asked. "I told him to be here by eight. It's already twenty after."

"No. About the letter."

"What? Yeah, drop off a copy later."

I handed him my draft. As he read it, he sat down slowly.

To the Murderer: I'm not going to tell you what you did is wrong. You know that. That's why you called me. You want to be stopped.

I can help you stop. You've chosen me to be your witness. You want to make it right for the person these women represent.

I'll help you make it right for her. But first you have to stop the killing. Then I will tell your story. Then you can be heard. But you have to stop killing.

Contact me through the paper. Leigh Girard.

When he finished, there was that tightness in his face I'd come to read as some struggle with inner demons.

"Not a good idea." He threw it across the desk at me.

"Look, the guy contacted me. Obviously he wants to use me for some reason. Maybe if I can engage him in a dialogue via the paper we can get some clue to his identity."

"You read too many mystery novels, Girard. And you don't know for sure the guy who called you is the killer." He had his game face on.

"It had to be. How else could he know about where Lisette's body was? C'mon Jake, you know it's a great idea. We have nothing to lose. You can write a disclaimer if you're worried about liability. Run it as a letter to the editor. I'll take full responsibility."

"It's too dangerous." He was running his long fingers across his chin where his goatee used to be.

"We're way past dangerous. He's going to kill again. I want to stop him."

"I'm telling you it's a bad idea. This guy's going to think you're his buddy."

"He already thinks that." I stared at my folded hands. "I can always go to another paper. I guarantee they'll print it."

He knew I was right. And he didn't look too happy about it.

"Leave the letter, I'll think about it. And get your feet off my desk."

All thoughts of lunch fled when I pulled up in front of the mobile home and saw Monroe Parks standing beside a rusty brown Olds convertible whose bumper was a little too close to the home's wooden steps. He was dressed in faded jeans, a black sweatshirt, and sneakers. His beard seemed to have crept further up his face. He looked as dark and dangerous as a grizzly bear.

For a second I considered turning around and leaving, but I needed to let Salinger out and grab something to eat before my interview with Brian McNaulty. Besides I wasn't going to let him intimidate me on my own turf.

Before exiting the truck, I dug in my purse, found the black cylinder of pepper spray and put it in my jacket pocket. As I slammed the truck door and started toward him, I kept the pepper spray in my pocket but turned its ridged top to the on position.

"What's this?" Parks asked, walking toward me. He shoved a copy of the *Gazette* in my face. He'd folded it back to my story on the sex offenders list.

"Old news." I pushed the paper out of my face and walked around him toward the stairs. I could hear Salinger scratching the door behind us. In another minute she'd be howling.

Parks moved his large frame in front of me, blocking the stairs.

"Get out of my way."

"The only reason I agreed to talk to you was because you said you wanted to show both sides. This isn't both sides." He rattled the paper in my face again.

"If you have a problem with the article, write a letter to the editor." I moved around him and walked up the steps to the mobile home. Salinger let out a high-pitched howl. I unlocked the door and pushed it open. Salinger bolted down the stairs and started circling Parks barking and nipping at his feet. I didn't stop her.

"I lost my job," he spat at me. His face was so transformed by rage, it was as if he had become another person. His dark eyes were slits of fury. "Because of you I lost my job."

"I'm not the one who screwed my patient," I said. "I had nothing to do with you being fired."

"The hell you didn't. They fired me because of that article. Businesses were threatening to cancel their advertising. They'd read your article. Shut that dog up." He kicked at Salinger. But she jogged sideways, avoiding the blow.

I ran down the stairs. "Stop that," I said, taking the pepper spray out of my pocket and pointing it at his face.

He looked at the pepper spray. "You think that would stop me if I wanted to do something to you?"

He turned away and walked toward his car. Salinger followed him, barking and jumping at him. As he opened the door, he kicked at her again. This time his foot made contact. Salinger let out a yelp and fell on her side.

"You bastard," I shouted, running to Salinger. I bent down and picked her up in my arms. She struggled against me as my hands searched her body for where he'd kicked her.

He got into his car, started the engine, and shut the car door. In a flurry of rocks and dust, he backed the car up, almost hitting several trees. As he pulled forward along side of me, he rolled down his window.

"Better watch your dog. She could get hurt."

Before I could disentangle my arm and spray his hairy face, he tore away, spitting up gravel.

I put Salinger down and checked her again. She let out a soft murmur when I touched her right hind flank. It was sore, but there didn't seem to be any damage. I let her go. She gingerly trotted up the stairs and into the mobile home. I looked down the long gravel drive where Parks's car had disappeared.

The doctor's dark side was darker than I'd guessed. And he had no alibi.

Brian McNaulty had the hunted look of a graduate student. His eyes were both wary and focused. His skittish demeanor seemed to be in contrast to his shaved head and football-player's physique, which made him appear pugnacious.

He hadn't wanted to talk to me and had given a number of lame excuses why we couldn't meet. Finally I reminded him that his colleague, Lisette Cohen, had been murdered and that finding her killer should be his top priority. It had been a reluctant assent. I wasn't sure if his reluctance came from a distrust of journalists or his own guilt.

He was dressed so similarly to Kolinsky, right down to the khaki vest, that I wondered if the professor issued the clothes like a uniform—fellowship, flannel shirt, jeans, khaki vest, boots.

"Like I told you on the phone, I don't know anything." He was standing with his hands on his hips looking out at Lake Michigan. He'd kayaked over to Newport Beach Park from the cabin. We were in the second shelter area near the entrance to Europe Bay Trail. Dry brown beach grass jutted up through the sand around the lone bench. The sand had a yellow cast to it, and snags of seaweed lipped the water. The sky was slate gray, but the rain had held off.

"Humor me. When did you last see Lisette?"

He made a deep sigh to let me know how put out he was. "In the morning. I was already up. Lisette had this habit of sleeping late. I think she did it so she didn't have to make coffee. Too demeaning." He used two fingers on each hand to indicate quotation marks. "Kolinsky let her get away with it."

"Skip the editorial, okay?"

"Why don't I skip this whole interview?" He leaned over and picked up his kayak paddle. Through his flannel shirt I could see his arm muscles tense against the cloth. There was a lot of power in his body.

I wasn't about to apologize. "Professor Kolinsky tells me you accused Lisette of stealing your research. Did you mention that to the police?"

"Get bent." He was still holding his paddle, but he hadn't moved toward the kayak.

"I'm sure you figured it out that the person who killed Stephanie Everson is probably the same person who killed Lisette, which means we have a potential serial killer. Do you want another murder on your conscience?"

He threw the paddle down so hard, sand shot up. "I didn't kill anybody. So don't guilt trip me. I'm going to tell you the same thing I told the police. Lisette left about ten that morning. I don't know why she went out in the canoe or why she went up the Mink. She had her usual stuff with her, field guide, backpack. I think she took a lunch because when I went to make a sandwich later, there wasn't any bread or meat. I left camp about noon and went into town for groceries. And plenty of people saw me there."

I figured the police had already checked his alibi. But that still left Kolinsky with no alibi after noon.

"What was she wearing?"

He pointed to his own clothes. "What we all wear."

If that was true, either she took a change of clothes or the killer undressed her and dressed her in clothes he brought. Either scenario gave me the creeps.

"How about her hair?"

"Her hair?" He looked quizzically at me. "A braid. One long braid. Like she always wears it in the field."

"And you have no idea where she was going that morning?"

"Nope. And for your information, she did steal my research. We were working on an article together and she got the credit. The only reason Kolinsky sided with her was he was banging her."

"He told me she had a crush on you."

He let out a loud snort. "He would say that to cover his butt. I think their thing was over by the time we got up here. I sensed a little tension, if you know what I mean. But something was going on before, I can tell you that. I caught them once in his office in a lip lock."

"Did you sleep with Lisette?" Something about his anger seemed more deep-rooted than research.

He picked up his paddle. "I've got nothing to hide. Yeah, I slept with her once or twice. Or should I say she slept with me? When I was no longer useful, she moved up the food chain."

He walked toward his kayak, then turned back toward me. "If you say anything to Kolinsky about what I said, I'll deny it."

"Why should I believe anything you've said?"

"Look, I told you what I know. Whether you believe me or not is your problem."

He pushed his kayak into the water, jumped in, and paddled into the gray horizon.

If I were to believe McNaulty, Kolinsky had lied to me about his relationship with Lisette. What else had he lied to me about?

My truck's headlights swept the woods like a searchlight as I pulled in front of the trailer home—green swatch of evergreens, gravelly drive, the trailer's silver side. Heavy cloud cover blocked the moon. But there was no rain. Nor anyone waiting for me.

I unlocked the door and let Salinger out. After a few short barks of complaint and reassurance, she tore into the woods. When she returned, she'd be wet and satisfied. If only my anxieties could be assuaged so easily.

I wasn't hungry, but I nuked a frozen dinner anyway. Chicken breast, wild rice, peas and carrots. What I really wanted was a long sleek glass of wine—rich yellow chardonnay or a wispy pinot grigio. Something to quiet the churning in my stomach and in my head. Something to ease me into sleep. There was no washing me clean of these murders. And once my letter appeared in Friday's paper, I would be in so deep there'd be no surfacing until this guy was caught. If he was caught.

I poured myself a tall glass of cranberry juice and took a sip. Tart and healthy, just like I wanted to be.

I looked at the phone. I could call Jake, but I was too bone tired to dodge the emotional turmoil of "us."

The buzzer went off on the microwave. I lifted the plastic film. Some carrots and peas were mixed in with the chicken breast and wild rice. I picked through the compartments, gathering the errant vegetables.

My hand was shaking, but I kept at it until every carrot and pea was in its proper place.

I could call Joe. I drank down the cranberry juice in three gulps. It felt like ice lining my throat and stomach. Then I got up and opened the refrigerator. The green bottle was almost spring-like, and inside was a yellow bouquet waiting to blossom.

What could one glass hurt?

It was important to breathe. Then it was important not to. I could see the deep rippled sand through the water. I could hear my heart pounding, asking for release.

I tried to lift my head but two hands were pressed against my skull holding me down in the water—making me see the ribbed sand, making me hear my heart pound.

I reached around trying to push the hands away, but they

only tightened on my head. So this is what it's like to die, I thought.

There was no white light at the end of a tunnel, no ancestors to greet me. Just the cold water and the absence of air. I took one long breath. The cold water flooded my lungs.

I awoke coughing, my body pressed against the metallic wall of the mobile home. My face felt frozen. I lifted my head. The pain blazed up at the back of my skull.

The darkness was shadowed with light. I nudged the curtain aside and gazed out the large window into the woods, into the true darkness where trees were a darker dark.

Right now the killer could be out there watching me. I got up, walked across the thin carpet to the door. I picked up the desk chair and hooked it under the doorknob.

I stumbled to the bathroom, opened the medicine chest and took out the bottle of migraine pills. I threw back two pills with water.

As I walked back to bed, I remembered the baseball bat I'd seen in the bottom of the closet. I reached in and grabbed it.

Salinger had kept the bed warm for me. I crawled under the quilt with the bat. If I'd owned a gun, it'd be under my pillow.

Chapter Twenty-Four

Saturday, June 3

The bar area of the River Supper Club was bursting with locals and tourists. The two murders didn't seem to have stopped anyone from going out. Maybe they figured as long as they avoided the Mink River they were safe.

Lydia and I had managed to grab a corner booth by the pool table while we waited for a table. I'd called Lydia that morning on the chance that she might be free for dinner. I wanted to have plans in case Jake asked me to join him and his daughter for dinner again. Lucky for me, Martin was away at a conference. Though Jake's dinner invitation had never materialized.

"This is really pushing it, even for you," Lydia said. She was holding a copy of the *Door County Gazette,* gesturing to my front-page letter to the killer. I was getting weary of people assaulting me with the paper. Jake had run an enlarged photo of me beside the letter along with a sidebar summarizing the Lisette Cohen case. Since the paper came out yesterday, I'd been assailed on the street, in the market, even in the library by people telling me they'd seen my letter and photo in the paper and asking what it had felt like talking to the killer.

Finally I'd gone home and buried myself for the rest of the day and evening in the complete stories of Flannery O'Connor. She seemed to understand the vagaries of human nature. A killer in her town would have only confirmed her ideas about free will and evil and the moral order.

"You gals want another round?" Candy asked, shouting over the bluegrass band that was sounding a lot better tonight. If she had seen the letter, and I'm sure she had, she wasn't saying anything.

"I'll have a Bloody Mary this time." I pushed my empty wine glass toward her. "No pepper. No . . ."

Candy stopped me. "I know. I know. No celery, olives. Got it. How about you, Lydia?" She pushed her Green Bay Packers' baseball hat higher up on her forehead with her pen.

"Just give me another Chablis." Lydia fluffed her chestnut hair and wiggled her nose like the debutante she once was. Since it was girls' night out, she was dressed down—a modicum of mascara, no eyeliner or shadow, just a touch of blush and lipstick, though she was wearing a V-neck chartreuse sweater and black jeans—the sweater was cashmere and the jeans designer. She had loops of silver chains of various lengths around her neck and silver hoop earrings. Lydia was always on the prowl.

I, on the other hand, was incognito—jeans, navy sweatshirt and baseball cap. If I thought sunglasses wouldn't draw attention to me, I'd be wearing them.

"I mean, Leigh, 'to make it right for the person these women represent. Then I can tell your story. Then you can be heard.' It's almost as if you're on this guy's side. And what does 'the person these women represent' mean? Where'd you come up with that? What do you think he's doing, killing these women in place of some other woman? Is this something you read somewhere or are you making it up as you go along? This is dangerous territory you're in here. You're dealing with a killer."

"I know what I'm doing." I fidgeted with my napkin, rolling it and unrolling it like a cigarette.

Lydia threw her head back again ruffling her lush hair. "This is just crazy. I can't believe Jake agreed to this."

"He printed a disclaimer. The paper's not liable." I didn't want to talk about the dangerous waters I'd dived into. I was only too aware of them.

"What's going on with you?" She gave me a sidelong glance. "Something up with you and Jake?"

Candy set our drinks down. "Your table should be ready in about ten minutes, ladies."

"Thanks," I said, picking up the red plastic heart pick that rested across my drink like a bridge and sliding one of the olives off. I popped the olive in my mouth savoring its briny taste.

"It's not because of Zoe, is it?" Lydia's green eyes opened wide with anticipation.

I didn't say anything.

"She's not a bad kid. Just overly protective of daddy. But hey, she hardly ever sees him." Lydia twisted a lock of her short hair. "Don't tell me Jake didn't tell you about her?" She was practically salivating. If she wasn't creating dramas in her own life, she was creating them in her friends' lives.

"Could we talk about something else?" I popped another olive in my mouth and stared at the giant plastic ice cube suspended over the pool table.

Lydia was not to be dissuaded. "If he didn't tell you about Zoe, then he probably didn't tell you the rest. His wife left him for another guy. Maybe seven, eight years ago. That's about all I was able to get out of him one night when we were both feeling lonely. And before you ask, no nothing happened between us. Just no chemistry there."

"Well, thanks, Diane Sawyer for filling me in." My stomach felt like lead. I took a long pull on my drink. "So where did you say Rob was this weekend?"

"Oh, some nature conference thing in Minneapolis." Lydia looked over my head and waved. "Look, there's Joe. Joe, over here."

I turned around to see Joe Stillwater and a small roundish woman approach our table.

Lydia shoved over and patted the seat. "Sit down and have a drink with us. We're waiting for a table."

The small dark woman sat next to Lydia. Joe slid in next to me. I moved so close to the wall, I could feel cold air through the wood paneling.

Joe cleared his throat. "Ruth, this is Lydia Crane and Leigh Girard. Ruth and I knew each other in medical school. She's up here visiting."

Joe smelled of a musky cologne. He was wearing a blue sweater and khaki pants. On his left hand was a gold ring with a red stone I'd never seen before.

"Medical school?" I blurted out.

"Long story," Joe said. "Not worth telling."

Ruth piped in, "Joe loves to talk but you ever notice you never find out anything about him." She had a perfectly round face framed by dark bangs and a bob cut.

"Apparently," I said, keeping my voice steady.

"We both dropped out of U of C the first year. University of Chicago. We decided about the same time that it wasn't for us. I ended up being a lab tech. And Joe joined the navy. How about you? What do you do?" Ruth asked me.

"I write for the *Door County Gazette*."

"Leigh's being too modest," Lydia said. "She also hunts down killers. Did you see today's paper?" Lydia shoved the paper in front of Ruth.

Ruth read the letter and then stared at me. "Gosh," she said. Her eyes were as dark as her hair.

Joe squirmed in his seat. "You want something to drink, Ruth?" he asked.

"Sure. Whatever's on tap that's American? But not light."

Joe got up and made his way through the crowd to the bar.

"What are you going to do if this guy answers you?" Ruth asked. Her bob cut gave her a girlish quality, though she had webs of fine lines around her eyes and mouth.

"I'll answer him. I'm hoping he gives something away about himself. Some clue."

"What if he comes after you?" Lydia asked. "This is not a good idea." She tapped the paper with her index finger.

"Lydia's right." Joe stood by the booth holding two beers. "You don't know what you're getting into." He put both beers down on the table and slid into the booth.

I could feel dampness on the backs of my legs. I wanted to jump up and run out of the bar into the cool evening air. I felt like I couldn't get enough air.

"I don't need a lecture from you," I snapped at him.

"You sure about that?" Joe answered in a tight, angry voice. I didn't think Joe did angry. He was staring straight ahead at the giant ice cube. He wouldn't look at me.

There was an uncomfortable silence. "Well, I think you're brave," Ruth said. "I could never do this."

"Crane, table for two," a voice called. "Crane, table for two."

"Finally," Lydia said. "You want to join us? All the tables seat four."

Ruth looked at Joe expectantly.

"Some other time," he said. "Ruth and I have a lot of catching up to do."

"I get it." Lydia winked at Joe.

Ruth and Joe slid out of the booth to let us leave. As I stood up, I met Joe's eyes. He looked away. I'd never seen him so angry.

"What was that about?" Lydia asked after we gave our orders.

"Lydia, don't you ever get tired of trying to create these mini-plays?" I was fuming. I didn't know if I was angry at Lydia or Joe or both of them.

"C'mon Leigh, I got to get my jollies somehow. These men are only so entertaining. And you are such a good source of entertainment. I swear if I don't talk to you every day, I miss something."

I bit off a piece of my roll and chewed on the soft, warm dough. I was not going to be baited. "Joe and I shared two horrible experiences. When we see each other, it brings it all back. Now I don't want to talk about it anymore. Or I'm outta here."

She shook her head, tousling her hair. "I don't know what you're talking about, but I was talking about you being pen pals with a killer."

I grabbed my purse and pulled out a twenty and put it on the table. "Lydia, I can't do this. I've got to get out of here."

I ran through the bar area with my head down so Joe wouldn't see me. When I climbed into my truck and tried to put the key in the ignition my hand trembled so much I had to use two hands. There was so much adrenaline pumping through my body I could have run home.

The soft light of twilight diffused the woods as I drove down the long gravel drive toward the silver house. In the dark I could just see the white, three-petaled flowers scattered like candles. As I pulled into the clearing, I rolled down my window, hungry for the lake's calming sound. I shut off the engine, closed my eyes and rested my forehead on the cool steering wheel, listening. Back and forth, back and forth—the lake's restless, ceaseless swell filled the truck, making me more edgy.

I lifted my head and peered into the night, trying to hear over the lake. But I heard nothing but the water rushing the shore and Salinger. A nerve was beating at the back of my head. It shot up from my spine and across my shoulders like a faulty wire. I rolled the window back up and opened the truck door.

As I jumped down from the cab and slammed the door, Salinger's barks turned to plaintive howls that echoed through the trees. The howls had an undertone of real distress. I'd been neglecting her. She was due some quality time.

I climbed the wooden steps to the door, put the key in the lock and started to turn the key. The door pushed in before I completed the turn. I froze for a moment. Had I locked the door? Yes, I distinctly remembered checking the door before I left.

I bent down and studied the lock. It wasn't engaged. I slowly edged the door inward and called to Salinger.

"Here, girl." She practically leapt into my arms. "Okay, okay," I said, running my fingers through her fur which seemed to be electric.

I reached around the door with my left hand and flipped on the light switch. The long room blazed with light. I had a clear view of the place except for the bathroom. With Salinger beside me I inched into the room, grabbing the baseball bat I'd left by the door. Holding the bat with both hands, I walked toward the bathroom, my heart doing double time. Shifting the bat to my left hand, I reached for the doorknob and slowly turned it. I quickly pushed the door in, then grabbed the bat with two hands. Empty. I stepped in and yanked the shower curtain back. No one.

I checked under the dinette table and the desk. Nothing. Then as I glanced toward the bed, I saw something on the pillow nearest the wall. A white envelope. And below the envelope was an indentation in the comforter. Whoever had left the envelope had knelt on the bed. Nothing was written on the outside of the envelope. It rested there against the blue pillowcase—white and potent.

I was about to pick it up, then remembered about fingerprints. I found a pair of gloves in the pockets of my down jacket. My gloved hands were sweating as I slit the envelope open with a knife. The typed letter was all in caps. At the top of the page was my name. There was no signature.

To Leigh,

Three times three. See if you can see me. Right before your eyes. The wheel is come full circle; I am here.

I spun around the room sensing someone behind me. The room was empty. Then I took a long, deep breath as if I'd just surfaced from under water.

Suddenly the phone rang cutting the room's silence. I didn't move. It rang again, then again. Then I heard my voice saying, "Leave a message."

"Leigh, I know you're there. Pick up." I sat down on the bed, the letter still in my hand. It was Lydia. "Okay, you don't want to talk. Look, I'm really worried about you. The way you tore out of the restaurant. You've had two horrendous shocks. I've seen this kind of thing before. Believe me, I know what I'm talking about. I'll bet you're not sleeping or eating and having nightmares and flashbacks, right? Listen, I know you. You think can you tough it out. But it doesn't work that way. You have to get treatment for this or it could destroy you. Okay, that sounded dramatic. But this is not one of my mini-plays, as you call them. This is a real disorder caused by severe shock. Please, Leigh, you need help. You know, you can call me any time day or night."

I waited for the machine to click off, then I erased the message and picked up the phone.

"You can't stay here tonight," Hallaway said annoyed. My call had pulled her away from a quiet evening with her children. She hadn't said so, but Ferry had told me as much when I called the station.

"We need to dust this place for prints. Don't know how long it'll take. The forensic guy's on his way. He should be here in half an hour. He was already in bed." She was acting like I was responsible for ruining everyone's evening.

My first impulse would have been to crash at Jake's. But not now. And I didn't have the energy to deal with Nurse Lydia fussing over my so-called dented psyche.

"Don't worry about me," I said.

Hallaway narrowed her eyes. "I'm not worried about you. This is what comes of meddling in police business. And don't think you've made contact with the killer." She pointed to the letter, which rested on my table in a paper bag. "This could be from anybody, probably some crackpot who saw that letter of yours in the paper. You know anybody who has it in for you? Maybe because of something you wrote?" Her face was stern, but it was obvious she was enjoying busting my chops.

"You mean like what I wrote about the two murders." Monroe Parks had it in for me and maybe Chet Jorgensen. Chet would never do something like this. There was no telling what Parks was capable of.

"Monroe Parks paid me a visit yesterday. He blames me for his losing his job. He vented his anger by kicking my dog."

Hallaway's one eyebrow went up skeptically. "Anyone else?"

"The killer. Of course, that could be Parks."

Hallaway crossed her arms over her neatly pressed, uniformed chest. She was in full uniform, right down to her holster and gun. I wondered if she wore it to bed at night. Probably the only way she could maintain her steel exterior. The only thing out of place was a smear of green magic marker on her cheek that reminded me again that I'd pulled her away from a quiet evening with her children.

"You're this close to being arrested, Ms. Girard." She held her thumb and index finger close together in front of my nose.

We were back to Ms. Girard. Had to be a good sign.

"You are not to print any more letters to the killer. You understand that? Because if you do, I'm going to make it my business to lock you up for hindering a police investigation."

"You can't do that," I said not sure if she could or couldn't.

"Just try me. You got a good cop suspended with your interference. You're not going to do that to me. Now get outta here."

"I need to pack a few things."

"Until we go over this place, everything's evidence," she said, grinning and showing her very white, very big teeth.

I called Jake on my cell phone from the truck. Whatever was going on between us, he was still the editor of the paper and my boss. He had a right to know.

"She can't have you arrested for writing an editorial letter," he said. "Where are you now?"

I was sitting in my truck at the end of the drive. "I've checked into a motel," I lied. Salinger was growling in the background. Her hackles were still up.

"We need to go over everything. Which motel?"

"Look, Jake, I'm tired and all I want is to get some sleep. We can do this in the morning. I'll meet you at the office at ten." Before he could answer, I hung up the phone. I turned onto the side road and headed for Highway 42 without a clue where I was going.

Chapter Twenty-Five

Sunday, June 4

"Hallaway called me around seven," Jake said. He had his chair swiveled toward the window, his back to me.

I took a bite out of the breakfast biscuit I'd picked up at the McDonald's in Sturgeon Bay where I'd also freshened up in the ladies' washroom before heading over to the paper. I'd spent the night with Salinger in the truck parked off one of the deserted gravel roads between Sturgeon Bay and Little Harbor near the site of the old Leathan and Smith Quarry on Highway B. I hadn't slept much. Some time toward dawn I'd finally fallen asleep and had overslept. So I hadn't had time to go back to my place. My mouth felt gritty and my clothes damp. This homeless feeling was starting to be a little too real.

"Am I on double-triple probation?" I asked, swallowing the last of the biscuit and picking up my jumbo coffee.

"You're way beyond that." Jake stared out the window, looking at the bay. This morning the sky was white. That overdue rain was imminent. "Hallaway reamed me out pretty good about your letter and interfering with her investigation. I reminded her about the first amendment. Not that it did any good. She's way beyond reason on this. Which makes her dangerous and impossible." He turned from the window and looked at me. "Kinda like you. But we do like to keep a working relationship with the police. So go easy."

"They find anything at my place?" I took a gulp of coffee and burned my tongue. This was my second cup. It was taking all my self-control not to pace the room.

"Nothing. Same goes for that letter. Whoever put it there knew what he was doing. Makes me think it's our guy. Which makes it imperative that you write him a response. I want to run it and the letter in Tuesday's paper."

"What about Hallaway?" I blew on the coffee and took a sip this time.

"I'll deal with her. Just write the letter. You got any idea about this last sentence? 'The wheel is come full circle; I am here.' It sounds like a quote from a poem or a play."

Whatever our differences, Jake was usually on the side of the righteous.

"It's from Shakespeare's *King Lear.* I Googled the line as soon as I got here. Edmund, Gloucester's illegitimate son, says it in Act V, scene iii. Why the killer referenced it, I have no clue."

"Great, a potential serial killer with a literary bent." He reached back instinctively for the ponytail that wasn't there. Realized it wasn't there and patted the back of his neck. "Get started on that second letter; I want it on my desk tomorrow morning. We're going to have to come up with a name for this guy."

"You mean like Son of Sam? Won't that send Hallaway into convulsions?"

"Should." He smirked.

"I'll work on it."

I got up to leave.

Jake stopped me. "But before you get into that. They've arrested Erik Ritter on statutory rape charges."

I nearly knocked over my coffee. So Janet Margaris had gone to the police after all. I wonder what had changed her mind. "Nothing like keeping the best to last."

"You know anything about this?" There was that blue gaze boring holes into my psyche.

I studied my running shoes for about a minute. "Yeah."

He didn't pursue it. I got the feeling he didn't want to know what I'd been up to during his absence. That way he could claim innocence if Hallaway grilled him.

"Burnson made the arrest early this morning. Margaris insisted the chief be in on it from what Chet tells me. Get over to the police station and see what you can find out."

He was still staring at me. "And when this is over," he began, then thought better of it. "Go home and change first. You look like you slept in your clothes."

Though Chief Burnson was as hard-edged and slick as any Chicago cop, he had that plain speech that made him accessible and well liked on the peninsula. The combination helped him rise through the ranks in record time. But his down-home attitude was at odds with his appearance. Gray at the temples, nondescript features, tall and dark-haired, he had the bland good looks of a politician, which was what he was angling for—to be the next mayor of Sturgeon Bay. I felt Chet's suspension had as much to do with Burnson's political ambitions as my interference in police matters. Maybe they amounted to the same thing.

I'd taken Jake's advice and gone home to shower and change before heading over to the station. My place was splattered with white and black powder. Any surface that was light had black powder on it. And any surface that was dark had white powder on it. It would take a day to clean it and was too dusty to leave Salinger. So she was sitting in the truck, window down, waiting for me outside the station.

Burnson had those shaggy eyebrows some middle-aged men get. They shadowed his eyes and made him hard to read.

"Jake told me he'd be sending you." Burnson's knotty pine office wall was a collage of photos of Burnson either standing next to a slain animal with rifle in hand or shaking hands with state politicians from the mayor of Milwaukee to the governor of Wisconsin. I guess as far as Burnson was concerned it came down to the same thing—bagging your prey.

Where Hallaway was hostile and confrontational, Burnson was friendly and helpful. "What can I tell you?"

"About Ritter, when and where did you arrest him?" I knew Burnson would appreciate my direct approach. Regardless of his country demeanor, at heart he was all business.

"We arrested him this morning around eight. Russell Margaris came in early this morning, filed a complaint with the desk sergeant at . . ." He put a pair of glasses to his eyes and read from a paper on his desk, "Six-ten. We arrested Ritter at that abandoned church he's living in on Washington Island."

"What are the charges against him?"

"Statutory rape of a minor under the age of sixteen."

"How old is Ritter?" I needed to know his age for sure.

"He's nineteen. Claims he didn't know she was fifteen. They all say that when they're caught. Don't quote me on that there."

"Has he been in any other trouble with the police?"

"The usual, a few misdemeanors for disorderly conduct, underage drinking, wild-oat sowing stuff. But nothing like this. He was pretty het up. But as I told him, don't do the crime if you can't do the time. You can quote me on that."

"So what do you think is going to happen to him?"

"If Margaris follows through with the charges, judging from the way he was ranting and raving when I got here, I'd say this kid's in for a whole lot of pain there."

"And my place? You find anything?"

"Clean as a whistle. We sent your letter to Madison for DNA analysis. Should hear from them end of the week. But if the guy was that careful not to leave any fingerprints then he didn't lick no envelope. That's for sure then."

He got up from his chair and stretched. My cue the interview was over. "That is, if it was the killer's work. You know, Leigh, you might have made some enemies there. Maybe someone thought this was their idea of a practical joke. If I were you, I wouldn't lose no sleep over it though."

By afternoon the rain had finally come. A soft, warm rain full of promise. It fell straight down with such force I could feel its spray as I huddled beside the wooden Indian on Margaris's front porch. I'd rung the doorbell three times. I knew he was there because his silver Range Rover was parked in the circular drive.

I rang the bell again. I wasn't going away. Finally Margaris opened the door.

"I suppose you're here for some kind of reward?" he said. His blue eyes were like granite.

A flash of temper shot through my body. But I had decided to take a Zen approach with Margaris, whose only emotion seemed to be anger. So I took a deep, cleansing breath and blew it out in his face. "I want to talk to you about Erik Ritter."

He turned and walked down the hallway.

I followed him, dripping water on his Navaho rugs and shiny hardwood floor. Margaris was dressed in urban black—trousers, golf shirt and those loafers with tassels. The only break in his camouflage was his gold Rolex. It shone on his wrist like a beacon of wealth and privilege.

The furniture in the great room was still sheeted. Though the sheet on one couch had slid down. Newspapers were scattered on the floor in front of the couch. I could just make out the *Gazette* masthead from Friday's paper.

Rain was running down the floor-to-ceiling windows, blocking the view of the river and making the room shadowy and dark. The air had that stale smell of abandonment. The one light that glowed in the far corner made the room even more bereft.

"I had that child molester arrested. End of story." Margaris stood in front of the wall of windows with his arms crossed and his legs spread as if ready for an assault.

I didn't see any point in giving away my advantage so I remained standing.

"Why did you wait a week?" I'd been pondering this question on my drive up Highway 42. I had told Janet about Ritter last Sunday. Either it had taken Janet a week to tell Margaris or a week for Margaris to decide to bring charges.

For a minute he seemed confused, then a realization came over him. My question was answered.

"How long?" he spat out. "How long did she know?"

"Ask her." This was getting off to a bad start.

"I'm asking you." He came toward me. "You make some deal with my wife?"

He wasn't making any sense. What possible deal would I make with Janet, and for what advantage?

"She told you, didn't she?" I answered.

He was so close to me, I could see gold glints of beard stubble. My Zen-ness had gone the way of the world.

"You," he said, jabbing his finger in my face, "should have called me, not my wife. Who knows what else this degenerate's done since? And just so you understand how my wife operates, she told me yesterday. She likes to make her own rules."

I wondered why she'd waited so long to tell him.

"And you came straight here?"

"She's my only child. That child molester violated her. Castration's too good for him."

He turned and walked toward the windows. The rain was

coming down harder, making pinging noises on the glass. Then he turned back to the room.

"When? When did you tell her?" He was keeping some kind of score against his wife. I didn't want any part of it.

I didn't say anything.

"Never mind. I'll find out. You're not doing them any favors by protecting them. That's what Janet does. She thinks she can protect Janell from me. She's under some sick illusion that if she hides things from me, they'll go away. Just like that." He snapped his fingers. "But it's always me who has to clean up her messes. Janell's barely fifteen. You've seen her. She's pierced and branded like a fucking cow. And Janet lets her do it. Behind my back. And those clothes. What did she think was going to happen? But this time she's gone too far. I'm going to put an end to all of it. And I'm starting with that piece of shit Ritter. Then I'll take care of Janet."

So that was it, a power struggle between Margaris and his wife over their daughter. I wondered if either cared about Janell. It seemed she was just the catalyst for their mutual antagonism.

The phone rang. Margaris looked at it, annoyed. It rang again. He crossed the room and picked it up. "Yeah."

As he listened, the anger seemed to melt from his face.

"When? What about the rape charges?"

"All right. Thanks for letting me know. I wouldn't call it luck."

Margaris hung up the phone slowly. He walked back to the windows and looked out at the unseen river. When he finally spoke there was a calmness in his voice I'd never heard before.

"They've charged Ritter with first-degree murder."

"What?" I asked.

"They found evidence at his place."

Chapter Twenty-Six

Sunday, June 4

I sat behind Jake's desk with my dog-eared copy of Shakespeare's complete works open to Act V, scene iii of *King Lear,* trying to decipher the significance of the quote from the killer's letter. "The wheel is come full circle; I am here." I'd been there for hours reading the play. Because it was Sunday night, I didn't expect to find anyone in the office. And I'd been right. I still couldn't face the arduous task of cleaning the mobile home.

I'd placed a chair by the window so Salinger could sit and watch for seagulls and errant squirrels. Her nose was pressed against the glass in fervent expectation. Already doggy nose streaks smudged the windows. The sky was white as paint and the rain, as the weather people say, was intermittent.

After leaving Margaris, I'd sped down Highway 42 to the Sturgeon Bay police department. Burnson was as charming as he was tight lipped. He wouldn't say what the evidence was or why they'd searched Ritter's place. But he did say it belonged to Lisette Cohen and was solid enough to charge him with murder.

Whatever Ritter was, I was convinced he wasn't the murderer. Besides, there was no way he'd written that letter. The closest a guy like him had ever come to reading anything literary was CliffsNotes. When I mentioned that to Burnson, he'd repeated what he'd told me earlier—anybody could have written that letter. Reminding me once again that I had enemies and the world was full of crackpots.

I had copied the letter last night before the police had arrived. The copy was sitting beside the open book. In my former life as a college lecturer, I'd taught some of Shakespeare's plays, not *King Lear* unfortunately, but as a Master's student I'd studied the play. It was one of my favorites. Though things turned out badly at the end, the play was hopeful. Like life, it showed we do get second chances and if we learn from our mistakes, there are opportunities for redemption.

As I leaned back in Jake's chair, I thought about the context in which the line appears. Edmund, the illegitimate brother, says it to Edgar, the exiled, legitimate brother, near the play's conclusion. Their father, Gloucester, has been blinded. Edgar reveals himself as his brother. The brothers reconcile.

For all Edmund's jealousy and conniving, he redeems himself at the end. He tries to save Cordelia, though it is too late. She is killed; Edmund dies as well as Lear. Typical Shakespearean tragedy—death also being another redemptive element.

What did any of this have to do with the murders of Stephanie and Lisette? Maybe the quoted line referred to where the bodies were found—"You know the place," the killer had said to me on the phone. "Where the circles end."

I leaned forward and put my elbows on Jake's desk, rubbing at my eyes and forehead.

Then there were the other sentences. Three times three. There had been two murders. Did the sentence mean there was another murder that hadn't been discovered? Or there was going to be another murder? Not if Ritter was the killer. But what if I was right and he wasn't the killer—or did the sentence mean there were to be nine murders? Three times three. Why a specific number? Did the killer think he could control his killing? That if he reached this magical number, he wouldn't kill anymore? Or did the number refer to something else?

The second two sentences seemed more transparent but equally disturbing. "See if you can see me. Right before your eyes." The killer was telling me that he was in plain view, maybe someone I knew. Someone right in front of me. But I, like Gloucester, was blind and couldn't see him. That would connect the two sentences with the *King Lear* quote.

I pushed away from the desk and stood up. My head felt heavy and my stomach was empty. When had I eaten last? This morning. I was falling into my pattern of not eating, of ignoring my body again. It was a dangerous habit I had developed after the cancer diagnosis. My way of denying a body that had betrayed me. I thought I was over that. All winter I'd opened my body to Jake. My body, not myself. But in my own defense, neither had Jake opened himself up to me. His daughter was proof of that. And then there was Joe. That had been a mistake. One I wasn't sure I could fix. Joe had said our coming together had been based on a mutual need. No strings attached. Then why had he been so furious with me at the restaurant? My stomach let out a rumble.

I grabbed my purse from the desk and rummaged through it. Not even a breath mint.

"C'mon, Salinger, we're outta here."

It was Sunday, so most of the weekend tourists had left the peninsula and only the locals were in the River Supper Club bar. Everyone was talking about the arrest of Ritter. I sometimes wondered why we put out the paper.

I'd ordered a white fish sandwich and bowl of corn chowder. Salinger was sleeping in the truck outside with her belly full. I'd stopped at the market and bought her a pouch of her favorite dog food—Butcher's Casserole. I was on my second glass of chardonnay. My head didn't feel any clearer, but at least I didn't care as much.

"Buy you a drink?" Andy Weathers was standing by my booth holding a beer and a glass of white wine. The pungent smell of tobacco exuding from him was like a vapor.

Where did he materialize from? I hadn't seen him at the bar when I came in.

"Do I have a choice?" I said none-too-friendly-like. I was weary of people shoving papers in my face and blaming me for whatever was wrong in their lives. Though I hadn't wronged him in any way I could think of, I was sure if he tried real hard he could come up with something.

He put the drinks down and slid into the seat across from me. "I hear they arrested Erik Ritter for the murders. Your letter have anything to do with that?" He crossed his hands and put them on the table in front of him.

He was wearing a black T-shirt and gray trousers. Over the T-shirt he had on a lightweight gray sport coat. The cut of the coat had the look of hand tailoring. In the breast pocket was a pipe like a strange boutonniere.

"I don't know any more than you do." I ran my hand through my hair, trying to comb out the knots.

"Oh, Ms. Girard, I find that hard to believe." He uncrossed his hands and took out his pipe.

"I don't want to smoke my dinner, okay?" The bar was littered with smokers. I was hoping he'd pick up on the fact it was him I didn't want with my dinner.

He slipped the pipe back in his pocket. "So you don't know what evidence they have on Ritter." He hadn't asked it as a question.

"What do you think?" If I hadn't ordered food and wasn't starving, I'd be making up an excuse to leave.

"I think you're surprisingly tenacious. Sort of like a pit bull." His eyes ran over me. "Though you have the look of a cheetah. Long and sleek and those same cheetah eyes, though yours have more green in them. Very striking."

"Where's Roz?"

He let out a laugh that sounded like an exhalation of air. "You think I'm coming on to you? Must be you're expecting me to. I've found that people often project on others their own expectations and hopes. So if you think I'm coming on to you, then it's what you're expecting or maybe hoping. Is the world just one big hard-on for you?"

I took a deep swallow of wine. Weathers had some business with me, and it was personal.

"Is there something you want from me, Mr. Weathers? 'Cause we don't know each other well enough to be having this conversation." Two glasses of wine on an empty stomach had loosened my tongue more than usual.

He put his hands together. The fingers were long and bony. Pianist's hands—except for the grease and the calluses. "Andy. You have to call me Andy. How are we going to get to know each other?"

"You must be projecting, Andy. Who said I want to get to know you?"

"Oh, but you do. You're just a little confused by the wine. Tomorrow you'll be kicking yourself for letting this opportunity pass you by."

Even through my wine haze I felt electricity run up my back. I stared at his dull brown eyes through the black-rimmed glasses. The pupils were tight like two drops of ink. "You like Shakespeare, Andy?"

"Not particularly."

"Ever hear the line, 'The wheel is come full circle'?"

" 'The wheel is come full circle,' " he repeated slowly. "Interesting. Can't say it rings any bells. Why you asking?"

"Just something someone sent me in a letter."

"So he answered you."

I twirled the stem of my wine glass. "He?"

"Come on, Leigh, let's not play games. You're not the kind who plays games. That's why that letter you wrote to the killer seemed so out of character for you."

"Again, Andy, projecting." I drained the glass and pushed it away.

"Like I said, you're tenacious, Leigh. But, you're also foolish. And you don't know the difference between a risk and an opportunity. But that's what I like about you. Consider yourself lucky that they got Ritter when they did. Because it's very dangerous baiting a killer. They're so unpredictable." The corners of his mouth went up, but he wasn't smiling.

"You're not drinking your beer."

"Have to keep my wits about me. Got a date later."

His hand went over mine. "Nice seeing you," he said as he slowly slid his hand across mine.

Monday, June 5

It was after two a.m. before I had rid the place of the black and white powder. The powder now resided in the vacuum bag at the bottom of my garbage can. My wine buzz had worn off and I was too wound up to sleep, so I grabbed my Shakespeare book and read *Macbeth* straight through, just for the fun of it. "Out, damned spot!" It seemed appropriate.

I put the book down and switched off the overhead light. Salinger was asleep at my feet. For the umpteenth time my encounter with Weathers started to unwind in my head, always ending with the same conclusion.

He had been telling me something. Under all the innuendoes and double talk was a message. Was his message, *I am the killer, catch me if you can?* Or maybe he knew who the killer was. Or were my nerves getting the better of me?

Even if he was the killer, there was no way I could prove it.

And he knew it. I had no evidence. My supposition was based on a gut feeling—the tone of his voice, the almost-smile on his face, his dead eyes and those waxy-white, callused hands. For some reason he wanted to draw attention to himself, and he wanted to know what evidence the police had on Ritter.

I rolled over on my right side to face the room. The baseball bat rested against the bed near my pillow. There was no way I was sleeping unprotected or with my back to the door.

Chapter Twenty-Seven

December, 23 years earlier

The reporter sat in the courtroom, his pen poised in his hand as the verdict was read.

The jury foreperson was a large woman with more middle than top or bottom. Her muumuu-like dress blossomed around her like a parachute. Her hand was steady but sweat glistened on her face.

"Guilty of first degree murder." She stood uncertainly for a moment. Then sat down.

"He didn't do it," Carol Sandinsky shouted at the jury. Her hands were wrapped so tightly around the banister separating her from her brother, they were white.

"He couldn't. Can't you see he's not right? He's slow. He's always been slow."

Her husband put his arm around her, but she shrugged it off.

William Gilman stood very still as the bailiff handcuffed him and led him toward a side door, an expression of surprise and wonder on his narrow, disheveled face.

The reporter wrote, "Probably thinking this was another dream."

Like the one he'd had about his niece, the reporter told himself. The dream where she was wet and muddy and cold. The one he'd told the police.

This story was writing itself, the reporter thought.

Carol pushed past her husband and two sons, walking fast

down the aisle toward the exit. "It's your fault," she shouted at her mother-in-law, who was leaving the courtroom. "You never liked him."

The reporter followed the woman and her family outside into the courthouse hallway.

"Look at me when I'm talking to you! You lying old hag," Carol shouted at her mother-in-law.

The woman turned around. "I told what I saw. It was the truth," she said, pulling herself up as she spoke. The curve in her arthritic back straightened momentarily.

It happened so fast the reporter didn't even see Carol raise her hand when he heard the slap. Then the gasp from the old woman. He watched as a red imprint of a hand rose on her cheek. Mitch Sandinsky pulled Carol away from his mother, who was weeping.

Now all the family members were in the hallway. The reporter was surrounded by them.

Helen Gilman, Carol's sister, yelled at Mitch Sandinsky. "You're a liar just like your mother."

Mitch yelled back, "He killed my daughter, you sick fucks."

Just then a bailiff emerged from the courtroom and tussled the parties apart.

The reporter glanced down the hall. Ashley's half-brothers stood against the veined marble green walls. One was staring at his shoes, his hands deep in his pockets. The other was looking down the long hallway toward the stairs. They both looked lost.

Chapter Twenty-Eight

Monday, June 5

As I waited for an SUV, squat and fierce as a tank, to pass the gravel drive before I exited onto Water's End Road, I glanced at my watch—eight-twenty. I would be late for the eight-thirty Monday morning staff meeting. I'd had a restless night full of nightmares. In the only one I remembered I was in the clearing by the Mink, once again kneeling beside Stephanie's body. In this dream she was still alive. I kept breathing air into her lungs until she pushed my hands away. Then I woke to daylight and the reality that Stephanie was dead and I hadn't been able to save her.

The SUV whizzed by, sending a spray of water over my windshield. As I turned and watched it head up the road, something white sticking out of Sarah's mailbox caught my eye. I got out of the truck, walked over to the mailbox, and pulled open the metal door. I slid the rest of the envelope out. There were no markings on the outside. But my hands were tingling. The first letter had come in the same type of envelope.

Two plops of rain fell from the trees onto the envelope. I wiped the drops off on my jeans and shoved the envelope into my front pocket.

I dashed back to the truck, jumped up into the cab, and shut the door. There was no doubt in my mind who the letter was from. I dug in the glove compartment for something to protect the letter from my fingerprints. I found a swatch of napkins from various fast food restaurants. Covering my hands as best I could, I slipped the envelope from my pocket, ripping it open with one napkin-covered finger. Just like before the letter was addressed to me.

Dear Leigh,

Three times three. Right before your eyes. See if you can see me. I am here like a river running through her soon you.

I carefully folded the letter and put it back into the envelope. I wrapped the envelope with the remaining napkins and placed the bulky package in the glove compartment. I sat for a moment listening to the raindrops ping the truck as the wind shook the trees.

You have two choices, I told myself—police or Weathers.

I dug my cell phone from my purse and the phone book from under the seat.

My fingers felt steady as I punched in the numbers.

"Can you tell me if Andy Weathers is working crew today? It's about a boat repair."

As I drove north, I thought about the new clue. I didn't need to do a Google search to know where it came from. It was a take off of Norman Maclean's book title, *A River Runs Through It.*

I'd never read the book, but I'd seen the movie. The title referred to the river that weaves through the story of two brothers. One brother, who leaves home and the river, prospers, and the other brother, who stays home and by the river, ends tragically. But the change in the wording from a river runs through it to a river running through her, changed the meaning. The river no longer runs through a particular story—the it in the title—the river runs through her. How can a river run through a person if the person is dead and her body is in the river? I reasoned.

But neither Stephanie nor Lisette had been put in the river. Was the killer referring to another murdered girl and another river? If so, what was the connection? One thing I did know, if the killer was referring to another murdered girl, she hadn't been killed by the Mink River. After Lisette's murder, I'd done a search on the computer. These were the first homicides committed in the vicinity of the Mink.

Not until I slowed the truck as I neared Rowleys Bay Resort did I allow myself to think about the rest of the killer's message and the threat directed at me.

"I want to rent a boat." I watched the white caps break over the lake through the grimy window of the marina boathouse. The air was humid and heavy. Joe was standing behind the cash register dressed in jeans and a yellow T-shirt that said Rowleys Bay Marina in black letters. I was trying to act normal. Whatever that meant. I hoped he'd decided to do the same thing.

"You want a canoe?" Joe didn't look up. He shuffled through slips of paper as if they were a deck of cards.

"Power boat." I glanced around the wooden boathouse. Paddles, life vests, a potbelly stove, assortment of fishing equipment. There was a glass cooler with various power drinks against the far wall. An assortment of live bait was in buckets on the floor.

"You know how to run one of those?"

"Can't be much different than a car. Got to be easier than a canoe." I dug in my back pocket for the driver's license and money I'd shoved in there before leaving the truck.

"Where you going, Leigh?" Now he was looking at me, and I wished he'd go back to ignoring me. His dark eyes had too much honesty in them.

"Washington Island."

"Why not take the ferry?"

"You going to rent me a boat or what?" I was tapping my foot with impatience. If he didn't rent me the boat soon, I was going to lose my nerve.

Taking the ferry was out of the question, because Weathers was crewing one of them and I didn't know which one. All I could get out of the ticket agent was that he was working today. It was imperative that he didn't know I was going over to the Island to search his house for evidence. If he was the killer, and my gut said he was, he had planted the evidence at Ritter's place. That meant that if he'd taken other trophies, they might be hidden somewhere in his house. I didn't know what evidence the police had from the Cohen murder or if they'd found Stephanie's hairbrush yet. But if they hadn't, it could be at Weathers's.

"Not until you tell me what's going on."

I reached into my front jeans pocket, pulled out the letter, and handed it to Joe. He read it and gave it back to me. I put it back in my front pocket.

"What is that?"

"The second letter from the killer. He left it in my mailbox. I found it this morning. I'm guessing he put it in there last night."

"Back up. As far as I know, Ritter's still in jail."

"Ritter's not the killer. The police arrested the wrong man. I'm pretty sure it's Andy Weathers. He's the one writing these letters. I ran into him last night at the River Supper Club. He all but told me." I had no real proof except the gnawing in my gut.

Joe bit his lower lip, his eyes down as he considered what I said.

"You look tired, Leigh. Why don't you go home and get some rest."

I put my driver's license and money on the counter. "I need a boat and I need it now."

He pushed my license and money back toward me. "Okay, you can have a boat, but I'm going with you. The waves are running high today. And you don't know the first thing about crossing Death's Door."

The boat was hitting the waves hard, the bow riding high in the water. The sky was more texture than color. Pebbled clouds broken here and there with blue. Though it was still humid, the air was damp and cold on the water. I was glad I'd brought my rain slicker. I huddled inside it watching Washington Island get closer and closer, the wind sharp on my face, ignoring my stomach, which seemed permanently lodged in my throat. The boat felt as if it were moving over the water, not through it.

Once we left the marina, Joe hadn't said much. I got the feeling he was doing this to humor me and prove me wrong. Sort of the way you guide a child's hand near a flame so they get the idea not to touch it.

As we passed Plum Island I saw the ferry coming in the opposite direction. For a Monday there seemed to be a number of people sitting on top. I wondered if Weathers was on board.

I didn't know how I was going to get into his house and search it. But one thing I had decided. Joe was not going to be a part of my breaking and entering.

We pulled into a slip at Detroit Harbor. A few tourists were lined up to take the Cherry Train to tour the Island. There was a husband and wife dressed in identical red crew shirts, white shorts, baseball caps and running shoes. A black station wagon was lined up for the return ferry, which was docked at the end of the pier.

I unzipped my slicker and jumped out of the boat.

"This won't take long," I told Joe who was tying up the boat.

"Have it your way," he said, turning his back to me. He was

tightening the rope around the pier as if he were strangling someone.

The house had a closed look. All the shades were drawn. Just in case the ticket agent had got it wrong and Weathers was home, I used the knocker and waited a few minutes. When no one answered, I tried the knob; it didn't turn. I walked around to the back of the cottage along a narrow grassy path crowded by yellowish fir trees and budding green shrubs. There was a side door, bottom half wood, top half multicolored blocks of green, blue and red glass. I peered through the colored glass, but the wavy design distorted the view. I tried the knob; it turned.

The side door opened directly into a kitchen. I closed the door behind me. Immediately the smell of tobacco filled my nose—pungent and thick. With the shades drawn and the tree cover, the room was shrouded in a yellow, dusky light. Directly across the room from the side door was another door that I guessed led to the upper floor.

The kitchen was reminiscent of an old farm kitchen with wide plank floors, whitewashed walls, a green-enameled wood-burning stove, a porcelain sink complete with well pump and an ancient white refrigerator. There were no cabinets. Instead, a large freestanding hutch held dishes, pots and pans and silverware. A small round table covered in a lacy cloth was pushed against a wall and flanked by two wood chairs. On the table was a bouquet of dried flowers in a glass vase sans water. There were no dishes drying in the dish rack, no newspapers on the table, no coffee cups in the sink. The room was fastidiously clean. The country décor extended to the matching red-and-white-checked potholder and dishrag neatly placed by the sink. For all its country charm, the room didn't look lived in. It was both authentic and sterile.

The only thing that broke the kitchen's magazine perfection

was something affixed to the refrigerator door. I walked over to get a closer look. It was an article from the *Gazette* dated August sixteenth. The story centered on a town meeting where Margaris and his lawyer defended his right to develop his land along the Mink River. The Nature Conservancy and a citizens activist group opposed development on the grounds that the river was habitat to the endangered Hine's Emerald Dragonfly. Martin had written the article.

Weathers had drawn a black circle around one of the people in the audience. The man was standing, his back to the camera. I squinted at the circled head. The man had dark hair, but it was impossible to make out his face. The magnet holding the article bore the Nature Conservancy oak leaf logo and said *Save the Hine's.*

I looked at my watch. It was after twelve. I didn't know when Weathers would be back, so I started searching the kitchen. After finding nothing, I went through the arched doorway into the paneled living room. I perused every title in his bookcase. Weathers had filled the shelves with those bound sets of the classics—Greek philosophers, American fiction writers, British novelists from the nineteenth century. All the books were arranged by category, then alphabetically by author. But there was no Shakespeare and no Maclean. I went back into the kitchen and up the back stairs. The steep wooden stairs dipped in the middle from wear but shone with a high slick varnish. They led directly into a large bedroom. Off the bedroom on the right I could see a bathroom.

I searched the bedroom first. Like the kitchen and the living room, it too had beautifully restored plank floors. But that was where the similarities ended. The bedroom was both sparse and messy. The twin bed had no headboard. A navy quilt was pulled sideways across the bed. The blue-and-white-striped sheets were rumpled. A white T-shirt and pair of black briefs were thrown on the floor. There was a shaggy white rug beside the bed that had dark lint tufts scattered through it. The bedside table was stained with water rings and littered with tobacco. There was a large yellow glass ashtray on the table filled with ashes and several dirty pipe cleaners. A gooseneck floor lamp arched over the bed. The black metal shade had been turned around, exposing the bulb.

Two bookcases overflowing with books took up one wall. Piles of books were on the floor in front of the bookcase. Again I went through every title. Unlike the carefully arranged bound classics, these books didn't have any common theme or order. There was such a diversity of topics from Abraham Lincoln to Impressionism to snowboarding to computers, I wondered if he had bought them in a lot sale.

He did have a volume of Shakespeare's complete plays and poems. A big, fat, blue book with gold lettering, copyright 1942. The original price tag was still inside, ten dollars. The edges were frayed and worn through. But no pages were marked or turned down. Though many of the plays' lines had been underlined. I found the Maclean book in one of the piles on the floor. The spine wasn't broken. It didn't even look like the book had been read.

I continued my search of the bedroom and then the bathroom—opening drawers and closets, looking under furniture. I went through his medicine cabinet, his dirty clothes hamper, and his wastebasket. Nothing was out of the ordinary. If there was any evidence at his house, he'd hidden it well.

I walked down the wood steps from upstairs into the kitchen and was about to leave through the kitchen door when I glanced back at the refrigerator. I walked over and studied the circled man. It was impossible to tell who he was. Not only could I not see his face, but the photo was grainy.

I held the magnet in place and slid the article out. It would be foolhardy to take it. But if I did, what proof would Weathers have that I took it? Carefully I folded it into fours and slid it into my jacket pocket zipping up the pocket.

As I approached the powerboat, I could see the ferry, *Robert Noble,* had just docked. Cars were embarking, people were walking off, and there was Andy Weathers directing it all, puffing away on his pipe. I put my head down and kept walking toward the dock.

When I reached the powerboat, I looked over at the *Robert Noble.* As if he'd been waiting to catch my eye, Weathers waved at me.

"Come here and take the wheel," Joe said as he maneuvered the boat away from the dock.

For the first time since the night we'd been together, I really saw him. His hair was longer, straight and shiny black, shot with white here and there. His features seemed sharper, his skin more burnished.

"Make sure you use both hands," he said, moving aside slightly.

I took the wheel and the boat pulled right. "Steady," Joe said, standing behind me.

His hands went over mine and steadied the boat. "Okay, now you try." He took his hands away.

I applied more pressure. He opened the throttle and water parted in front of the boat, circling behind us.

"You find anything at Weathers's house?"

"Not what I was looking for."

"You mean a trophy of some kind?" There was an undertone of sarcasm in his voice.

I ignored it. "I did find something else. I'm not sure what it means. Unzip my right jacket pocket. It's in there."

Joe unzipped my pocket, reached in, and pulled out the

article. The article flapped in the wind as he held it. "What's this have to do with anything?"

"I don't know yet. I got this strange feeling about his place. Like he knew I was coming. And he put that article there for me to find."

"Hmm," Joe murmured.

"You think I'm wrong about this."

"You got to follow what you believe. Doesn't matter what I think."

"Am I headed in the right direction?" I could see Plum Island coming up on my left.

"I'll let you know when you're off course. Just avoid the big stuff like ferries and land masses."

"We straight then?" I was asking about more than the direction of the boat.

Joe took a deep breath. "I've got no right being mad at you. I'm really sorry about the way I acted at the bar."

"Joe." I kept my eyes forward.

"Let me get this out. I've got no right. But I am, mad at you. That's the long and short of it. I can't pretend that I'm not. But I'm even madder at myself. For letting it happen that way."

I turned back to look at him.

Every word seemed to be costing him something. "Not that I'm sorry it happened. Just that it should have been different."

"Different?"

"There was a lot of death in bed with us that night. I wanted us to be about joy. And this has nothing to do with Jake. I don't care about Jake. I know how that sounds. But that's his problem. And I suppose yours too."

"You done?" I asked, turning my head to look at him. "We . . . I made a mistake. It won't happen again. So stop beating yourself up, and me, for that matter. Now do I get to dock this thing or what?"

I didn't need to look at him. I felt his body pull away from me.

The red light on my answering machine was blinking when I got home. I pressed the button and listened to the metallic voice tell me I had two messages. I slipped off my running shoes and flopped on the bed.

The first was from Jake. "You're expected for dinner. Seven sharp. My house. No excuses. And be on time for once in your life. And speaking of excuses you'd better have one for missing the staff meeting."

The second message was from Andy Weathers. "Find what you were looking for, Leigh?"

Chapter Twenty-Nine

Monday, June 5

It was 7:30 when I pulled my truck into Jake's drive. He had the good fortune to have a cottage adjacent to Newport State Park. So he was surrounded by open fields that backed to protected woods.

Behind his limestone cottage was a spectacular display of large, tumbling clouds against a cobalt blue sky. New grass was greening in the fields round his place. I shut off the engine and sat for a moment taking it all in. On the drive over, a guy had pulled off Highway 42 to snap the sunset, reminding me once again why I came here. Sunsets so moving they made people pull off the road; people so moved by sunsets they pulled off the road.

Well, I could only delay the inevitable so long.

I knocked on the carved wood door. Zoe opened it.

"Hi, Ms. Girard. C'mon in. Dad's in the kitchen."

"Leigh, call me Leigh." I could smell the familiar scent of Asian cooking—Jake's specialty. Peanut oil, mushrooms, onions, shrimp, celery, garlic and his secret ingredient, turmeric.

Jake stuck his head around the corner. "Zoe, get Leigh a glass of wine. It's in the fridge."

Zoe went into the kitchen. I could hear the low murmur of voices and Jake's laugh. Talk about feeling like a fifth wheel.

Zoe came back. Again I noticed how she shared her father's lean bones. She was all angles. Her jeans barely hugged her hips, and her tight, blue knit top revealed small, high breasts. Around her neck was a leather strap holding a silver leaf pendant. She had silver studs in her ears. And there was that scarlet halo of hair.

"You starting college next fall?" I asked, taking the glass of wine from her.

She sat down on a chair, putting one foot under her. She wasn't wearing shoes. Her toenails were painted a lipstick red.

"Well, actually, it's my second year," she said, laughing. "I skipped a year."

Smart and cute. Ugh. "Where?"

"Northwestern." She played with the leaf around her neck.

"What are you studying?"

"Theater. You ever teach there? Dad says you used to be a college teacher."

Theater? She also shared her father's love of the artistic and impractical. Another dreamer who'll have to find a day job.

"Uh, no. Not there. They wouldn't hire the likes of me."

"Oh." She looked up at the ceiling. "What's up with you and my father?" She had the decency to flush when she asked the question.

"Not much right now," I said, taken aback by her directness.

She nodded her head up and down slowly. "That's what I thought. Except, sometimes he's awful sneaky about stuff. He thinks he has to protect me from things. But if something's going on, you should just tell me. I can handle it."

"What's your dad say?"

"You work together. But I know there's more. I could tell that day on the beach."

I put my glass of wine down on a side table. I didn't see any point in lying to her. "We were involved over the winter. But we're not now."

"Dinner's ready," Jake said. I wondered how long he had

been standing in the doorway.

"I don't know who's pulling your chain," Jake said. "But I'm not running this or that other one now that Ritter's been arrested." I had played Weathers's message for him, given him the second letter from the killer to read, and detailed my encounter with Weathers in the bar, omitting my suspicion that he might be the killer. I wanted Jake to make the connection.

Jake continued. "I have to agree with Burnson on this. To run this would be irresponsible."

"Ritter didn't do it," I said, pushing my plate away. My appetite had soured. An assortment of carrots, celery and mushrooms, and a clump of rice were still on my plate.

"Says you. Still can't do it." What with Jake's cautious attitude and his new haircut, I felt like I was talking to a stranger. At least he was wearing his usual blue work shirt and jeans. Maybe he could be saved.

"Jake, there's no way Ritter wrote that first letter. And that second letter, which is almost identical to the first, came after he was arrested."

"Doesn't mean he didn't do the murders."

"What's his motive?"

"Sometimes there doesn't have to be one. Some people just get off on killing."

I knew that only too well. "He's not a killer. He prides himself on sexual conquest the old-fashioned way, by lying and manipulation. He considers himself a stud. And this second letter gives us another literary clue."

Jake rolled his eyes. "You mean the title of Maclean's book, *A River Runs Through It?* Where's the clue, everyone knows the murders happened near a river."

Jake was purposely being dismissive. "The letter doesn't say, 'a river runs through it', it says 'a river running through her, soon you'. The only way a river can run through a person is if the person is dead and her body is in the river. Neither Stephanie nor Lisette were found in the river. And since these are the first homicides committed in the vicinity of the Mink, I think he's referring to another murdered girl and another river?"

"C'mon, Leigh, that's reaching. Like I said some guy is yanking your chain."

"Dad, I think maybe you should listen to Leigh. If what she says is right, this guy who left the letters is sort of like stalking her. Even if he isn't the killer, he's got serious problems. And that one part about a river running through her sounds like he wants to hurt her." Zoe dropped her voice. It was obvious *hurt* was the wrong word.

She was an unexpected ally. But I wasn't sure she was helping my cause. "Let this go. Zoe's right. Who knows what this guy's agenda is. Take the second letter to the police. If it's Weathers sending the letters, let the police deal with it. I'd tell you to take the tape to the police, but then you'd have to explain your breaking into Weathers's place."

"I didn't break in. I walked in. What do you know about Andy Weathers?"

"Not much. He's lived on the Island for about ten years. Nice enough guy. He and Roz have been together a while."

"You don't find it strange his leaving that message on my machine? Or the way he acted last night in the bar?"

Jake gave Zoe a look. She started cleaning up the plates. He waited until she disappeared into the kitchen.

"Leigh, this time I'm going to play by the rules. No heroics from you. Let the police handle it. I don't know if Weathers is playing with you or if your imagination is getting the better of you. You've been through a lot lately. You probably should take some time off. Take a trip. Get away from here till things settle down. As for the letters, who knows? After all, you put yourself out there last fall with the Peck case. Granted, you were right. But you can't keep doing this kinda thing. Eventually your luck's going to run out."

I was furious. "What kinda thing would that be?"

"Sticking your neck out. I don't know if Ritter is the killer or not. But I don't want you involved in it."

"Seems you don't want me involved in a lot of things." I pushed back my chair from the table.

"Okay, is that what this is about? I apologized. I was wrong not to tell you about Zoe. I gave you some space. Now let's get past it." He'd pushed his chair back as well.

"I'm investigating the murder of two young women. That *I* found. How do I get past that? You put me on the story. And I intend staying on it until I think it's over. As for the rest, don't flatter yourself. I knew what we were about from the beginning. Like you said on the beach, I haven't told you everything either."

I stood up. "Thanks for dinner. Tell Zoe goodbye."

Jake followed me to the front door. "Leigh, c'mon. You look like hell."

"You're not the first person to tell me that today," I said, storming out the door.

Chapter Thirty

Tuesday, June 6

"Chief Burnson, Leigh Girard. Did the forensics report on Lisette Cohen come in yet?"

I was sitting at my desk. Marge was on the other line talking to one of our distributors. Today she was a little bit country: big hair, high-waisted floral dress, and brown knee-high boots with three-inch heels.

I heard the rustle of papers. "Got 'em right here. Pretty much what we expected." Burnson paused.

"You mean the same person who killed Stephanie Everson killed Lisette Cohen."

"I'm not going to speculate until all the evidence is in." His usual slick gregariousness was gone.

"What about the clothes? Were you able to determine if they were hers?"

"Can't say."

"Can't say or won't say?"

"As far as you're concerned—same thing."

He had every right to withhold certain details from the press, but I had every right to try and weasel those details out of him.

"Was she sexually assaulted?"

"Nope."

Something in that nope sounded too quick and too definite. "What about sexual intercourse? Did she have sex prior to death? You can tell me that at least."

He let out a deep sigh. "I'm not saying one way or another."

"Okay, but if she did, you'd be able to compare the DNA from the semen with Ritter's DNA."

"That's the way it usually works."

"And if it didn't match up, then—"

Before I could finish, he said, "Doesn't mean he didn't kill her."

I hung up the phone and blew air out through my mouth. That was the second frustrating call of the day. I'd tried to pry from the ferry line's secretary whether Andy Weathers had worked crew on May twentieth and May thirtieth—the days Stephanie and Lisette were murdered. I'd made up some bogus story about Weathers claiming he'd worked on my boat those days and I wanted to make sure he wasn't bilking me. The woman had told me that Andy would never do that and hung up.

"Marge," I said. "You know when Martin's getting in?"

"Hon, staff meeting's at nine. Rescheduled. You forget again?"

I had forgotten.

"I guess you got a lot on your mind. What with finding both those poor girls and then that phone call. Gives me the shivers. Bet you're glad they caught the killer. What would make a person do something like that?"

Marge had lived in Door County a long time and knew how not to ask a question while asking it. There was another question under her question.

"Before you tie your tongue up in knots, I'm not convinced Ritter is the murderer, if that's what you're asking."

"Aren't we touchy today? Isn't Jake's daughter a nice girl?"

"You know, Marge, you missed your calling. The CIA could really use your talents."

"Now there's no need to get like that, Leigh. Someone's got to look out for you. God knows these men are useless." For all her newfound freedom of self-expression, Marge still thought that women needed protecting. And that only men could provide that protection.

"Speaking of useless," I said.

Martin had just walked into the office. Marge giggled.

He was wearing a red short-sleeve shirt that clashed with his shockingly red hair. He went to his desk, sat down, and flipped on his computer, completely ignoring me.

"Got a minute?" I asked. "I need to show you something."

He looked over at me as if I'd just appeared out of thin air. "If it's a body, not interested."

"Real funny. It's about an article you did last summer. The one on that town meeting protesting Russell Margaris's development along the Mink."

He made a face as if I was speaking a foreign language.

"What about it?"

I unfolded the article and held it up. "Who was at that meeting besides Margaris, Guy Connors and the board?"

Martin made a big deal out of pushing his chair back, standing up and walking over to my desk.

"Why do you want to know that?" He took the article from my hand. As he stood over me holding the article, I could smell a piney scent. Either he'd been rubbing elbows with trees this morning, or he'd overdone the cologne.

"I'm just following something up."

"Nothing to follow up. The whole thing ended up in a so-called compromise. Which means the bad guys won. Margaris gets to develop the land if he stays upland and dedicates the breeding area in perpetuity. Problem is, it doesn't matter if he doesn't build along the breeding area. The fact that he's building near it will impact it negatively. The damned thing should be left just as is. It's the only known breeding area of the Hine's Emerald Dragonfly in the US besides a few remote places in Illinois and Minnesota. The Hine's is federally endangered. Not that anyone gives a damn."

I'd heard all that from Kolinsky. But I threw in a few nods to let him think I was interested.

"Was Andy Weathers there?"

"Andy Weathers?" He craned his neck back. "Why do you want to know about him?"

"This has nothing to do with the murders. I just need to know if he was there."

"You really do think I'm that stupid, don't you?"

"Okay, it might have something to do with them."

"News flash. The police caught the killer. You know different?"

"Weathers? Was he there?"

Martin put the article back on my desk and pointed to the circled person standing with his back to the camera. "That's him. And the only reason I know it's him is that I sat behind him. He was part of the citizens group protesting the development. Just like everyone else there, except Margaris, his lawyer and our nearsighted board."

A thought just occurred to me. "Was Stephanie Everson there?"

"I don't remember seeing her, but her father was there. And Kolinsky and his group. You're not trying to connect those girls' murders up with this?" He straightened up.

"Who shot the photo?"

"You're whacked, Girard. You know that?"

"The photo, who shot it?"

"I did."

"You take any others?"

"Why should I let you see them?"

"Martin, does everything between us have to be a pissing contest? I just want to see the photos. It might come to nothing.

Or, like the thing with Sarah, it might come to something."

He didn't like it. But there was no escaping the facts. I'd saved his ex-wife's life. "I'll get them to you tomorrow. If I have time." He stressed the *if*.

"And this one. I need it blown up."

"Don't push it."

I refolded the article, grabbed my purse and put the article inside.

"Where you going? We've got a staff meeting," Martin said.

I didn't answer.

"Jake's not going to like this," Martin called after me.

"He'll get over it."

Chapter Thirty-One

March, Nineteen years earlier

The *Chicago Times* reporter sat in the tiny dark apartment watching Carol Sandinsky light her third cigarette. The room smelled of smoke and grease and something else, heavy and imbedded in the faded, patchy wallpaper—cheap food and despair.

If it was possible, this place was worse than the last one, he thought. Instead of five rooms, there were only three, not counting the bathroom—a living room that probably doubled as a bedroom, a tiny alcove that doubled as a closet, and a kitchen. He wondered if the boys were still with her and, if so, where they slept. In that little alcove under the coats and dresses, on the kitchen floor, in the bathtub?

"Eddie's at work. I don't know where Bobby is," she said as if reading his mind. "It's like he dropped off the face of the earth." She pushed up on her sweater sleeves, looked at the crook of her left arm, and then quickly pulled the sleeve back down. "Just like Ashley."

But he'd seen them anyway. The track marks—lines of yellow and purplish bruises leading nowhere. Carol's clothes hung on her emaciated body like on a hanger. Her stringy hair was dull and dirty. There were shadows under her eyes dark as smudged ashes. Though he knew she was in her forties, she looked sixty.

"Like they was never here." Her eyes drifted off. There was a sheen over them that looked like glass. "You want something to drink? I got coffee or we could have something stronger. If you wanted to go out and get something. There's a market round the corner. On Main."

"Carol, I talked to the woman who runs the clinic. They have an opening. But you have to take it by the end of the week or they'll give it to someone else."

"Did you talk to that lawyer friend of yours?" Carol said, pulling the front of her sweater together as if a wind had come up.

"You have to accept the fact that he did it. There's no getting around the evidence."

She stubbed out the cigarette in the overfilled plastic ashtray on the side table. "I asked you to talk to that lawyer. That's all. Just talk to him. See if we can get him out on some technicality. He is mentally deficient. Maybe when he comes up for parole, we plead for mercy because of his mental deficiency."

She swiped across her nose with her sweater sleeve. "My brother would never hurt anyone. Let alone kill Ash. I thought you were on my side. All them articles you wrote. You know, I got a scrapbook filled with them. All them articles show you understand."

"I am on your side. That's why I'm telling you to get help. Or you're going to kill yourself."

"You know what he said to me before he took off? You know what he said?" Two circles appeared on her cheeks like dabs of rouge.

The reporter had heard the story before about the ex-husband who had abandoned her and the boys. But he sat quietly and let her tell it once again.

"He said I was just like him. Just like my brother." Her body seemed to cave in on itself. " 'Yeah,' I said. 'I am just like him, innocent.' That's what I told him."

"Then he packs up his suitcase as if he's going on some trip. Right in front of the boys. I'm making lunch for them and he's leaving us. Well, I showed him. I took that soup can and threw it right at his head. I missed him by a hair. Glass everywhere. The can went right through that kitchen window. A piece hits Eddie right here. Right above the eye. Blood running down his face.

" 'See what you made me do,' I says. That's when he makes the crack about Bill and me being alike. 'You didn't stand up for him in court,' I says. He goes upstairs and packs that damn suitcase. Comes down, puts his coat on.

" 'Stand up for him,' he says. 'He killed our daughter.' 'Her killer's still out there,' I says. 'Her killer's right where he belongs,' he says, 'in a cell.' There's blood's on the table, on the green linoleum floor. And Eddie's just sitting there like nothing's happened.

" 'I got nothing left for you,' I says. 'Look,' he says, 'look what you did to your own kid. You're just like your brother.' He said that to me. All the pain I'm in and he says that to me in front of the boys." She was coming to the end. Her speech had slowed. She was worn out with the telling. "You know I found bits of glass for months. Got one in my foot. It's still there."

"Carol, I'm going to leave the clinic's number and the name of the woman you should talk to. If you don't follow through this time, I'm not coming back." He stood up to leave, smoothing the front of his trousers.

"Yeah, go ahead, leave. Just like all of the rest of 'em."

Chapter Thirty-Two

Tuesday, June 6

If it was possible Annie Everson appeared even thinner. Her face was so hollow it seemed as if it had collapsed in on itself. Her thick brown hair was lifeless and dull. She looked like she was wearing a bigger woman's clothes.

The quickness was still there, but it didn't seem to have a focus. She was wiping at the kitchen counter with a dishcloth. She'd been doing that since I'd sat down at her kitchen table.

"I've been meaning to call and thank you." She wiped her hands on the cloth. "It's just so hard. That's no excuse, I know."

"Annie," I began. I didn't know if I should tell her about my conviction that Ritter didn't kill her daughter.

"I just find it all so hard to believe. That Stephanie's dead. I expect her to walk in here any minute, and say, 'Hi Mom, what's for dinner.' And Erik Ritter. I still can't believe he would do that."

"What do you mean?"

"I knew his mom. She took one of my weaving classes. Sometimes Erik showed up after class to take her back to the Island. He was a nice kid. But I know after his mom left, he had some problems. But to turn into a murderer. Maybe you never really know people or what they're capable of. So much of ourselves are kept hidden."

She put the cloth down on the counter. "I haven't even offered you something to drink. Where's my manners? You want coffee or soda?"

"Just some water." I wasn't thirsty, but it would give her something else to occupy her hands with for a while.

"Annie, do you remember that meeting protesting Russell Margaris's developing the land on the Mink? Do you know if Stephanie was there?"

"Why you asking me about that?"

"I don't want to say. In case I'm wrong."

She put the water down on the table and sat down. There was so much pain in her face as she looked at me, it took all my strength not to look away.

"Yes, she was there. Ben and she went. She was part of that citizens group. She was pretty hyped up about that development. I remember how upset she was that night. Telling me about the meeting. She wanted to do something to stop the development. Move stakes, stuff like that. How she felt sorry for Janell with a father like that. That she could see why Janell was like she was. Stephanie always saw the big picture. And so kindhearted. I always worried about that. Her being so kind, so caring." Annie was crying. Two lines of tears running down her sallow face.

"I'm sorry, Annie." I reached out for her hand.

She let me take it. "Nothing to do. That's what the pastor told me. Just let it come when it comes. Don't fight it. As if I could."

"Was Stephanie especially friendly with anyone in that group?"

"Not that I know of." She withdrew her hand. "You don't think Ritter murdered Stephanie, do you?"

I shook my head. "No, I don't."

"You have an idea who did?"

"Yes."

"I'm not going to ask you who. I can't bear to think of it

right now. But you find out one way or another. Then let me know. Okay?" The tears were back.

"I haven't forgotten my promise."

I grabbed the baseball bat as I heard the wheels crunch on the gravel drive. When I opened the mobile home door, it was in my right hand held high like a club.

Martin's black pickup truck was outside. Salinger let out a series of barks and bolted out the door. She greeted Martin with a combination bark and jump. Her tail was wagging shamelessly.

Just when I thought the day couldn't get any worse, I told myself, leaning the bat back against the wall.

After leaving Annie's place, I had returned to find Jake gone for the day. Marge's only comment was, "If it's important, call his cell."

He'd left me the stringer's notes from several town meetings along with a curt directive. "Write up." Below that order was another: "Edit feature column and sports. E-mail me when you're done."

"E-mail him?" I'd thought. He must really be mad.

In addition, the rain had left everything glistening and gloomy. Or maybe it was just I who felt gloomy.

Martin didn't wait to be invited in. He bounded up the steps past me and into the mobile home. He was still wearing that obnoxiously red shirt. Clumps of dried mud from his boots trailed him across the beige carpet.

"Make yourself at home," I said sarcastically.

He pulled out a chair from the dinette and sat down. A sense of irony was not a part of Martin's makeup.

He was carrying a manila envelope, which he opened and emptied on the table. A pile of black-and-white photos spilled out.

"I printed all of them. Nothing interesting here."

Though he had said he would print up the photos, I hadn't really expected him to do it, let alone so soon. That is, not without my asking him several more times with a few grovels thrown in. My guard went up immediately.

I picked out the blow-up of the picture Weathers had left on his refrigerator and studied it.

"Some of the quality was lost," Martin said as he petted Salinger on her head. She was salivating all over him. "But that's what happens when you blow it up."

The photo was grainy. But aspects of it appeared that weren't noticeable before. Margaris had a strange expression on his face. His jaw jutted sideways and his eyes were closed. He looked exasperated and maybe wary.

"What do you make of the look on Margaris's face?"

I put the photo in front of Martin, pulled up the other chair, and sat down. "He's pissed."

Martin picked up Salinger's ball from under the table and threw it across the room. Salinger ran after it, scurrying back and depositing it at his feet as if he were the one who fed her.

"Yeah," I said slowly, "but there's something else there."

"Look, he spent most of the meeting shooting angry stares at the audience and whispering to his lawyer." He smirked. "Say, maybe he's your murderer."

"Humorous. You remember what Weathers said?"

"Unfortunately, I do. He made this rambling speech about the importance of rivers. Which wasn't the point of the protest. I kept thinking, why doesn't this jerk sit down and let someone who knows what's going on talk. We weren't trying to save the Mink, we were trying to save the Hine's dragonfly. Though I suppose it might amount to the same thing. But the point was the Hine's is endangered, not the Mink."

"What'd he say their importance was?" I was thinking of the

letters and what the killer had said about a river running through her and soon me.

"I tuned him out. He was rambling all over the place. He did more to hurt our cause than help it. Weathers can be such a pompous ass sometimes. There's a guy who can't accept the fact that he fixes boats and crews a ferry for a living."

"You got something against Andy Weathers?" I asked.

"Me? At least I'm not trying to pin two murders on him. That's what this is about, isn't it? The police have Ritter dead to rights, but you think they're wrong. God, what an ego. Solve one crime and you're cock of the walk. And why Weathers? He offend your feminist sensibilities in some way? I would have thought you'd a gone for one of those sex offenders. Too obvious?" He was squeezing Salinger's ball in his hand.

"You're the worst kind of journalist, you know that, Girard? To you journalism is an excuse to air your own biases. In fact, you're not even a journalist. That piece of crap you wrote on those pervs. Talk about bias." He had squeezed Salinger's ball so hard, it had collapsed in his hand. Salinger slunk to a far corner of the mobile home, her tail between her legs, her ears down.

"Then why'd you bring me the photos?" His rant seemed to have materialized out of thin air—or had it been hovering between us for a long while? "Needed a reason to come here and dump all over me?"

His face went as red as his shirt. I thought he was going to take a swing at me.

"I want to see you go down in a blaze of glory. And if these photos can help, why not?" He threw the ball across the room. It hit the wall and landed on the bed with a dull thump. "And it's going to happen. Jake told me about those letters you got. Somebody has it in for you."

I could feel the heat flush my face. "You mean someone like you?"

He laughed. "Yeah. And I murdered those girls too."

"Woman," I said. "One of them was a woman."

"Girls, woman. No matter what you call them, they're still dead."

"Why don't you get the hell out of my place."

He leaned back in his chair and stretched out his legs in front of him. He was looking at the wall.

"Sarah's place," he said in a low voice.

I followed his eyes. He was staring at Sarah's charcoal sketch taped to the wall. A few sailboats, a pier, a man looking out to the horizon—all done with strong lines and an eye for what's important.

So we were back to that. Rob Martin's obsession with his ex-wife Sarah Peck. The fact that she'd rented her mobile home to me, that I was sleeping in the bed they had probably made love in, had sent him over the edge.

"Look, you don't like me. I don't like you. But we have to work together." I was going to offer an olive branch, or in this case, maybe the whole tree if it would work. Martin and I were never going to be friends. The most we could hope for was civility.

"Do you think we could bury the hatchet for a while? And not in each other?" I asked.

Salinger slunk back across the room and sat between us.

Martin leaned down and ruffled the white fur on Salinger's chest. "I got nothing against your dog," he said.

"Is that a yes?"

He continued ruffling Salinger's fur. "What do you want?"

"I don't know if Weathers is the murderer, but he's connected in some way. Either directly or indirectly. That I'm certain of. I won't go into my reasons until I am certain. But it all centers on rivers. And according to you, he had a lot to say about rivers at that protest meeting."

"You got copies of those two letters?" he asked.

I walked over to the bed, picked up the Shakespeare book, and took out the two letters.

As I sat down, I put them on the table in front of Martin. He picked them up and read them. Then placed them side by side on top of the photos.

"You sure that second letter was put in your mailbox after Ritter was arrested?" Martin tapped the letter with his index finger.

"About as sure as you and I are never going to be buddies."

"What about the sex offenders? I could see these coming from one of them." He rubbed at his goatee. I was used to Martin's mercurial personality, one minute raging, the next reasonable. But even for him, this was an abrupt about-face.

"Monroe Parks paid me a visit. He was so angry he kicked Salinger. Though I'm sure he wanted to kick me too."

Martin bent down, picked up Salinger, and held her over his shoulder like a baby. "You okay, girl?" His voice had gone up an octave. I wanted to puke.

"I know how to take care of my dog," I said, resisting the urge to grab Salinger out of his arms.

After a few minutes, he put her down on the floor. "Could be him. Could be a lot of people. But, if, and it's a big if, the police do have the wrong guy, these could be from the killer."

I nearly fell off my chair.

"*Could* be," he stressed. "Regardless of who it is, you're on his hit list. So maybe it's time to back off."

I clenched my jaw. "I'm not backing off." If one more person told me that, I was going to scream.

Martin laughed—a deep full-bodied laugh that relaxed the lines in his face.

"Like I said, blaze of glory." He did a spiral downward move with his finger.

I glared at him, my body pulsing with antagonism, because he was right. I could go down in a blaze of glory. And this time I might not be so lucky. Why was I doing this, risking my life? I could tell Annie it had become too dangerous—that I'd done all I could do. She'd understand.

As I stared at Martin's florid face, the quicksilver of emotions so evident, I understood for the first time what was really driving me. What had been driving me all along. Danger had become an addiction to me. I craved its adrenaline rush. It kept my dark cancer thoughts at bay.

Martin picked up the letters again. "Like a river running through her. A river running through her soon you." He put the letters down. "You know, I always thought rivers were like people. Unreliable and unpredictable. You can never count on them. Too susceptible to their environments. And that's especially true of the Mink. When the water level's low in Lake Michigan, the water level's low in the Mink. Cause and effect. The river depends on the lake. The lake even controls the Mink's tidal current. Every thirty minutes or so the water moves upstream, then downstream. That's what makes it an estuary."

"And this means what?"

"You're so smart, you figure it out."

Chapter Thirty-Three

Wednesday, June 7

The afternoon was bright and sunny. Everywhere flowers were burdening the fields with spring's fragile colors—lilac, white, pink, blue—here today, gone tomorrow. But the green had finally settled into itself. Even the evergreens had turned from sallow yellow to emerald. But all that was lost as I watched Patrolman Seeger work the hydraulic lift on his truck's tailgate, drag a dead deer up on the lift, and pull the lever. The deer's eyes had lost their color, and a cloying scent rose from its carcass. I turned away and looked again at the field.

Jake had assigned me a personal-interest story on Patrolman Seeger's job, which was to drive around the county five days a week and collect road kill. I didn't know if this was meant as a punishment or some kind of ironic lesson. This guy made his living from finding and disposing of bodies. I, on the other hand, just found them.

"It's mostly deer," Seeger explained, pushing his patrolman's hat up off his forehead. He was a middle-aged, broad-shouldered man with hands like sauté pans, or maybe it was the gloves he wore that were like sauté pans. He hadn't taken them off the entire afternoon. He even drove with them on.

It was after six. Seeger covered 250 miles a week. It felt like we'd driven that much in the five hours I'd been with him, and I still had to write up the story before heading home. I didn't expect to get home until after dark.

He had a lot of enthusiasm for his job that I racked up to making an eight-hour day of picking up dead animals seem meaningful.

"Just got to dump 'em, then I can drop you off at your truck," he said, slamming the tailgate shut.

"I'm on deadline. You think you could drop me first?" I asked, walking around the side of the truck and opening the door.

"Out on the way," he said. "This shouldn't take long. Besides, gotta see this for that there story of yours. Else it won't be complete."

I sighed and got into the cab.

As we sped down a side road, I thought about which Shakespeare play I'd read tonight. Reading *King Lear* had reminded me how much I enjoyed Shakespeare's insights into the human psyche. Maybe *Antony and Cleopatra*. Last night I'd tackled *Hamlet*—the boy angst play—until the wee hours. I had closed the book keyed up. Really, how confused could one adolescent be? Harboring incestuous feelings toward his mother, passing on the lovely Ophelia, and taking five acts to avenge his father's death. How many visitations did this kid need from his father's ghost to convince him? By the play's end, when the stage is scattered with more bodies than a Florida beach at spring break, I wanted to throw the book across the mobile home in sheer frustration. Teenagers and trouble seemed to be synonymous. Hadn't this whole thing started with Janell Margaris's tryst with Erik Ritter? Now two young women were dead.

The truck came to a stop by a dirt road. Seeger put the truck in reverse and backed down the road.

As he turned off the engine, he said, "Hope you're not squeamish."

I climbed down from the cab and waited for Seeger to unload the deer and various other smaller animal carcasses in front of a large trench. Already the trench was half full of decaying animals. My stomach did a flip-flop. I pulled out my notebook and clicked my pen.

"Soon as the weather gets warm, you can smell 'em," said Seeger as he hauled the animals into the trench. "That's when I use the lime. Helps with the decomposition and the stench."

I jotted down his quote and started doodling. Big petaled flowers with leaves like hands or sauté pans.

It was late and I was tired as I pulled up in front of the mobile home. Before I turned off the engine, I saw it—the door standing open like the entrance to a cave—dark and empty. The only sound was the water—its slow sloshing back and forth—and my heart's quickstep. The moon was lodged in a bank of clouds casting a cold silvery light on the trees, on the metal house.

Salinger was nowhere in sight. I jumped down from the truck.

"Salinger," I called. "Here, girl."

Not even a rustle in the grass. Fear rose up in my mouth. It tasted cold.

"She's here," I told myself, walking up the steps to the mobile home. "She's just run off into the woods. She'll be back when she hears me."

I reached around the door and flipped on the light switch. Everything looked just as I had left it. My clothes strewn on the floor, bathroom door ajar, breakfast dishes piled on the counter. Martin's photos scattered on the table. I looked over at the bed. Nothing. No note on either pillow.

But someone had opened the door and let Salinger out, or . . . I didn't want to think about or.

I scurried down the steps toward Sarah's artist studio. Even before I reached it, I saw the open door. Someone had sprung the lock. I walked inside. The moonlight threw long shadows across the room. Against the wall the stacked paintings looked like dark areas of profound absence. An easel stood in the center of the room facing the wall of windows. On the easel was propped a canvas. Something was drawn on the canvas. I hadn't been in the studio, so I didn't know if Sarah had left it there.

I walked toward the easel. Even before I reached it, I knew Sarah hadn't drawn it. On the canvas was a crude drawing done with black magic marker. It was a sketch of a dog. The dog was hanging from a tree. It's tongue dangling from its mouth, its eyes large and bulging. Below it in large block letters were the words Death's Door. And below that in smaller letters were the initials A. W.

"No," I cried. "No!"

As I drove toward Rowleys Bay, I listened to the beep of Weathers's answering machine.

"Pick up, you sick bastard," I said. "If you hurt my dog, I'm going to kill you." The machine clicked off.

I dialed again. Waited for the beep. "I've called the police. You better not have hurt her."

I had called the police. To my surprise, Chet was on duty. I was too frantic to ask him if he'd been reinstated. He said he'd be there in about an hour. Not to worry. That Salinger had probably run off. I told him about the drawing, the initials, who had taken Salinger, and that I was going after him. He told me to wait until he got there. I had hung up on him.

Andy Weathers had Salinger. This was the next move in whatever twisted game he was playing with me.

The marina was deserted except for a few boats listing in the harbor. The night was warm and a slight breeze ruffled the water. I pulled into a parking space closest to the boathouse. No one was around. I knew where Joe kept the keys to the powerboat. I'd seen him take them from a hook behind the cash register.

In a duffel bag, I'd brought an assortment of tools to break the Yale lock on the worn wood door. I pulled out a hammer and a chisel and positioned the chisel on the lock. With all my strength I brought the hammer down on the chisel. The lock, along with a piece of wood, split from the door.

I threw the hammer and chisel into the duffel and slung it over my shoulder. Then I pushed the door in. The odor of fish and damp wood filled my nose.

I went behind the counter. The keys were on the hook. I grabbed them and ran toward the boat, replaying in my head how to start the engine. The duffel banged against my shoulder as I ran.

Once I reached the boat, I threw the duffel in and unwound the rope that held the boat to the dock. I slung the rope into the boat and jumped in.

The boat listed in the water. I pulled out one of the life jackets from under the seat, slipped into it, zipping it up and pulling on the side straps to tighten it. I took a jagged breath and turned the key in the ignition. The engine started on the first try. I eased the throttle forward and moved away from the dock. The moon had emerged from a cloud bank and was riding high over the water, illuminating my way. I reminded myself that once I entered *Porte des Morts Strait* to look for Plum Island. As long as I kept it in sight, I'd be heading toward Washington Island. The green and blue buoy bobbed in the water. Somewhere in the distance a bell sounded deep and clear.

I pushed the throttle further. The boat jerked forward and rose in the water. I was having a hard time keeping the boat steady, but I didn't want to cut back on my speed. Salinger could still be alive. She had to be. Weathers wanted me. He wasn't interested in Salinger. He was toying with me. What had he said in his last letter—*a river running through her—soon you?* I looked down at the duffel. That hammer would come in handy.

★ ★ ★ ★ ★

It was 10:35 when I maneuvered the boat into one of the slips at Detroit Harbor. I pulled the throttle back and turned off the key. Then I tied up the boat, took off the life jacket, and slipped the rope attached to the key around my neck. Before I climbed up on the pier, I took the hammer out of the duffel.

The dock was empty. The ferries rocked against the pier, making a dull thudding sound. The moon, cloaked in clouds, shadowed itself, rippling and silvered.

I sprinted up Green Bay to Weathers's cottage. As I ran down the grassy driveway, I could see a faint glow in one of the second-floor windows. I bounded up the steps to the front door. It wasn't locked. I pushed it open. No lights were on in the living room.

I heard faint murmurings, like someone crying coming from the back of the house. I held the hammer tight in my right hand.

Following the cries that I prayed belonged to Salinger, I walked through the dark living room. As I entered the kitchen the murmurings turned to howls. Salinger was alive.

I ran my hand over the wall, searching for a light switch and knocked over a chair. My hand finally found the switch. I flipped it up.

The overhead light cast a yellow glare around the kitchen. The howls became cries again. They were coming from the closed door on the left side of the room. I walked over to the door and turned the knob. But the door wouldn't open. I put the hammer down on the floor and pushed against the door. It wouldn't budge. Something was propped against the door, keeping it shut.

I pushed again. The door opened a crack. I peered through the crack but couldn't see what was against the door. I took a step back, put my shoulder down, and shoved against the door with my full body weight. The door jerked open so fast, I lost my balance and almost fell over him.

Andy Weathers was staring up at me, his body a stiff tableau at the bottom of the stairs. The brown irises were blank and watery. His mouth was frozen open, a trickle of blood at the corner. And his fingers were curled and tight, as if he had fought his way into death. There was no need to touch him. Andy Weathers was dead.

I stepped over him and looked upstairs.

Salinger was straining against a rope tied round her neck and looped around the banister. She let out a plaintive bellow and jerked forward. Instantly the rope cut her cry to a strangled gurgle. I ran up the stairs to her.

Chapter Thirty-Four

Thursday, June 8

Hallaway arrested me. She had the decency not to lead me away in handcuffs. The charges were stealing a boat and breaking and entering. I'd been fingerprinted, mug shot, divested of my shoes and socks, and put in a holding cell. There was only one other female in the cell. She'd been arrested for drunk driving. At least that was my guess, because she'd slept through my lock-up and odors reminiscent of a brewery were exuding from her.

I knew when they went over Weathers's house, they'd find my fingerprints everywhere. What Hallaway thought about Weathers's death, she wasn't saying. But once they heard my message on Weathers's answering machine threatening his life, she'd have every reason to suspect me. My only hope was that he was already dead by the time I'd called.

I had explained repeatedly to Hallaway before she arrested me what I was doing at his house.

"How'd my dog get there?" I'd asked her.

"You brought her."

"You've got to believe me. There was a drawing."

She had raised one eyebrow.

The police hadn't found the drawing. Which meant someone had come back and taken it. Weathers was already dead. So who had taken it? And why? How had he or she known there was a drawing? Unless that person had left it, or Weathers had told him or her. Was that person the killer? Had I been wrong about Weathers?

"It was in Sarah's studio," I'd insisted. "A drawing of a hanged dog. Under the dog was written Death's Door and the initials AW. Why would I make this up?"

There was that eyebrow again.

"Right now," she'd said, jutting out her jaw, "you're looking at breaking and entering and theft. Until bail's posted, you'll be spending the night with us. Maybe after a night in jail, you'll tell us what you really were doing at Andy Weathers's house."

"You can't think I had anything to do with his death," I'd said as she escorted me out of the interrogation room.

Hallaway had wanted to put Salinger in the animal shelter. But Chet had offered to take her home with him until things got sorted out. I could have hugged him.

I sat up against the cold brick wall on the steel bench, listening to the middle-aged woman snore. She had coal-black hair that showed an even line of gray at her roots. Her face had that unhealthy, reddish glow of long-time alcohol abuse. She was wearing a loose, flowery dress she'd pulled over her legs and feet. I wondered what had set her life down that path.

As if she could hear my thought, the drunken woman let out a loud snort that woke her up. Her blurry eyes blinked open.

"Who you?" she asked.

"Leigh," I answered. "And you?"

She closed her eyes and went back to sleep.

I had made my one phone call to Lydia. She had assured me she'd have me out before morning. I wasn't assured.

Hallaway had given me the full criminal treatment, from making me lean up against the station wall while she patted me down, to having me stick out my tongue so she could check for a concealed weapon. She had stopped short of a full body-cavity search. She had me where she wanted me, and she was enjoying it. And it was all legal.

There were no windows in the cell. The only light came from the hall. I couldn't sleep. It had become clear to me that I'd been set up. From beginning to end. But was it Weathers who had set me up? I'd been so sure about him. But who had disposed of the drawing? And why? What was this all about? I was beginning to think that maybe I'd been wrong. Maybe the two murders weren't the work of a serial killer. Maybe there was a motive behind them. And somehow it involved Margaris's development of the land and the Hine's Emerald Dragonfly. But how did Weathers fit into all that? Was his death an accident, maybe even caused by Salinger, or did it just look like an accident? Had someone pushed him down the stairs? One thing I still felt sure of—he had written those letters to me. He'd been leading me somewhere. But where? Maybe Burnson was right. Maybe he was just a crackpot. Maybe he got in the way of the real killer.

I could feel the pressure of a migraine building in my head. They'd taken my purse along with my pills. I lay back on the cold bench and massaged my forehead. At least Salinger was safe.

I must have fallen asleep, because the rattle of keys woke me. For a minute I didn't know where I was.

"Girard, let's go." Hallaway held the door open.

I sat up and the pressure in my head pulled, tightening like a vise. I padded after Hallaway down the hall in my bare feet. It must be morning, because light was coming through the windows. I put my hand up to my eyes to block it.

"Jorgensen, give her her stuff." Hallaway sounded weary and angry.

I was shielding my eyes from the dots dancing in the light. "I can go?"

"For now," Hallaway said.

"What about Weathers?" I asked. "Do you know what time he died?"

She put her hands on her hips. "Your friends are waiting. One of them saved your meddling ass. We'll expect you in here for more questioning. You be here tomorrow morning at seven."

Lydia was waiting for me in the reception area. "You okay?" she asked. "You look kinda green."

"You ever spend a night in jail?" My head was so tightly banded, I felt nauseous.

"Well, thank you too." Lydia held the door open for me.

"Sorry," I said, walking into the spring day. "Where'd you park?"

"Over here." She pointed to a truck across the street.

I hesitated. Joe was leaning against the truck.

"Who do you think convinced Hallaway you didn't steal that boat?"

By the time Joe dropped Lydia at her shop in Fish Creek, my nausea was roiling. I didn't know if I could make it home. I kept swallowing and concentrating on the sky.

As we passed a dairy farm off Route A, I called out, "Joe, pull over quick."

Joe jerked the truck onto the shoulder. I jumped out of the truck, bent over, and vomited into the grass. I tried to straighten up, but the nausea rolled over me again. This time my stomach retched up bile. I didn't think I could feel this bad and be alive. I knelt down in the grass and sat back on my heels waiting for the nausea to pass.

Joe got out of the truck and came around to where I was kneeling. I bent over again to vomit. Joe reached down and pulled my hair from my face. I pushed at his hands and tried to stand up. Then everything went black.

A faint lemony smell woke me. Everything seemed both too

dark and too light. Then my stomach contracted and it all came rushing back. I put my hand over my eyes.

"You're awake," Joe said. He was sitting in a rocking chair beside the bed. He leaned toward me, a bottle of pills in his hand.

I moaned and turned my head away from him. On the bed stand was a lamp and a cup. Its lemony scent made the bile rise up in my mouth again. I swallowed hard.

"Take that away," I said, turning back toward the room.

Dark blue walls, one small dresser, dark wood, matching bedstand, braided rug in front of the bed, and the rocking chair where Joe sat looking at me as if I were a bug under a pin.

"I'll give you one of these for your migraine, but you need something in your stomach first."

"I can take care of myself." I sat up and reached for the pills.

Joe pulled away from me. "Jeez, Leigh. Don't you ever stop fighting people?"

"Where's Salinger?" I asked. "I've got to get her."

I threw off the blanket and put my feet on the cool wood floor.

"Where are my clothes?" I asked, shivering in my underwear. My head spun. "I need my truck. You gonna drive me?" I held my arms tight, trying to steady myself.

He came around the bed and knelt down in front of me. "It's okay, Leigh. It's okay."

"It's not," I said, biting the side of my mouth. "It's not okay. Nothing's okay."

"I know," he said. "I know." He knew enough not to touch me.

A cold sweat broke out over my body. I felt as if everything—the two murders, Weathers's death—had rushed to the surface of my skin and I was drenched in them.

I sat there with my feet on the floor and Joe kneeling in front of me for what seemed like a long time. Finally Joe got up and walked to the door.

"I'll pick up Salinger and bring her here," he said. "But you have to eat something first."

I lay back on the pillow and stared at the blue ceiling. There was a faint glow of stars pasted on it.

"Don't leash her," I called after him.

Chapter Thirty-Five

Friday, June 9

Hallaway was doing the talking. Chet stood in the corner listening. I got the feeling he was there not so much to observe me as to observe Hallaway. They were giving him a second chance.

Salinger and I hadn't returned to the trailer home until late afternoon. There'd been a message on the machine from Chet reminding me to report to the station at seven sharp.

"That there's seven in the morning," he'd said.

Hallaway, Chet and I were back in the gray windowless interrogation room. As Hallaway spoke, I watched the creases around her full mouth tighten and relax. The creases matched her uniform's creases. Only those never seemed to relax.

"For now we're treating Weathers's death as an accident. But that could change." There was a threat in her statement directed at me. Her almond-shaped eyes became slits.

"What were you doing at his house?"

"I already told you this," I said, exasperated. "There was a drawing in Sarah's studio signed A.W. As in Andy Weathers." This morning I felt equal to whatever Hallaway was dishing out. It was amazing what vomiting your guts out and a day's sleep did for a gal.

"As I already told you, we didn't find any drawing," said Hallaway smugly.

"Someone took it after I left. But there was a drawing."

"We didn't find any drawing," Hallaway repeated. "But we

did find your fingerprints all over Weathers's house. What were you looking for?"

I glanced over at Chet. He had taken my frantic phone call. He had to know I'd been telling the truth. His face was stern. There'd be no help from him.

"I had reason to believe that he was involved in the murders of Stephanie Everson and Lisette Cohen." I was going to tell Hallaway as much of the truth as would get her off my back and allow me to continue my investigation without her interference.

Hallaway slammed her fist down so hard on the table I jumped. "You must have some mental defect, Ms. Girard. Erik Ritter is in jail for those murders. We have evidence to prove he did them."

"Evidence can be planted." I steeled myself for another fist-slamming. Instead Hallaway suddenly grinned. "Okay. Okay. You want to play it that way. We'll play it that way. Tell me why you think Weathers murdered Everson and Cohen."

I was no longer convinced that Weathers had murdered them. The missing drawing complicated that theory. But until I figured how it all fit together, I was sticking with my original belief that Weathers was the killer.

In excruciating detail I went over the two letters, my meetings with Weathers, his taunting me. I didn't tell her about the article. I could see by her puckered mouth and slight head nods that she wasn't buying any of it.

"Now if I understand your reasoning, Weathers was giving you clues, in the hopes of . . . ah. What? Having you catch him?"

When she said it, it sounded ridiculous. "No, not catch him. He wanted someone to witness what he'd done. For what reason, I don't know."

"Did you hear that, Deputy Jorgensen? There's something Ms. Girard doesn't know." She winked at Chet.

"Well, what about those letters? I got the second one after Ritter was arrested."

Hallaway turned around and looked at Chet. "Officer Jorgensen. How do we explain that?"

Chet cleared his throat. "We think you wrote the letters, Leigh."

"Chet, you know me better than that. What conceivable reason would I have for doing that?"

Hallaway waited for Chet to answer. "It's a good story."

"You think I made it all up for a story? I wrote letters to myself for a story? And then I guess I faked those phone calls to Weathers, too. And stole a boat and dragged Salinger to his house. For a story?" I was incredulous.

"The letters, yeah. The rest maybe not made up exactly. You're just too hell-bent on proving the police wrong there. Kinda like before then."

"I was right before." I glared across the table at Hallaway. "Then why don't you arrest me? You're so sure I set this thing up. I must have killed Weathers too. Right? Makes a good story."

"You got lucky there, Leigh," said Chet. "Coroner puts time of death before you made them phone calls. Weathers was already dead."

"Whew, that's a relief," I said, running my hand over my forehead. "You done with me? I've got work to do."

Hallaway lowered her voice so much, I had to lean in to hear her. "The next time you interfere with this investigation, or any police investigation in any way, I'm going to press charges. And your friends aren't going to be able to help you. I'll see to that. Got it, Girard?"

I didn't answer. I was looking at Chet, who was looking at his shoes.

Chapter Thirty-Six

Friday, June 9

Who had taken the drawing? I asked myself as I left the police station. Had I been wrong about Weathers? Maybe he wasn't the killer. But maybe he had known who the killer was, and it had cost him his life. I'd been so sure it was Weathers.

I needed to talk to Weathers's girlfriend, Roz. If anyone had any insights into Weathers, she would. It was midmorning. Death's Door would be open.

As I drove up Highway 42 to Gills Rock, I popped a tape into the truck's cassette player: *Mozart for Your Mind,* guaranteed to boost your brainpower.

I mulled over Hallaway's ludicrous accusations. I didn't think Hallaway really believed I'd written the letters or faked Salinger's kidnapping. It was all a strategy to intimidate me. To scare me off the case. Her threats and accusations only made me more determined.

But what troubled me was, if she didn't believe I'd faked the letters and the kidnapping, then what did she think? Had she convinced herself that Weathers was some nut with an axe to grind with me? For what reason? For all her rigidness, I felt she was a competent policewoman. As head of the task force investigating the deaths of two young women, and with tourist season just beginning, I knew she was getting a lot of pressure from her superiors. Being female didn't help. She couldn't bend. She had to play by the book. And above all, she had to keep the press at bay. But she was wrong about the murders. Ritter wasn't the killer. If nothing else, Weathers's death convinced me of that. I could understand Hallaway's position, but in no way was it going to alter what I had to do. She had her job and I had mine.

But what troubled me even more than Hallaway's accusations and seeming indifference to other murder suspects was the missing drawing and all it implied. Had the person who took the drawing also been the person who put it there in the first place? If so, for what reason—to lure me to Weathers's cottage, to implicate me in his death? Or if Weathers had left the drawing and taken Salinger, then the person who took the drawing had been at the cottage before Weathers's death. Maybe even had been the cause of it?

The swirling mind-boosting symphony ended as I turned right off the ferry ramp road and parked in front of Death's Door restaurant. A closed sign rested against the front window.

I pulled out the directory from under the seat, found the restaurant's number and called it on my cell phone. Roz's message said the restaurant was closed until further notice, due to a death in the family. Her voice had that monotone sound that sudden death and grief brought.

I flipped through the white pages and found her home number. Her home message was a little more forthcoming. She'd gone to Washington Island and left a number where she could be reached. Even if I hadn't recognized Weathers's number, I didn't need a crystal ball to know where she'd gone. I called Weathers's house. Roz told me she planned on being there for a couple days to get things in order.

I told her I couldn't wait that long. I had to talk to her about Andy. I didn't elaborate. I let her think it was for a *Gazette* obit on Weathers.

Like a good citizen, this time I took the ferry over.

All the front windows in the cottage were open. A boisterous breeze ruffled the white curtains. The place seemed lighter somehow.

Roz wore a black apron over red spandex pants and a tight black scoop-necked T-shirt. Across the front in white letters were the words *Don't mess with the Chef.* Her mules had those three-inch block heels that looked like cartoon shoes. I didn't know how she could walk around in them, much less clean a house.

"He told me he was leaving everything to me about a year ago. 'It's not much, Roz,' he says, 'but it's yours free and clear. No encumbrances.' Yeah, right." She smacked the dust cloth she was holding against the desk. A rush of dust rose and twirled in the light.

She continued moving around the room with the dust cloth. "At the time I was surprised, but didn't really think much about it. I mean, we've been together for a few years, but neither one of us wanted anything permanent. I've been down that road twice, and Andy just wasn't the marrying type. Anyway, soon as everything settles down about his death, I'm going to sell the place. It'll sell quick. Probably to some tourist. This is prime real estate. Besides, tourists will buy just about anything if the price is right." She stopped dusting, her eyes darting around the room. "What the hell am I going to do with all these books? You should see upstairs. There's even more."

The police in their search had scattered the books everywhere. The floor was so littered, it was hard not to step on them.

"You can always donate them to the Sturgeon Bay library," I said.

She nodded her head absently. "That was the only thing I never understood about Andy. He was never happy just to do his job and have a good time. He always had to be reading about something. He'd go on and on about this and that. Half the time I didn't understand a thing he said. But I'd just let him talk. I'd be going over what I had to do at the restaurant in my head. Don't get me wrong. I really liked the guy. I could always count on Andy. If he said he'd be there at eight, he'd be there at eight. He was real reliable. Never let me down. My exes had a problem with commitment. I could really pick 'em. But Andy wasn't like them. He was real steady. You can't say that about a lot of 'em. Can you?"

"I suppose not."

"You want to sit down? You look tired."

I was standing by the fireplace.

"No, I'm fine. Did Andy ever say anything about his family?"

"I asked him about them early on when we were getting to know each other. He said he didn't have any. When I asked if they all were dead, he said, 'Might as well be.' When I tried to find out more, he got real angry and said something like, 'What's my family have to do with anything?' I let it drop after that."

"He ever say where he was from?"

"Nope. He was real secretive about before he came here. I always got a feeling something had happened to him. Something life changing. Maybe something tragic. But I learned from two marriages when a man don't want to tell you something, he's not going to tell you. Or he's going to lie to get you off his back. So you might as well let it drop."

Ignorance is bliss. I could see why it would be easy for men to lead secrets lives with Roz. I wondered if on some level she knew that.

"He ever say why he decided to live on the Island instead of the peninsula? He could have just as easily lived there and repaired boats and worked for the ferry line."

"I think he liked the isolation. Especially in the winter, when Death's Door froze over. He got a kick out of bucking the ice in winter. That it could take six hours to cross Death's Door. 'It should always take that long,' he'd say. 'If people slowed down, then they'd think about what they say or do to each other.' That's when I got the idea that all his talk was covering up the fact that he was a loner by nature. Not that he wasn't sociable. 'Cause he was. But sometimes he just needed this distance between people. Like a rest or something."

Maybe he'd been running away from himself, I thought. If so, no distance would ever have been enough.

"Didn't you think it strange then when he joined that protest against Margaris's development along the Mink?"

Roz smiled wistfully. "That's because of me. I talked him into it. He was against the development and all. But he wasn't going to do anything about it. I told him that once in his life he should stand up for something and not be such a loner. I showed him all the stuff from the Nature Conservancy. About what that rich guy Margaris was going to do. There was this article on Margaris in *The Windy City Reporter* with his picture and all. It told how he bought these run-down housing developments in Chicago and was building high-rise condos in their place. When Andy looked at that, it seemed to change his mind."

"Any chance you still have the article?"

"Funny you should ask. I found it this morning when I was cleaning out Andy's bedroom. He had it in, of all places, a box of garbage bags. It fell out when I took one. Can't imagine why he put it there. But that's Andy. Was Andy. Wait a minute. I'll get it out of the trash."

She walked back to the kitchen. I heard her rustling around. When she came back, she handed me the article. It was all rumpled and had a dark stain in the middle. But the photo of Margaris was pristine. He was dressed in an expensively cut suit and was standing beside the mayor and two aldermen. Margaris was about to plant a ceremonial shovel into the ground. The caption read: "Developer Russell Margaris breaks ground on new high-rise condominiums." There was a sidebar story with the headline: "Many former residents homeless."

"You mind if I take this?"

"It was in the trash."

I was hedging about asking the next two questions, because I knew that once I did Roz would probably hate me, and that would put an end to her cooperation. But I had to know.

"Roz, one more thing. Was Andy with you on Saturday, May twentieth between twelve and seven, and on Tuesday, May thirtieth between say ten-thirty and five?"

"Why you asking me about those dates?"

I didn't have to answer, because she figured it out. I don't think I ever saw anyone change demeanor so quickly. Her whole body went rigid with rage.

"You get outta here. Now." She was on her feet.

"I have to know, Roz. Annie Everson's daughter was murdered. Lisette Cohen was murdered."

"I knew I shouldn't have talked to you. I kept telling myself, 'You're making a mistake. This woman found Andy. How do you know what really happened? But the police said he fell. That it was an accident.' Why don't you tell me what you were doing here that night?"

I explained once again everything, from the first letter to the drawing. It was like watching bullets bounce off steel.

But something must have gotten through. "He wasn't with me. Those dates you said. I don't know where he was. Like I said, we didn't have that kind of relationship."

Then I got it. For all her protests to the contrary, he'd kept her at a distance she hadn't wanted. In the end, he was just like the rest of the men who had hurt her—leading separate lives that didn't include her. Doing who knew what.

"Now I want you to leave." She pointed to the door. Her red fingernail polish was chipped near the tip.

"If you think of anything else, anything out of the usual, call me."

I put my card on a table.

I read and reread the *Reporter* article on the ferry ride back to the peninsula. Margaris really was an opportunistic scumbag. He'd paid the city off to free up the housing development sooner than the residents had been promised. Which made it difficult for the city to find them suitable housing in time. Many had ended up in homeless shelters. Those were the lucky ones. Others were on the streets. I wondered why this article had turned Weathers from a recluse to an activist. He hadn't seemed like the kind who cared about issues larger than himself. And the coincidence of him being the person who found Margaris's daughter? How did this all connect to Weathers murdering two young women near the Mink River? If he had murdered them. And had Weathers accidentally fallen down the stairs, or had he had some help? If so, who had reason to kill him? And was that the person who took the drawing?

As I watched one of the crew in a navy windbreaker loop a rope thick as a boa constrictor around the dock, I made up my mind that too many trails were leading back to Margaris.

On my way back to the office, I stopped by Margaris's house. He wasn't there. I tried the front door, but it was locked. I walked around the back and cupped my hands against a window. The room was in total disarray. White sheets were on the floor, falling off the furniture. Dishes, papers and clothes were everywhere, but no Margaris.

I turned around and looked upriver; here and there the red-banded development stakes were newly planted.

Disgusted, I walked back to my truck and called his number. When the answering machine beeped, I left him a message.

"Leigh Girard. I have to see you as soon as possible. An article about you was found in Andy Weathers's cottage. He was the man who found Janell. In case you don't know, he's dead. The police are calling it an accident. But I have reason to believe his death is tied to the two murders. We need to talk."

That sounded provocative and cryptic enough to elicit some response. In the meantime, my stomach was doing the two-step. My newly reformed self was going to have lunch.

I stopped at the Harbor Café off Highway 42 in Egg Harbor. The restaurant seemed to change ownership with each tourist season, which probably contributed to its food being mediocre. But regardless of ownership, the view remained splendid. And each new owner had kept the early bird breakfast special—two eggs, bacon or sausage, hash browns, and toast for $3.50, making the view almost free in my opinion.

I was too late for the early bird, so I ordered a BLT, bacon crisp, on wheat toast, with an iced tea. No fries. Fruit salad. It was a hard sandwich to mess up.

The Café was on the second floor of a building that housed a bookstore and a real estate office. Almost every table in the restaurant offered a view of the harbor. Towering arbor vitae crested the windows. The revolving owners always kept them below the ledge so as not to obscure the customers' appreciation of why they tolerated the so-so food—Green Bay's teal waters.

This afternoon a few boats bobbed against the pier. Out on the water a jet skier was pushing the season, and a sailboat was moving north at a leisurely pace. The sky blued the water; not a cloud anywhere.

I had brought the article, the envelope of photos, and a magnifying glass with me. I placed the article at the top center of the table and then took out the photos. The blow-up with

Weathers standing I centered on the table. Then I took out the four other photos. One photo was of Guy Connors, the Nature Conservancy ecologist. He was standing by an easel, which held a plat map of the Mink River area. I used the magnifying glass trying to decipher what Connors was pointing at. It was Rogers Lake, where the Mink River emptied.

The next photo was of Margaris's lawyer, who also was standing by the plat map. He, too, was pointing, but at an area farther down river where I guessed Margaris planned his development. The third photo was a group shot of the men and one woman seated at the table: Margaris, his lawyer, Guy Connors, and the three-man, one-woman county board. Someone in the audience must have been addressing the group, because they all were looking in one direction except Margaris. He was touching the Rolex watch on his wrist—a look of boredom on his face. He knew he was going to win. He always won. It was just a matter of waiting for everyone else to understand that. The fourth picture was of the audience. Martin had tried to focus on a few individuals to represent the whole. The shot was dark, and two of the individuals had their faces turned sideways, but I recognized Kolinsky, Brian and Lisette. At least it looked like it was Lisette. She was talking to someone beside her. But that person wasn't visible. I moved Weathers's photo next to the audience photo. There it was. The person next to Lisette was Weathers. Lisette was smiling at him.

"You look like the cat who swallowed the mouse," the waitress said, putting down my plate.

"More like the mouse who swallowed the cat," I said.

She gave me a quizzical look and left.

I took a bite out of the BLT. The bacon slid out of the sandwich. A rubbery, undercooked slice. I pulled the slice from my mouth, put it on the plate beside the curled orange slice, and opened the sandwich. Okay, an LT was better than no lunch.

"Marge, how do you do a trace search on someone?"

Marge had opted for an eclectic look today. Her silvery hair was teased and sprayed into a beehive. She had on spike heels and a shoulder-padded emerald-green pant suit. Her white ruffled collar blouse also must have had shoulder pads, because from the back, her shoulders resembled a linebacker's.

"That only works if they have a record. For example, you could do one on yourself. Your person been arrested?"

"One of these days, Marge, you're going to push me too far."

"You know I'm only teasing you. You're my hero, Leigh. You inspire me to be daring."

"Okay, enough."

I did a trace search on Margaris and Weathers—which turned up zilch. Then I did a bio search on them. As expected, nothing came up on Weathers. Margaris's bio contained the usual PR stuff. The ruthless developer came off sounding like Mother Teresa providing shelter for the indigent. If you considered people who forked over half a mill for a condo indigent.

I printed up Margaris's info and shut off the computer. It was near dinnertime.

"I'm heading out," I told Marge. "If anyone calls, give them my cell number."

"Anyone in particular?" Marge asked, patting the top of her stiff hair.

"Russell Margaris," I said. "In particular."

"Okay. You going home then?"

"Yes, ma'am. Got another date with a King tonight."

"They all think they're kings," Marge said.

"Ain't that the truth."

★ ★ ★ ★ ★

The light lingered over the lake making me take my microwaved dinner outside. A vegetarian chili potpie made from soy products that I was trying not to look at too closely. The important thing was—it was healthy and tasted sort of like ground meat. I'd passed on wine in favor of a glass of water with a slice of lemon. I wanted a clear head. There was something I was missing in the killer's literary clues, some common thread that explained why he'd chosen those two literary references.

Both referred to where the two murders had taken place. The line, "The wheel is come full circle," echoed the killer's words to me on the phone, "You know the place, where the circles end." "A river running through her, soon you," was a take off on the book title, *A River Runs Through It,* and specified the murder site, in this case, the Mink River.

Both the play and the book dealt with two brothers. But only one of the clues used the actual words of one of the brothers. So those words or that character had some special significance. When Edmund says those words, the two brothers who've been estranged throughout the play, are revealed for who and what they are. And Edgar finally accepts his brother.

I shivered. The light was nearly gone. Salinger, asleep by my feet, was also shivering.

Weathers, the well-read psychopath, would not have chosen the line for its surface meaning alone. He identified with Edmund. Now all I had to do was to find his Edgar, his "good" brother. Or was it the other way around? Was Weathers the good brother and the other brother the killer? If there was a brother, good or bad, it would explain who had taken the drawing. No, I was sure Weathers was the killer. His last words to me had been "nice seeing you." Was I pushing it to make my case? Lots of people say nice seeing you.

The light faded over the water; the sky smudged violet. He'd been there all along. Right in front of me. From the very beginning. On the river that runs through her. Now through me.

But who was this she that Stephanie and Lisette, so similar in appearance, had represented? Someone significant to Weathers? A girlfriend, a sister, his mother? Someone who had died? More likely been murdered.

And was there a brother?

I gathered up my dinner container, drank down the rest of the water, and walked back to the trailer home.

When I pulled out of the driveway, Salinger was sitting in the passenger seat. I had to talk to Margaris. There'd been too many coincidences involving Weathers and Margaris. Weathers finding Janell. The evidence linking Ritter to the murders found after Margaris had filed the rape charge. Margaris's development along the Mink River where the murders had occurred. The protest meeting. And the two articles in Weathers's house.

But there'd be no faking out Margaris; he was too smart for that. I'd have to have proof—irrefutable proof that there were two brothers linked by some tragedy equal to a Shakespearean play. If they were brothers.

Saturday, June 10

I was on my fourth cup of coffee. The caffeine was keeping me awake, but it was also making me jumpy. Even though it was the middle of the night and I was in Jake's office at the back of the building, I hadn't turned on the lights. Even with the blinds drawn, my outline would be seen. If some insomniac decided to take a stroll along Green Bay, I didn't want him or her knowing someone was in the office. So the only illumination was the computer screen, a light much like a television's in a dark room—harsh, unforgiving, disturbing. Conducive to my bad thoughts and self-doubt.

Salinger was having the same reaction and kept moving around the room, not able to settle anywhere.

Because I had so few concrete facts, and the time period involved was so large, and since both Weathers and Margaris were in their early forties, my only choice was to meticulously comb through the Wisconsin and Illinois major newspaper archives for the last thirty or so years. I figured I'd start with those states under the assumption that the killer would stay close to home. After hours and hours of reading the worst that people did to each other, I was no nearer to finding what I was looking for. My stomach was sour with coffee and disgust.

Only the *Chicago Times* archives remained to be checked. The archive went back twenty-five years. I typed in murderers/women, murderers/children and the year. A list of murders of women and children appeared. Each had a headline and a brief description. I scrolled down the list.

There had to be an easier way. Maybe my theory was all wrong. Maybe Weathers was just a crazy nut job who got off on murdering young, yellow-haired women and dumping their bodies by the Mink River. And Russell Margaris was just another greedy developer. Even so, if Weathers was the killer, and I was convinced he was, Erik Ritter was innocent. I didn't like the guy, but he didn't deserve to be sent to prison for life for two murders he didn't commit.

I leaned back in Jake's chair and caught my reflection in the small mirror on the opposite wall. My naturally wavy dark hair was a frizzy mass. My hazel eyes were dark and hollow. I looked haunted.

I typed in another year. Another list of murders of women and children appeared. I scrolled down the list and noticed the reporter Wallace Bernard's name appeared throughout the list. His name had appeared in the first list. I typed in another year. Again Bernard's name peppered the list. I jumped the chronology five years, then ten years and Bernard's name appeared in each year's list. He seemed to have covered a great many of the major crime stories for the twenty-five-year period I was checking. Maybe I was going about this all wrong.

I closed out the *Times* window and returned to the search engine. I plugged his name into the computer. A list of Wallace Bernards appeared—from wine experts to golfers. I scrolled down until I found Wallace Bernard, *Chicago Times* reporter. I clicked on his bio. He was still alive, retired and living in Chicago. It was a long shot. But I was out of ideas.

I looked at my watch. It was 3:30 in the morning. Even granting him senior sleeping habits, I doubt that he'd be up yet. I'd wait a few hours. I switched off the computer, grabbed Jake's beat-up leather jacket from the hook, and stretched out on the floor. Salinger crawled into my body's curve, finally settling down.

Chapter Thirty-Seven

Saturday, June 10

"The *Door County Gazette,* huh? Jake Stevens still editor?"

"You know Jake?" That was a surprise. I rubbed at my eyes, as if that could clear my head. I'd waited until seven to call Wallace Bernard after drifting in and out of sleep.

"One of my interns, years ago. Great investigative instincts." Bernard had one of those deep bass voices that seemed to grow more full-bodied with age. "You tell him Bernard still wants to know when he's going to take a real job. And stop vacationing."

"I'll tell him." Another piece in the Jake puzzle.

"So you want to know about a murder or murders I may or may not have covered in the thirty years I was with the paper involving a blond girl murdered by a river or left by a river." When he said it, it sounded even more absurd.

"I'm following up a hunch. And I don't have anything else I can give you. I know it's a long shot. The two murders up here follow the profile of a serial killer, but the person they arrested for the murders doesn't. As I explained, those two letters I received, one of them was sent after the guy was arrested."

I'd explained the whole sequence of events from Janell's disappearance to Weathers's fall down the stairs. Bernard had listened silently.

"You're not thinking that a serial killer has come out of hiding after twenty-some years to start killing again?"

"I don't know."

"Not likely. Serial killers usually follow a profile. If they got away with it, they'd probably be too old to be still practicing their trade, so to speak. Though there's always the exception that proves the rule." He paused for a moment. "You're probably right, though, about the victims representing someone to him. And the fact that he strangles them means he needs to show his physical superiority. He gets some kind of relief using his hands. Whether the guy sending you those letters is the killer, hard to say. But it would be consistent with his need to show his superiority."

I forced down the image of Stephanie's bruised neck.

"Any guesses what sets these guys off?"

"Could be anything. If you buy into the psychological mumbo jumbo, it's some stressful event they can't handle because they were abused as kids. Which is a load of crap, in my opinion. Lots of people have stress and lousy childhoods and they don't turn into killers. Fact is, there are people out there walking around who are just plain evil."

It was a bleak view, but one I shared.

I could hear him take a sip of coffee. "But getting back to your question. There was one case that seems similar to what you're describing, except the guy wasn't a serial killer. And he's still in prison. His name was William Gilman. He murdered his niece, Ashley Sandinsky. Strangled her after he sexually assaulted her. Left her body in the Des Plaines River. Two canoeists found it on a sand bar."

"When was this?" My heart was beating in my ears.

"About twenty-three years ago. I remember it so well, because it was the first murder of a kid I covered. The mother, Carol Sandinsky, was convinced Gilman hadn't done it. You see, he was her brother. She kept saying he wasn't smart enough to hide the body, that he was mentally challenged, which wasn't true."

"Was there any doubt he was the killer?"

"None. The police had strong forensic evidence. And he'd taken a trophy—the girl's hair band, a purple rubber band with a purple ball attached. She'd been wearing it the day she disappeared. They found it in his room. And what made it worse for Gilman was he told the police that he'd seen his niece in a dream. This was before they found her. He described her body as being wet and muddy. No doubt he did it. The whole thing split the family apart. At the trial Carol slugged her mother-in-law outside the courtroom. The mother-in-law had testified against Gilman. She said she'd seen him hug Ashley in that way. Those were her exact words."

I was breathing fast. "The Sandinskys, they have any other children?"

"Not the Sandinskys. But Carol did. Two boys from a previous marriage."

"You remember their names?"

"That I don't remember. But you can check the *Times* on microfiche at the local library under the year I gave you. It's all there. I think there's a photo of the family at their apartment, keeping a vigil. That was before they knew she was dead. Probably the reason you didn't find it before is that it never made front page. It was in the metro section. The archives only cover major stories. But it should be on microfiche."

"You know what happened to the family?"

"I don't usually keep tabs, but like I said, it was my first murder of a young girl. The father, Mitch Sandinsky, he left. Abandoned the family. After that Carol went downhill, started drinking, taking drugs. She'd call me from time to time. I'd send her some money. She ended up dying of an overdose. The two brothers, I'm not sure what happened to them. Probably left Chicago. That's what I'd do." A somberness had come into his voice. "One other thing I do remember Carol telling me was one of the boys had gotten a scholarship to college. Some school out east. She was really proud of that. Though the last time I saw her, one of the boys had taken off. Can't remember which one."

My mind was clicking off the similarities. "I didn't mention it. But when I found Stephanie, there was a purple hair band with a purple ball on her ring finger. The same for Lisette Cohen."

He let out a long breath. "Jeez, you got to be kidding. That can't be a coincidence. It's someone familiar with the case, maybe someone who was affected personally by it."

"I'm fairly certain Weathers is the killer and one of the brothers. And I think the other brother is up here too."

"What makes you think that?"

I explained about the quote from *Lear.*

"You might be reaching. And this guy Weathers could've been pulling your chain. Purposely misleading you. He could have nothing to do with the killings."

"I don't think so. I think he wanted me to find him, so I could admire his work. See how clever he was. Then I would write about him. If Weathers was one of the brothers, he was pointing me toward his brother. Something about his sister's death needed to be revealed."

"Like I said, there was no doubt the uncle did it. I'm convinced of that. You have any candidates for the other brother?"

"One or two. You know anything about Russell Margaris, the Chicago developer?"

"Just that he's on the mayor's A list. You're not thinking he's the other brother? I find that hard to believe. How could he have covered that up?"

"You ever meet the guy?"

"No, but I know the kind of scrutiny the mayor's office would have given his background."

Bernard might be right.

He continued, "Though people lie on their resumes all the time and never get caught. If he changed his name and lied about his background, he might have slipped through."

"And he would have everything to lose if this all came out."

"That he would. If he's your guy. Which, I've got to tell you, seems pretty far-fetched."

"Maybe."

"However this turns out, give me a call and let me know. I have to live vicariously now." He paused. "Jake must be jumping out of those extra large shoes of his. Story like this."

"Something like that," I said, hedging.

"Give me your number. If I think of anything else, I'll give you a ring."

I gave him the number at the paper and my cell phone number.

"Can I give you one piece of advice?" He didn't wait for my answer. "Don't make the mistake I made early in my career. I was following up a hunch just like you are. I was totally convinced I knew who had committed this murder. But as it turned out, I was wrong. And the person I had trusted ended up being the killer. It almost cost me my life."

"I'll keep that in mind."

As soon as I hung up, I grabbed my purse and dashed out of Jake's office with Salinger on my heels. I had an hour to kill before the Sturgeon Bay library opened, but I was too hopped up to stay in the office. I circled Sturgeon Bay's business district and headed back to Green Bay Road and breakfast. The McDonald's was packed inside, so I went through the drive-up. I rewarded myself with a breakfast biscuit, hash browns and a large coffee. I broke up bits of biscuit and bacon and fed them to Salinger as I stared out the open window at the Dollar Store across the parking lot. Under the red-lettered Dollar Store sign was another sign, Discount City, just in case you weren't sure you were getting a bargain.

Two women carrying four bags of food and one full drink holder walked to the car parked next to my truck.

"He goes, I don't know, man," the one carrying the drink holder said. She put the holder on the roof and opened the door. "He goes, I don't know."

The other woman climbed in and put the food bags on the floor.

"Yeah," she answered, lighting up a cigarette. "That's the same thing he told me."

"I hear you, sisters," I said as they drove away. "They never know."

By 8:55 a.m. I was parked across from the library on Fourth Avenue. At nine sharp Ida Reeves, the new reference librarian, unlocked the front door. I slammed the door and bolted up the stone steps, leaving Salinger crying with her nose out the window. I gave Ida a quick hello.

She knew me well enough not to engage me in conversation when I had that determined expression.

All she said was, "I'll keep an eye on your dog."

"Thanks," I said, heading for the microfiche area.

There were five articles on the Sandinsky murder. Even in the first article, which had been reported as a missing person, there was a strange aura of resignation about the mother's comments. As if she knew her daughter was already dead. The second article reported the discovery of the girl's body by two canoeists on the Des Plaines River.

The third and longest article involved the arrest of William Gilman. There was the dream Bernard had told me about. The fourth article covered the trial and conviction of Gilman for second-degree murder. Bernard went into some detail about the family rift and the assault of the mother-in-law by Carol Sandinsky. The last article was short and factual, relating the sentencing of life in prison.

I printed all five articles. The photo of the family outside the apartment building was too distant and grainy. The two brothers were in it, as well as Carol and her sister. They were identified as Edward and Robert Thomas. One brother was standing alone by the door with his hands in his pockets. The other was sitting next to his mother. There was no definition to their features. They could be anybody. One of the brothers had light hair—most likely blond.

I stuffed the articles in my purse and headed out.

When I got in the truck, I checked voice mail on my cell. No message from Margaris.

I'll stop by the house for a quick lunch, I told myself. Leave Salinger, then drive over to the police station. I'll show them the articles and tell them what I'd learned from Bernard. If they arrest me, so be it.

But surely, they'd see there was enough evidence to at least cast doubt on Ritter's guilt. Meanwhile, I'd have to find a way to get Margaris to talk to me—in person and in a public place.

As I put the key in the truck's ignition, again my hand was shaking so badly I had to steady it with my other hand.

"Too much coffee, not enough sleep," I told Salinger, who tilted her head sideways as if I were speaking a foreign language.

Chapter Thirty-Eight

Saturday, June 10

As I walked toward my truck, I heard the crunch of tires on the gravel drive and saw Margaris's silver Range Rover emerge into the turnaround in front of the mobile home. The SUV made a sharp left turn and pulled up behind my truck.

My gut immediately tightened around the turkey sandwich I'd just eaten. Margaris had decided to make a personal visit, which seemed out of character for him, and I didn't like it. Not to mention that he'd effectively blocked my truck with his SUV. As if echoing my frantic thoughts, Salinger was barking and throwing herself furiously against the mobile home door.

As Margaris slammed the SUV door with a loud thud, I shifted my keys to my left hand, pressing the envelope that contained the Margaris article and the five Sandinsky articles close to my chest as I fished the pepper spray out of my purse and shoved it into my jeans pocket.

"You got my message," I said as he came up beside me. He was standing so close, I could smell a musky dampness exuding from his clothes; and his green rain slicker and waterproof pants were blotched with mud, as if he'd been walking in the woods all afternoon.

"Is that the article?" he pointed to the envelope. There was an amazing calmness about him that made me even more nervous.

As I opened the envelope and shuffled through the articles, it started to rain again, a warm rain that felt capable of bringing anything to life.

"I saw the stakes along the river." I was taking my time finding the article. I needed to gauge what I was dealing with. "When do you break ground?"

He was staring at me as if I were the entertainment. "Monday."

"You don't waste any time."

"Time is money."

I eased the article out and handed it to him, closing the envelope flap.

As he glanced at it, there was a flicker at the corner of his mouth. He gave it back to me. "What does this have to do with anything?"

"Andy Weathers, the guy who found your daughter on the ferry and who is now dead, had this article hidden at his cottage."

He shook his head. "So?"

"You have to admit it's quite a coincidence. And Weathers had another article about you and the protest meeting against your development."

"And this proves what?"

I wasn't about to tell him what I'd learned from Bernard about the connection between the Mink River murders and the Sandinsky murder, or the meaning of the Shakespeare quote and my hunch about the two brothers. Not here, not in this isolated place where no one would hear me if I screamed.

"Like I said in my phone message, I think Weathers's death is tied to the two murders," I said lamely. "I'm still following up leads."

"You do that."

He started to walk away, then stopped. When he turned back, something had changed in his demeanor—something subtle, like a slight shift in temperature; nothing you could see, only feel.

"Aren't you going to show me what else you have there?"

Before I could react, he yanked the envelope from me. My hand reached into my pocket and clamped round the pepper spray.

He leafed through the articles briefly as if he were bored, then thrust them back at me.

"What's that about?"

I had to give him credit; he did look puzzled.

"Like I said, following up leads."

For a moment, we stood face to face, his expression as blank as the rain, mine questioning. Then he abruptly turned away and walked toward his SUV. I let out a long deep breath. If he was one of the brothers, he'd hidden it well, his exterior as unreadable as steel. Maybe I was wrong about Margaris.

I shoved the soggy articles into the envelope and reached for the truck's door handle when I suddenly heard the crunch of gravel. I reached for my pepper spray and then everything went black.

There was a rocking motion that seemed to be coming from the base of my skull. I rolled over on my back. The rocking dropped to the pit of my stomach; I was going to be sick. I opened my eyes to a gray sky and rain pelting my face. I tried to sit up but my hands and feet were tied.

Margaris was kneeling in the back of the canoe vigorously paddling, as if someone were chasing him. His butt rested up against the seat. The hood of the green rain slicker was pulled over his baseball cap and tied tightly under his chin. His face was flushed, his mouth a hard line, his eyes slate blue.

"I'm going to be sick," I said.

He stopped paddling, slid the paddle inside the canoe, and

inched forward on his knees. He grabbed my shoulders and yanked me to a sitting position.

"Puke in the river," he said, moving back to his position against the seat.

I leaned over the side, but the wave of nausea passed. The water was metallic and molten—the rain falling relentlessly in sheets. My blouse, jeans, underwear were drenched. My hair hung in rivulets around my face. Though the sun hadn't set and the air was warm, I was cold. Dampness seemed to have settled into my bones.

"What are you doing?" I asked. If I'd had any doubts about Margaris and Weathers being brothers, they were gone.

He was paddling hard, switching sides, struggling to keep the canoe moving straight ahead. The seiche must be against him, because he didn't seem to be making a lot of progress. Rain dripped off the rim of his black baseball cap and down the front of his rain slicker. He wore the same green pants, but he'd changed his sneakers for heavy work boots. One of the laces was untied and dangled in the brown water that pooled around his feet. On the floor between us was a red and gray backpack, whose strap circled the center thwart.

"That's up to you," he said, breathing hard.

My head pounded and my hands and feet tingled with numbness, but I tried to stay focused. "That reporter, Wallace Bernard, the one who wrote the articles on the Sandinsky murder, I talked to him this morning. He knows about you," I said. "If I turn up dead or missing, he'll go to the police."

"And tell them what? What do you think you've figured out? Some ridiculous theory about Weathers killing those girls and my being his brother? That's your theory, isn't it? The problem is there's no proof. As far as the police know, they have their killer. Face it, you're the only one who won't let this go."

He was right. "What do you want?" I didn't think Margaris

was a psychopath like his brother. But would he kill to keep me quiet?

He kept paddling, looking side to side with each stroke as if he expected someone to appear on one of the shores. "Silence. You let this thing go. In exchange you get to live. I thought about bribing you. But then, money's not much of a temptation for you, is it? You're all about feeling good at the end of the day."

He stopped paddling a moment and pushed himself up on the stern seat. He nudged my foot with his boot as if I was a prize fish he'd just caught.

"What did you make as a teacher, huh? Couldn't have been much. I know you don't make squat as a reporter for that hick paper. Ah, but there's that promise you made to Annie Everson. You willing to die for that?"

How did he know about my promise to Annie? I wondered.

"Don't look so surprised. Annie told me all about it. She thinks you're going to find the 'real' killer. She's convinced that Erik Ritter didn't do it. I wonder where she got that idea."

He bent down, picked up a water bottle and took a long drink. He closed the plunger and threw the bottle behind him.

"She's another do-gooder like you. Look what that got her—a dead daughter. People like you never get it. You think the world is run by good deeds. But that's where you're wrong. The world is run by power. Power and money, which amount to the same thing. The powerful call the shots. The powerful win. And their daughters don't get killed by lunatics."

I was astonished at his callousness. "How?"

"How do I know about your pathetic life? You're not the only one with sources. Your life's an open book. If you have enough money, you can read it. I even know about the cancer. A shame you'd have to die like this. After everything. But hey, life's just full of those kinds of ironies. Like that Cohen woman. Girl gets fellowship. Girl gets murdered. Go figure." He grinned. "So how much do you value your life? Enough to live with a little guilt?"

The nausea was back. I leaned over the side and this time I vomited. All my good intentions about health over the side. When I was done, I sat back against the front seat and faced Margaris. The hard seat dug into my spine. If I didn't cooperate, he was going to kill me. That was now clear. Or was he just going to kill me regardless?

"Was it you or your brother who did the murders?"

"You answer me first. Silence or your life?" The canoe was listing back downstream. He began paddling again.

"How will you know I'll keep my end of the bargain?"

He laughed. "We're getting close to the place. So what's it going to be?"

I looked over my shoulder. I saw the Nature Conservancy path upriver on the right. Margaris veered the canoe toward it.

"I can't make that kind of decision without knowing if you killed those young women."

"What possible motive would I have to kill them?" he scoffed.

"They discovered something about the Hine's dragonfly that would have stopped your development."

He laughed again, this time putting his head back. The sound echoed through the forest. "The only thing they discovered was that my brother's a killer."

"Like your uncle?" I asked. "Or was your mother right?"

"Andy, or should I say Eddie, didn't kill our sister, if that's what you're asking. Good old pervert Uncle Bill did that. But Eddie might as well have. After they convicted Bill, Eddie told me he'd known all along Bill had killed Ashley. I told him he was crazy. He said he'd seen Ashley's purple hair band in Bill's car after she went missing. When I asked him why he didn't tell the police, he said family doesn't turn on family. I said that was lame, considering Uncle Mental had killed our half-sister. Kinda makes you wonder if murder runs in families. Like maybe there's a gene for it. For your sake, you'd better hope it doesn't."

The shore was getting closer. I knew once I set foot on it, I'd be walking to my death.

"What about your brother's death?"

He shoved the paddle into the river so hard water splashed over the side of the canoe. "What do you care about him? He was a murderer. The world's a better place without him."

"Did you kill him?"

As if he were explaining something difficult to a child, his voice softened. "He wouldn't listen. I told him he had to stop baiting you, that he'd get caught. I couldn't keep covering up for him. I begged him to stop. I even offered him money if he'd leave. 'Go somewhere else,' I told him. 'Get a fresh start.' He laughed at me. Told me he wasn't leaving until he finished what he started. That's when I knew I couldn't let the dumb fuck live. Eddie always thought he could outsmart everyone. Even me. Why couldn't he just stay up here and live out his useless life riding back and forth on that ferry he loved so much? Why'd he have to ruin my life? He wouldn't listen. So, he had to die. In business, we call that downsizing. My brother just wasn't productive. So he had to go."

"You know the police will eventually figure it out. And killing me will only make it worse for you."

"They'll figure it out, all right. I'll make sure of that. But they'll figure it out wrong. That's where you come in. That's the beauty of my plan. Or should I say, Eddie's plan." The canoe was within feet of the shore.

"They'll think the killer struck again. They'll realize the killer's still out there. Which puts my brother in the clear. And, unfortunately, that piece of shit Ritter. But I'll deal with him later."

He wasn't making sense. "I don't fit the pattern of the other victims."

The canoe's nose bumped the shore lodging in the mud. Margaris stopped paddling and reached down for the backpack. He unzipped the top compartment.

He took out a long, yellow-haired wig and dangled it in front of me. "Who do you think my brother's next victim was, Ms. Girard? I found this at his house after his unfortunate fall. That's why he took that damned dog of yours and left that picture. He was luring you to him. He hated you. Seems you reminded him of that reporter Bernard. The one he blamed for our mother's death. Too bad for Eddie, I happened by and spoiled his plan. You should have seen his face when he opened the door and saw it was me and not you. He bragged to me about his plan to kill you. I saved your pathetic life. Now's your chance to save yourself."

"What about Erik Ritter?" I asked, desperate to break through to him. "If I keep quiet an innocent man goes to prison."

His mouth tightened. "Ritter raped my daughter. That son of a bitch belongs in prison where he'll learn what it means to be raped."

I didn't believe he'd let me go. My agreeing to silence was his way of winning. He wanted control not only over my body but my soul. The ultimate power trip.

I had nothing to lose, so I decided to test my theory. "Okay, I'll keep quiet. I'll let it go. You're right, Ritter belongs in prison."

He laughed. "I knew it. I knew you'd cave."

"You got what you want. Now let me go."

He shoved the wig in the backpack, zipped it up and threw it on shore. After securing the paddle under the thwarts, he jumped onto the muddy bank.

"Time's up," he said.

He reached down, untied my feet and yanked me up by my

shoulders. "Now. Out of the boat."

I pulled away from him, falling back onto the seat. "I said I'd keep quiet. You can walk away from this. Just let me go." I'd been right about him. This was all a power trip.

He dragged me out of the canoe by my arms and pushed me up the bank. My running shoes sank in the squishy mud, but I managed to stay upright. In front of me was the two-mile hiking trail that led to the Conservancy parking lot. To my right was the trail leading to the clearing. I gazed straight ahead, willing someone to be walking toward us. But all I saw were woods glistening green in the quiet light.

"Too late. You should have stayed out of this," he said, picking up the backpack.

Chapter Thirty-Nine

Rain splashed down on me from the densely packed trees mudding the path. My clothes were beyond wet. They hugged my body like a second skin, a cold and clammy skin. A thick mist shrouded everything, making seeing difficult. But I didn't need to see; I knew the way. The yellow tin circles once again led me to the clearing where Stephanie Everson and Lisette Cohen had been murdered.

Margaris walked behind me with a knife at my back. Every once in a while, I felt the knife's edge through the thin fabric of my blouse. He'd taken out the knife, a flashlight and a pair of latex gloves from the backpack at the river's edge. The wig was still in the backpack, which was now draped over his shoulder. The latex gloves were on his hands.

After he had put on the gloves, he'd searched me and found the pepper spray in my pocket. He had shoved it in the back pocket of his jeans. When I had asked him to untie my hands so I could keep my balance walking the rocky trail, he had laughed, asking me if I thought he was stupid.

I struggled down the trail, trying to avoid the slick, mossy rocks, each step bringing me closer to death. I thought of Stephanie and Lisette and hoped their deaths had come without warning. That there had been little time for this awful dread I could taste in my mouth. Every breath a reminder that my breaths were numbered.

As I rounded a bend, I tripped over a tree stump and fell

forward, smashing my knees on a jagged rock. Margaris swore and yanked me up by my blouse, ripping it open and popping the buttons. I could feel the warm ooze of blood inside my jeans.

"Move," he said, again poking me in the back with the knife.

As we snaked deeper into the forest, the flashlight's eerie halo bounced from tree to underbrush to tree, adding to the macabre atmosphere that was a prelude to my death.

I hadn't made the mistake Bernard had warned me about. I hadn't trusted the wrong person. My mistake was I hadn't trusted anyone. No one knew where I was. There would be no help; I was on my own. And other than Salinger, there was no one who was counting on my return tonight. And now I was going to pay for it if I didn't think of some way out of this.

The flashlight beam hit the tree in front of me, illuminating the yellow Nature Conservancy circle. In the near distance I could see the edge of the clearing.

"You still didn't tell me how your brother did it," I said through chattering teeth. My shoulders and arms ached. I couldn't feel my fingers.

"Just keep moving. We're almost there." He pressed the edge of the knife in my back again. This time it pierced my skin. The warm adrenaline of fear spread through me.

I walked into the clearing. An image shot across my brain—Stephanie's body, its strange position, the blond hair so carefully arranged. I closed my eyes and forced the vision from my head. I had to keep clear and steady if I was going to survive this.

"Okay, over there." He pointed to the exact spot where I had found Stephanie and Lisette. Strips of yellow police tape were on the ground, some fluttered in an evergreen like bizarre tinsel.

I tried once more to persuade him not to kill me. "Your brother had everyone fooled, especially the police. There's no way any of this can be traced back to him or you. I'm the only one who cares. And I'm not going to say anything."

Margaris put the flashlight down on the ground, directing its beam to the murder spot.

"Kneel down," he said.

"Why?"

He put the knife to my throat and nicked my skin. I could feel the sharp burn of the blade and then the blood.

I knelt down on my bleeding knees.

He walked behind me, tied my feet together and untied my hands. I could hear him unzip the backpack. When he stood in front of me he was holding the wig in one hand. The other hand held the knife close to my throat.

"Put it on. And make sure your hair doesn't show."

I reluctantly took the wig, pulled it over my head, and shoved my wet and dripping hair underneath. Cold water ran down my back.

"Stand up," he said, satisfied.

I stood up. Time seemed to have disappeared. Already I could feel myself wanting to slip out of my body. I told myself not to.

"It was the resemblance, wasn't it? That's why he chose them. I saw a picture of your sister." I was talking fast. "Stephanie and Lisette both had long blond hair and were slender like her. But what set him off? What made that rage inside him turn on?"

Margaris was looking at me with an expression of both wonder and horror. He reached out with one hand toward my face. Through the glove, his hand felt ice cold as he rubbed it against my cheek. Not with tenderness, but as if he could erase me with the motion. I stood as still as stone, meeting the cold blue of his eyes that seemed to have shut down.

"Janell," he said, his cold fingers pulling down my neck. "She's the one who looks like Ashley. A dead ringer." He laughed at the joke. "That's what Eddie said to me. 'She's a dead ringer for Ashley.' "

Now his hand was pressing down across one breast, then the other. The pressure was so intense on my remaining breast I wanted to cry out but didn't. The blouse was hanging off my shoulders. He ripped it off and threw it on the ground.

I kept talking as if nothing had happened. "Eddie was the one who found her on the ferry. But that was after he murdered Stephanie. What set him off?" I asked, willing myself not to feel his hand as it pressed down and caressed my stomach.

His blue eyes stared into mine as if he were seeing something there unnamable.

"Irony of ironies. All of it. As if fate had some plan to fuck up our lives. Eddie saw Ritter pick her up from the ferry dock that Friday night. He had no idea she was my daughter. He told me it was like a dream. 'There was Ashley,' he said."

His hand stopped moving. "And then the grand irony. He would be the one person in the whole world who found her. I didn't even know he was living up here until that damned protest meeting. You know what he told me when he found Janell? 'It was as if it were happening all over again. Ashley disappearing. Ashley dead. And our uncle killing her. Only she wasn't dead. And I saved her. My sweet, beautiful, unobtainable Ashley.' That's what he said. I almost felt sorry for the poor deluded bastard. But then he said, 'I didn't touch her. I wanted to, I really did. But I resisted.' That sick fuck. I had to protect Janell from him."

"And yourself." That's why he had to silence me. No one could know that his uncle was a killer and now his brother. When he'd realized that Weathers was the killer, it must have been like watching a house of cards fall. His whole world, the one he'd built out of lies and hard work, tumbling down.

His hand was on my crotch now. Not moving, just there, warm and unwanted.

"I had to fix it. I had to take control."

"By planting evidence on Ritter's boat?"

"And it all would have worked. If Eddie hadn't written those damned letters. He wanted power. He wanted you to give him that power. And you fell right into his trap. He used you. And if it hadn't been for me, the good brother, he would have killed you."

I resisted pointing out to him that the so-called good brother was about to kill me. "Before all this started, why didn't you help him? You knew last summer he was living up here. You could have done something for him. Then maybe none of this would have happened."

"Help him? You mean like he helped the family by not turning Uncle Mental in? If he had, maybe then our mother wouldn't have spent the rest of her life convinced her brother hadn't murdered her daughter. He was a sick loser. I'm the only one who made something of himself. Who didn't let this thing beat him. And it's not going to beat me now."

His hand moved away from my crotch.

"Turn around," he said, looking around for the rope to tie my hands.

I didn't move. "What about the hair band?" I was frantic, stalling, saying anything to stay alive.

"What are you talking about?"

"Both victims had a hair band on their ring fingers."

"You're lying."

I couldn't believe he hadn't seen it. "Didn't you see it on Stephanie's finger? He put one on Lisette too. Both the same. A purple rubber band with a purple ball. Like the one your uncle kept as a trophy and your brother found."

He looked down at the spot where the bodies had been. Then he seemed to go inside himself.

"Shut up," he said, pushing me hard.

I fell backwards with such force that my head bounced on the soft earth. There was a ringing in my ears. He knelt down, his legs straddling me. The knife was no longer in his hand. I couldn't see where he'd put it. I tried to look for it, but suddenly his gloved hands were on my throat, tightening. I pulled at his fingers, trying to peel them away from my throat. But they wouldn't budge. I reached up and scratched at his face. But he didn't seem to feel it. He had closed his eyes. I was gasping for breath, taking short jagged breaths. I tried to jerk my legs up but his weight held me fast. My hands kept clawing at his face. I could feel his skin under my nails. It was taking a long time to die. I turned to the side gasping for air.

Then I saw something—there in the soft mud, a large rock sticking up from the leaves. I reached toward it and pulled it from the mud. It was jagged and heavy. I grasped it tight in my hand and thrust it at his head with my waning strength, aiming for his temple.

His hands fell from my throat and he fell backwards, momentarily stunned by the blow. I crawled out from under him, my fingers fumbling at the rope round my ankles. Margaris was reeling on the ground in front of me, blood oozing down his face.

I untied the first knot and was working on the second when Margaris grabbed my foot.

"You bitch," he shouted through his pain. "You fucking bitch!"

I kicked at him so hard, I freed my feet from the rope. I jumped up and ran out of the clearing. As I stumbled down the path, I could hear Margaris behind me cursing and shouting.

The woods were a green smoky maze. I ran in the opposite direction from where we had come, looking for the yellow circles. Trees lashed across my face, underbrush tugged at my running shoes, but I didn't fall. My throat burned. But I was breathing in the dank loamy air, and it tasted good.

I reached the shore just ahead of Margaris. I shoved the canoe in the water and jumped in the back, paddling furiously. He dove into the water after me. I pulled hard on the paddle, digging it deep in the water and switching sides every four strokes. I was moving fast. The current must be with me. But that meant the current was also with Margaris. I turned around once quickly and saw that he was gaining on me.

I calculated it must be several miles downriver to Rowleys Bay. I had to get distance between Margaris and me before I made it to shore. If I didn't, he would easily overpower me before I could make it to the safety of the marina.

I was paddling so hard my arms were starting to feel rubbery, but I kept at it. Shoving the paddle in, bringing it back and out, and shoving it in again. But as hard as I was paddling, I could still hear Margaris's splashes coming closer and closer. How could he keep up with me? I thought. He had to be inches from the canoe.

Suddenly I felt the canoe dip low in the river from behind. I turned and saw Margaris, his fingers inside the canoe's rubber-tipped end. I struck his fingers with the paddle. He howled and let go. But he came back for more. As the moon emerged from a cloudbank, I saw clearly for the first time the bloody mess of his face.

As Margaris grabbed the canoe's end again, his weight tipped the canoe left. I tried to hit him, but the canoe was listing left too much. I leaned right and paddled trying to stabilize the canoe. Margaris let go of the canoe's end.

For a moment I thought he'd given up. The canoe was moving swiftly toward the river's mouth. Just a little farther and I'd be through the mouth and into the bay. Maybe I was safe.

Then I saw him swim wide around the reach of my paddle past the front of the canoe. I tried to paddle around him, but the current was moving too fast. The canoe was heading right for him. I back paddled but it was too late. As the canoe came abreast of him, he grabbed onto the bow plate. I swatted the paddle at him, but I was too far back in the canoe to reach him. Before I could get to him, he had his one leg and one arm over the canoe's side. I scrambled forward and whacked him with the paddle, but he managed to swing the rest of his body in.

The canoe was rocking and swaying as I scurried toward the back of the canoe. The paddle was still in my hand. I held it at him like a lance. But he kept crawling toward me. Suddenly he stood up and lunged for the paddle. The canoe pitched sideways and over, throwing me into the water.

The cold shock of water pulled me down. I told myself not to breathe, not to panic. I felt myself descend. My feet touched the river's bottom with a soft thud. I forced my eyes open, looking for Margaris. But I didn't see him, only the dark outline of the canoe overhead. I pushed off with my feet kicking like crazy, and felt my body rise toward the surface. Like a cork, my head sprang up out of the water. I took in one deep breath after another, coughing and sputtering, kicking my feet and flailing my arms to stay afloat. The cool night air stung my face. The overturned canoe was drifting beside me. I threw my arm over the canoe and held on for dear life. It was only then that I turned my head around looking for Margaris. He wasn't there. And I was only yards from the river's mouth and Rowleys Bay.

Holding onto the canoe, I kicked my legs and headed toward the bay. I kept telling myself that the worst was over, that I only had to maneuver the canoe around the point to the marina. But that sleepy cold was numbing my senses.

As I rounded the point, I could see the silver lights from the marina shimmering on the waves. I tried to kick harder, but my legs seemed heavy and weighted. The lights were starting to dance, and I wanted to close my eyes. But I kept kicking and holding on.

When I reached the marina, my body was so cold I could barely stand up. So I crawled on my hands and knees up the shore toward the boathouse. The door was closed but it wasn't locked. Joe hadn't replaced the broken lock. I went inside. Behind the counter was Joe's dry bag. It took me three tries, but I finally was able to open it. Inside was his extra set of clothes. I stripped off my sodden jeans and underwear and put on Joe's flannel shirt, wool socks and sweatpants. I placed the wet clothes and wig on the counter. Somehow the wig had stayed on my head. There was coffee in the coffeemaker. I flipped the switch to on and reheated the stale coffee. After I drank the entire cup and stopped shaking, I dialed the police.

I opened my mouth to talk but nothing came out but air.

"Door County Police," the dispatcher said over and over. "Please state your business."

Finally I put the phone down, left the boathouse and started up the road toward Rowleys Bay Resort. The sharp cold was gone from my body. But I was still shaking inside Joe's fleece jacket. There were a million stars newly washed by the rain that had stopped hours ago. A large cloud was backlit by the moon. It lumbered low in the sky. A few cars buzzed past me. Nothing seemed real.

At the Resort I hit the front desk bell until the desk clerk, whose nametag read Kenny and who looked all of sixteen, emerged from the back office. I showed the suspicious Kenny my throat and gestured for a piece of paper and pen. I wrote down my name and that he should call the police. About forty minutes later Deputy Chief Hallaway, trailed by Chet Jorgensen, stormed in, all spit and polish and aching for a fight.

"What is your problem?" she yelled at me.

I unzipped the fleece jacket and once again pointed to my

throat where fingerprints had purpled my skin.

Hallaway turned toward the desk clerk. "Why isn't this woman in a hospital?"

Epilogue

Sunday, June 18

The Mink River shone with splintered light. Right now the seiche was moving its green-gray water upstream—the river at the mercy of the wind and the lake.

I stood on the Margarises' pier, watching an eagle wing across the river and land in a birch tree. The cathedral windows behind me would be reflecting the eagle, the river and me.

I looked upstream, the red-flagged stakes fluttered in the warm spring air, making a gentle flapping sound. There was a For Sale sign at the end of Margate Lane. I'd seen it when I drove in. Janet was asking an exorbitant amount for the house and land.

"She'll come down. Soon enough," was what people were saying.

The peninsula was breathing a collective sigh of relief with the murders solved. After Hallaway had taken my statement, the police had searched Weathers's house again and then his boat. On the boat they'd found a hairbrush laced with blond hair and several purple hair bands—six to be exact. The hair in the brush matched Stephanie Everson's DNA. The six hair bands plus the two found on the victims' fingers and the one left on my doorknob equaled nine—the number Weathers had mentioned in his letters. I was convinced that had Andy Weathers lived, there would have been six more dead women. And if Margaris hadn't been lying, I would have been one of those six women.

Wallace Bernard supplied the significance of the number nine. Ashley Sandinsky was born on March third—three times three.

Whether Stephanie and Lisette had met their deaths because of a chance meeting by the Mink River or whether Weathers had lured them there, I'd never know.

Janet had dropped charges on Ritter. He'd been released and already left Door County.

As to Russell Margaris, there was nothing directly linking him to the two murders. Of course, Margaris could have planted the evidence on Weathers's boat as he did on Ritter's. But it didn't fit his character. His crimes were crimes of expediency—framing Ritter, killing Weathers and then trying to kill me. In his mind these had been necessary steps to keep his past secret. He probably thought if it got out that both his uncle and his brother were killers, the scandal would have ruined his business. Or maybe he just couldn't live through that nightmare again.

I still didn't know whether he'd succumbed to hypothermia or hit his head when the canoe went over. His body had yet to be recovered.

"He'll wash up one of these days then," Chet had reassured me. "They always do."

And in a couple of weeks the Hine's Emerald Dragonfly would emerge to breed. And life's cycle would start all over again.

"You been waiting long?" Joe asked.

I'd been so lost in my thoughts I hadn't heard him come up behind me.

"Long enough," I said. "How's the river look to you?"

"Good, real good."

ABOUT THE AUTHOR

Gail Lukasik was born in Cleveland, Ohio, and was a dancer with the Cleveland Civic Ballet Company. She has worked as a choreographer and a freelance writer. Lisel Mueller described her book of poems, *Landscape Toward a Proper Silence*, as a "splendid collection." She also has been published in over sixty literary journals, including *The Georgia Review, Carolina Quarterly,* and *Mississippi Valley Review.* The Illinois Arts Council awarded her a literary award for her poetry. She earned her M.A. and Ph.D. from the University of Illinois at Chicago, where she taught writing and literature. *Death's Door* is the second book in the Leigh Girard mystery series.